As the Hague Ordains

THEY PUT ALL THE OFFICERS IN ONE COMMON WARD FOR THREE DAYS

As the Hague Ordains

A Novel of Japan at the Turn of the
Twentieth Century

Eliza Ruhamah Scidmore

LEONAUR

As the Hague Ordains
A Novel of Japan at the Turn of the Twentieth Century
by Eliza Ruhamah Scidmore

First published under the title
As the Hague Ordains

Leonaur is an imprint of Oakpast Ltd

Copyright in this form © 2012 Oakpast Ltd

ISBN: 978-1-78282-002-4 (hardcover)
ISBN: 978-1-78282-003-1 (softcover)

http://www.leonaur.com

Publisher's Notes

Contents

To Emily E.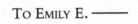

THE HAGUE 1899
CONVENTION WITH RESPECT TO THE LAWS AND
CUSTOMS OF WAR ON LAND
Annex: Section 1—Belligerents.
Chapter II— Prisoners of War.

Article VII. The government into whose hands prisoners of war have fallen is bound to maintain them.

Failing a special agreement between the belligerents, prisoners of war shall be treated as regards food, quarters and clothing, on the same footing as the troops of the government which has captured them.

CHAPTER 1

Europe

Thursday, June 16th.

The blow so long dreaded has at last fallen, and, after crouching away from it for weeks, it is almost a relief from the long tension of emotion and fear to have had it happen—to know the worst.

It was not the unexpected either; since, from that day of awful shame and stupefaction, when everyone turned his eyes away from his friend's gaze in humiliation at the defeat of our army at the Yalu River, and its flight from the yellow hordes—since then, we women at home have had our minds filled with the worst presentiments.

Vladimir, while out on a scouting expedition with a few Cossacks, has been captured and taken to a prison in Japan!

That was a strange enterprise surely, for a staff colonel, the diplomatic adviser and legal aide, whose presence at headquarters was solely to make rulings in international law and draft the treaty,—strange for him to be off on a scouting trip. Had they no young Cossack officers for such work?

I was wakened early by Anna drawing the curtains noisily and throwing the strong daylight in my face. Evidently the telegraph messenger had given her an idea of the contents of the official message he brought, for with great excitement she said: "It is news from Manchuria. Oh! read it quick, *barina*."

I only thought of death or wounds, and could scarcely tear the paper apart to read:

Prisoner—healthy. Write Matsuyama, Japan—Vladimir.

My heart leaped and stopped beating, all my life currents seemed streaming out from my cold finger tips, and I could not think. Slowly the words, as I stared at them, brought their full meaning to me. As if

9

present before me, I saw Vladimir led along a road by soldiers, a cord tied to his clasped hands as I had often seen convicts led through the streets in Japan—vividly I saw the disconsolate figures in faded, salmon-pink clothes, and peaked straw hats like their thatch roofs and fences, half concealing the faces. I heard the clank of fetters, and then I shrieked with horror, with anger, at the mere idea. How dare they? How dare they?

In a fury of excitement I dressed, drank my coffee standing, while Anna held the tray and followed me around the room, blankly, dumbly, wondering. I almost ran to the A——s to tell them.

Of course I should go at once to Japan. Of that there was no kind of doubt. With no family, no children, no estates, no people or duties to hold me here, how could it be supposed for one moment that I should not go to Japan? Should I sit here in Petersburg, and Vladimir live in prison in Japan? Not at all. Not at all.

I dread the Red Cross meetings, because some women always talk of Japan, as they do of England, with the view of deriding and insulting me, it would seem. At that last meeting, Sophia and Hilka Belogotrovy were discussing whether it would not be better to be killed outright in battle, than to be tortured and starved to death in a Japanese prison. I kept still with difficulty, and Sophia was malicious enough to see it, and rant the more for my benefit. They will not understand that there is any difference between Japan and China, and I long ago found it of no avail to try to set them right about Japan and the Japanese. They called me "*Japonski*" if I attempted to tell them anything about Japan. They prefer an imaginary barbarism to the highly civilised Japan that exists.

This hideous war has resulted from just such Russian ignorance of Japan; and then, it is cruel, after my long and loyal championship of Japan in all countries, that this blow should come to me from it. I can laugh now, almost to hysterics, to remember how I besought Vladimir to throw all his influence, to strain every point of mercy when it came to the treaty-making; to be merciful to the spirited, sensitive people who could not comprehend what they were so madly rushing upon. And how I threatened to rush across and join him in Tokyo, when a triumphant Russia should be making peace terms there! I counted upon the negotiation and all that occupying a long time, and I wanted to be there again—to see the old pine trees on the grey castle walls, the pink and white lotus in the long stretches of the castle moats— and to soften the hearts of the conqueror to the Japanese, whom I have loved so long and so much. And now, on what an errand I go to Japan!

At first, they thought it madness for me to think of going to Japan, and opposed it. "They will imprison you too and who knows what tortures they have in their filthy prisons.—Oh! They will make both of you work in their nasty rice fields," said the Princess Tilly, who was never clear in her mind that Japan was not a province of China.

I wanted to leave that very night, but the trans-Siberian line was impossible because of the delays and the impasse at the Manchurian end, and the Suez route was not to be faced in midsummer. Nicholas A—— explained to me quietly about my passport for leaving Russia, in the first place; my letter of credit for funds to travel with, in the second place; besides the necessity of sending requests to take leave at Tsarskoe, and of the grand duchesses, and of resigning from the Red Cross Committees.

All my world of Petersburg came to the station to see me off, with flowers, lamentations, bonbons, books, and cheers for my long voyage. It was little like that going away of the troops early in the year with gay promises of "On to Tokyo!" My "On to Tokyo" was sad enough.

I slept and I woke, and changed carriages at the frontier. I slept and I woke at Berlin, and changed to the Ostend train, and I came into London one afternoon at the end of the season, and found such a strangeness in all its familiar scenes that a chill struck me. The change was in myself, not in London. The newsboys in the streets held billboards announcing:

Another Japanese Victory. The Russians in Retreat as Usual. Kuropatkin still 'luring them on!'

And everyone grinned to read the lines. "And bally well they deserve all this," said a man in the street in my hearing.

Barclay's rushed my credit through; I left my jewel box and all Vladimir's papers with them, and I added something for faithful Anna to my will at the solicitors'. Anna, who has followed my fortunes so faithfully for these dozen and more years, made no protests against this strange trip; and as she is German and is good in her English, and is unsurpassed as a courier, will be invaluable. I drew every rouble of credit I had in St. Petersburg, by Nicholas A——'s advice, for he says he foresees only trouble—riots and revolution ahead, a Reign of Terror, if the fortunes of war do not quickly change. All these disasters have inflamed the people, who now resist mobilisation, and it is a question if they can be kept down if any more troops are taken away for the front. The Tsarskoe crowd are furious with Kuropatkin that he does not land his armies in Japan.

Now, I have only to sit still for these weeks to come, and think and think, while the machinery does the rest and takes me on and on— until I stand at the prison door and try to see Vladimir. I wonder if I shall have to sing under the window like Coeur de Lion's little page, to find him and let him know I am there! I telegraphed of course, from Petersburg, and again from London, that I am coming, and he must know that I am now on my way to Japan. To Japan! the trip that we have so often talked of taking together!

How strange it will be for me to find myself again in Japan! A changed Japan, and a changed Sophia Ivanovna too! I wonder if there will be any one there who knew me before, eighteen, nineteen, twenty years ago? I fear not, and I shall be glad to have it so. Of course the name is different now, and I was such a child then. Certainly these ten years of quiet happiness and a contented heart with Vladimir, have made me another being in another world. I wonder how real the past will seem; if the horror of those days of revelation, disillusionment, and degradation will come back? if, in the same scenes, I shall see the bloated figure, the satyr's face of Paul before me? and remember again, how his hideous nature was revealed to me too late? how his grossness, his coarse pleasures, his cruelties crushed me? I often used to start from dreams in a cold chill of terror, having lived again in the dark, gloomy, little Tokyo house, my bruised body aching, my ears ringing with Paul's drunken voice.

I could not endure to stay in Russia after that. Everything Russian was unpleasant to me, and England and my mother's kinsfolk seemed my only home and attachments. Then followed the winters abroad with my invalid uncle, the meeting with Vladimir, and last our happy life in Rome. In the first years, when Vladimir found it necessary to go back to Russia each summer, I used to wonder why I was so indifferent to Russia. Why I felt myself so aloof, such an outsider and spectator, really only a critic, when I was in Russia. Although everyone was so kind to me in Petersburg, the sovereigns were so gracious, and Vladimir so fortunate, I found myself caring less for, almost disliking the Russian life. It seemed to me that the whole thing was a sham, a thin veneer of western civilisation, a clever imitation up to a certain point. The government denied too much to the people, and the want of education in the masses appalled me. Vladimir has always believed

12

in compulsory education, in fewer prisons and barracks and more schoolhouses.

That quaint old American minister, who came to Madrid after Petersburg, used to say that he had only changed jails, as far as he could see; only that he as a diplomat had a little more liberty than the shackled people in either country. "What Russia needs most is more soap and spelling books; fewer princes and more country schoo mas- ters; fewer diamonds, on the bare-backed court ladies in Petersburg, and more broken stone on the country roads." "Then, as for Spain!" he said, "she wants fewer priests, more soap, and more schoolmasters too." He longed to get back to "God's country," as he called America, "Which smelled neither of leather boots nor garlic." A droll old fellow, who quite bewitched my Vladimir.

CHAPTER 2

America

June 30th.

It seems ages to me since I left Petersburg that hot June day, and almost as long since the hotter day that I sat and stood five weary hours on the docks of New York. The Americans claim to be a civilised people, but the difficulties they made us, the restrictions they laid down as to our landing in their free country, would disgrace Abyssinia or Persia. We answered innumerable questions on board the ship, signed papers, and paid an entrance fee of five roubles to gain the land of liberty! What a misnomer! It must be a bit of American humour, or rather a gibe of France, to have erected that great statue of Liberty Enlightening the World at the mouth of the harbour. Oh! Liberty! what crimes are committed in thy name—in America.

When I went through America years ago, we had a diplomatic privilege, a *laissez-passer* for the Customs, and all that. It was all bows, courtesy, effusive politeness. Today, Anna and I are only two cabin passengers,—nationality, Russian; occupation, blank; ages, forty and forty-two; not paupers, criminals, nor lunatics, as they closely inquired; not suffering with any contagious disease; possessing at least one hundred *roubles* each,—so that we shall not become a charge on the charitable institutions of the country!

We were alone. I had kept entirely to myself on the ship, and we had no one to appeal to from the brusque and surly officials. There was no *café* or waiting-room, and, with all the richly dressed Americans, we were driven down on the dock and sat there among cargo boxes to wait for our luggage. America did not smell of leather or garlic that day. *Niet. Niet.* How that close warehouse on the dock smelled of low-tide and horses! Phew! my head swims now, as I recall it. It was a heathen, a savage and uncivilised, a bureaucratical, tyrannical America I found to my sorrow. America quite the perfect person forsooth to throw stones at poor Russia! Certainly we do not treat prisoners worse in Russia than the Goddess of Liberty treats the arriving sea passenger in America.

So, we sat on boxes of merchandise "in the foul *étape*," as their writers always speak of Siberian prisons. We were hungry, without food or drink, and could not pass the cordon of guards to seek it outside; and Anna stood for two hours in the queue of convicts waiting to draw a number for a customs officer to search our luggage. Heavens! how much better they do it in Wirballen and Eydtkunen on our frontier! and at Odessa! Constantinople even would blush to have such a *douane*.

In the long hours on this ill-smelling, stifling wharf, the passengers greedily seized the newspapers, and again their laughter was for Russia's misfortunes in war. Nothing was lacking to make me completely miserable. But, at last, an official came toward me with a letter, followed by a man who was plainly a Russian from the toes of his boots to his blonde-white hair. "Lady, are you Mrs. *Van Till?* because this man from the Russian Consulate has been hunting you all over the docks." And then our troubles ended, for the consul's clerk knew how to manage the dreadful Americans. I don't know how much he had to pay in fees and tips to get us off; but anyhow, he soon had our boxes corded and sealed, and we crossed by a ferry to the city, and went to a mammoth hotel—a skyscraper, they call it. From my windows on the fifteenth floor, I looked out to other fifteen- and twenty-storey buildings in every direction. The sea breeze blew in my face and there was no sound from the street far below.

The consul came and dined with me. He had been cabled his instructions from Petersburg, and had sent his man to meet me; and he had taken passage for me on a fast ship, which was to cross the Pacific in twelve days! Think of that! after the twenty-eight days we spent in crossing to San Francisco, such a little while ago.

The war has given the consul much work to do and keeps him in town, and even the embassy is tied fast at the capital for the summer. The newspapers in New York were full of praises of Japan, and the same absurd stories about Russia that always fill English newspapers. It is still a mystery why the American people have so suddenly forgotten the long traditional friendship between our two countries, and the gratitude they owed us, turned from us, and lost their heads so completely over the Japanese. It is a sort of insanity just now, and ever since the Japanese have won a victory over that silly Zakaroff on the Yalu River, the Americans seem to think Japan has conquered all creation, for all time. One must wait until events bring them to their senses; and make them quite ashamed of themselves too, I should think.

When I came to leave New York, a company of seventy Chinese was marched into the station, counted off like convicts, and locked into a car. "This is the land of freedom, you know," said the consul, "where they do not punish the Jews, no matter what they do. These Chinese are rich merchants going to China and intending to return to America. They count them, lock them up, and guard them, exactly as we do convicts going to Siberia. Someday, the Chinese may get tired of their treatment and make an uprising. Then the Americans will 'get busy,' as they say, and mend their manners."

I should think so, for the great republic is by no means the paradise we hear about in Europe. One encounter with pure Liberty will do for me. I long to meet again certain Americans who have made me blush for poor Russia. I shall make any one's salon a battle ground, if I can but meet again some of the American critics who taunted me in Rome. And that M. Georges Kennan! Ah!

The consul bade me goodbye as to one setting sail for the unknown. I felt like M. Andre starting on his airship. "We cannot send word ahead, or do any more for you now. Your own tact and sense must direct you. Go at once to the French minister in Tokyo, and he will do what he can. Drop Russian speech from this hour; and, as your name is so German, and your maid has Westphalia printed on her face, you can go without suspicion. But remember, there are always spies and informers about and you must be discreet. God be with you." And then I lost all touch with all Russia, and really embarked for the unknown.

On shipboard, while we were crossing the Atlantic, I had written fully to everyone and warned each one to be careful of what he put in letters to me. In New York, Anna washed every European sign and hotel label from our boxes. The four days on the train went by very quickly, and we saw a rich, contented, prosperous country day after day. Only once on the far western plains did we see a soldier in uniform, a suggestion of war; but there were bulletins at the railway stations, and everyone grinned at fresh discomfitures and defeats for Russia. The passengers on the ship were few and uninteresting; it was cold and foggy; and I spent the time in my deck cabin, and tried to picture the landing in Japan.

16

Tuesday, July 19th.

It was a hot, steamy, rainy morning when we anchored at Yoko-hama, and we quickly went ashore to the hotel and asked for rooms. I wrote my name with hesitation in the visitors' book, the innkeeper said: "This way, *Madame*," turned into a little room, and closed the door. In alarm, I felt that Japanese fetters were about to be put upon me, when he lifted his hand and said: "Oh! the Princess Sophia! Princess Sophia! My God! What are you doing here, *Madame la Princesse?* Go back to the ship. Quick! Quick! It is too dangerous, too dangerous. You cannot spy here. Go quick. I cannot let you stop. I cannot go with you. It is too dangerous." As he clasped his hands again, I recognised D——'s old steward, one who came to my rescue many times in my Tokyo days, and once really saved my life, when Paul was more drunk and more brutal than usual.

This steward at the Legation house was the only one to whom I could appeal and speak openly, and I always suspected that he was told off by D—— to keep an eye on the No. 2 house, and to save me, if necessary. It was this faithful M—— who concealed Paul's many disappearances; who found him drowned in the villa lakelet in the distant quarter across the river; and who closed my house for me, and got me away from Japan. All of that past life came before me in successive scenes, like a panorama. I stood quite speechless with all that the sudden appearance of M—— brought before me.

M—— now owns the large foreign hotel, and, sending Anna into the breakfast room, he himself served me in a private room, as the boy passed in the dishes. All my troubles were truly ended. Ministers and consuls could not advise nor do more for me than this faithful M——, who knew every link in the long diplomatic chain of events leading up to the war's beginning. He had seen the Rosens and Princess Kitty go away; and he had watched the flag hauled down from the consulate. He knew, too, all about the arrangements with the French Legation in Tokyo.

That good soul took me to the bank and got me money on my London letter. "Keep your English notes and gold," he advised, "for we cannot know what may happen. Keep enough of them always with you to pay to get you away, if you have to escape suddenly from Japan." He took me to Tokyo, and we saw the French minister, who at last gave me word of Vladimir, but—how terrible. "He is on the hospital list, you see," he said, showing me the paper. "He arrived from Dalny only a week ago, and the consul in Kobe came back from Matsuyama the day before yesterday, and sends me these reports. He has without doubt seen him, and after a few days you might go to Kobe and see the consul!"

"After a few days! *Mon Dieu!* No! at once, today, by my same steamer! It goes to Kobe."

"But, *Madame,* I have not any permit for you to see your husband yet. You must apply for it."

"But, your Excellency, I do not need any permit to see your consul. He has seen my husband. He can tell me of him. Ah! how could I wait here an hour? No! No! It is cruel to stop me now. Let me go to Kobe and wait there. It is nearer. Let me go."

The minister drew his shoulders a little, and then had me write an appeal to the Minister of War to be permitted to visit my husband in the hospital of the prisoners' quarters at Matsuyama, and that I might be permitted also to take up my residence at Matsuyama, and have frequent access to the hospital. "They will grant it. Oh, yes. I am quite sure of it. Be quite tranquil," he said.

All this took time, and we drove rapidly back to the station, past a long open park space beside the moat, now bare of its lotus plants, in a glare of light and heat insupportable. The thought of Vladimir, wounded and in a prison hospital, drove everything from my mind, and I but vaguely remember what was said and done in the chancery, nor did I notice what we passed as we hastened for our returning train. Great buildings, as in a European capital, stretched along vast park spaces; and I remember seeing, as if in a dream, as if in a mirage in the noon heat waves, the quaint, little, white towers perched high on the castle walls.

"Look!" said M——, who rode facing me. And there was the familiar old Legation building, with its loggiaed verandah, the steep, green garden, the rustic parasol of a summer house at the angle of the compound overlooking the old parade ground. How often did we stand there laughing until weak at the drill of the would-be army, the little manikin caricatures of European troops going through goose-step marches! I cannot yet understand or find the clue to the miraculous creation of the formidable army they must really have in the field, when I remember the travesty of manoeuvres that used to take place on the Hibiya parade ground. Our old legation was shuttered and silent, the flagstaff bare, the grille closed, and a policeman in a white uniform sat in a tiny sentry box by the *momban's* house. It was a sad sight.

Oh! War! War! how cruel and unnecessary are the sufferings you bring in your train!

Oh! Bezobrazoff! Bezobrazoff! What have you not brought down upon the hapless sovereign who trusted you? And upon his innocent subjects! All Vladimir's worst forebodings, since the day he followed the timid Nicholas in Alexander's funeral train, have more than come true. To think that Russia, with her great destiny, should come to this!—Halted in her great march to the Pacific by these puny people!

CHAPTER 3

Japan

Sunday, July 24th.

It was late in the afternoon before we could get ashore at Kobe and reach the French Consulate. The tri-colour of la Republique seemed as dear to me as our own, as it lifted now and then in the faint south wind that blew up the Inland Sea. My own excitement must have moved the door-man, for he abruptly ushered me into the cabinet where the Consul was quietly writing at a desk.

"*Madame?*" said the consul, rising to bow and receiving my card inquiringly. But I could not command my voice, and at last he spoke. "Well! I see it is Madame von Theill, for whom *M. le Colonel* has asked at Matsuyama. I had the pleasure to meet him but a few days ago. He is improving, they say, since his arrival, and since he learned that you were coming from Russia. It is a very long journey that you have made. You must telegraph him now from Kobe."

"I have, I have. But what—what—tell, tell me quickly the news of him, I implore you."

"Calm yourself, *Madame*. He is ill, he will recover. He has suffered much, but he is safely in the best hands now. A few wounds, some flesh wounds, you know. Many bandages and all that, but he is not in the quarter of the serious cases. His arm does not permit him to write, but he talks with much spirit, and he has begged me to charge myself with you when you shall have arrived in Kobe."

"Oh! Yes! You can go to Matsuyama and live there near him, and they will let you visit him each day. But first you must have a permit from the Minister of War. Have you such.? No? Then you must wait until it arrives, and in the meantime you can arrange for your *ménage* in Matsuyama. There are no foreign hotels there, in fact no good tea houses. There is a little community of American Protestant missionaries, and they will aid you."

I told how M—— was arranging for a courier-boy and cook, and that my maid was a *bonne à toute faire* herself, along with her many talents, and I begged to go at once.

"But, be tranquil, *Madame*. First, the permission. Then the steamer which will go from Kobe to the ports of Iyo province. There will be one on Monday evening, and for that you must wait. It is only five days, and you can send a telegram, and get direct answer from *M. le Colonel*. Ah! what pleasure for all those poor exiles to have you arrive! It will be a day of *fête* in Matsuyama for them to see a countrywoman again."

And then I dragged through long days, and longer nights, of suffocating heat. But, if it was hot for me in the foreign hotel, with all the accustomed comforts of Europe, what could it be for my poor sufferer so far away at the end of the Inland Sea? Each morning I went to the consulate to ask if the permission had come. Each morning, I sent a telegram to Vladimir, bought more stores and supplies. After all that Vladimir has endured in Manchuria, and suffered since, no amount of luxury can atone.

It seemed a good promise for other *agréments* of civilisation, when the consul told me I need not take lamps, since they had the electric light in Matsuyama. It seemed hard to believe that such a little place on the map, away down in the provinces of Shikoku Island, could be entirely up to date like that.

I was so dazed, so distracted that brief morning in Tokyo, that I hardly noticed Japan,—the new Japan—this modern Japan that has come up like magic in the years of my absence. There are the same bare-legged *coolies* in mushroom hats running their *jinrikishas* as before, but they run beside electric trams now; and we saw more carriages on the street those few hours in Tokyo than we used to see in a week or a month. The Japanese people continue to wear their own national dress more than I had expected they would, and the women still run around with their babies tied fast to their backs, and other babies play in the streets with still younger babies tied to their backs. It is a quaint, picturesque, charming Japan, to one who looks only at the tableaux of street life and sees no further.

But each time that I see here a Japanese soldier in uniform, something strikes me stone still—my heart stops, a terrible sense of dread, some kind of fear overpowers me; a sickening revolt at the idea of Vladimir shot, struck, wounded, and dragged in triumph, as a trophy of war, by such another soldier as that! Oh, it is maddening, sickening, horrible, humiliating, impossible. I never thought—no one can think—of these people as soldiers in the field, at war, like real soldiers, like the troops of a European country. And to be defeated by an army of these brown toys! Europeans to be held prisoners, helpless, beyond all remotest chance of escape by such Lilliputians as these! It is too much! War is fearful, war is hell indeed, as the Americans say. Many French people, in 1870, suffered misery and agonies of humiliation in being defeated and imprisoned by the enemy—but it was not a humiliation like this. Not this. Not this. I am sure I could stand it better if Vladimir were imprisoned anywhere else—by Germans, English, or Austrians, for they are our own race—even in Turkey, for the Turks are nearer to us, to me, to our customs, to the ways of Europe, of the West.

Yesterday, a train of soldiers on their way to the front was stopped on the railway embankment in the midst of the foreign settlement. There was a soldier's head or several heads out of each window; all were in new uniforms waving flags; and the streets were crowded with people waving more flags and cheering them—cheering them, with that peculiar *Banzai! Banzai! Banzai!* which they always shout with a rising note, both arms up- lifted, as if it were an invocation. It is as thrilling, as intense and vibrant of the martial spirit as the "*Aux Armes! Aux Armes!*" of the *Marseillaise*, and while under other conditions, in another war, elsewhere, it might fire me with a splendid, joyful enthusiasm, it deals me now blow upon blow, gives me shock, and sickening sense of misery. The cheers of a conqueror—of a triumphant people! and we! *The Russians!* the conquered ones! Defeated by Asiatics!

I find myself often wondering if in a few weeks I shall not be in Kobe again under other circumstances, cheering Russian troop-trains as they roll through the country and on to Tokyo! General Kuropatkin has promised that he will dictate the terms of the treaty of peace in Tokyo, and Admiral Alexeieff has promised everyone, for a year past, that he would give a New Year's ball in the Tokyo palace. Some sudden *coup* may even effect this. God grant it come soon!

But will anything ever atone to me or to Vladimir for his sufferings, and the agonies of humiliation of this present situation. For no matter how short a time it endures this Matsuyama incident in our lives is already graved and ground into the depths of my soul, with chagrin and bitterness unspeakable.

Tuesday, July 26th.

The official permit arrived. The consul himself brought it to me, and committing me to the charge of his assistant, embarked me on the tiny steamer. It was a suffocating afternoon. All the harbour was a grey blue, the hills were steeped in sodden grey and violet haze instead of shadows, and the very sky sulked in a dull, streaked canopy of weary clouds.

The consul and his assistant looked amazement at the mountain of boxes the courier was guarding. "Have you the intention of living in Matsuyama forever?" was the question. "God forbid!" my fervent answer.

The consul himself was sending down three pianos, a violin, a mandolin, and many stores—tea, red wine, and cognac for the miserables, so that all the visible cargo of the vessel seemed ours.

It was a trim modern little ship, with electric lights, electric bells, and boys, in the uniform and buttons of the European pages, to wait on one—and to prevent one from defiling the soft green velvet carpet of the salon with one's base, European shoes. In the comfortable straw chairs on the open deck we found air to breathe, when the little steamer got under way through the darkness that fell so fast. After the long summer evenings of Russia I had just left, there was always something sinister and uncanny in the early blackness that came upon the world of Japan, after the last clear beam of the sinking sun. It was always to me like an eclipse, or the terrible darkness that fell upon Pompeii at midday. We stopped in the night once or twice, and chattering passengers clattered off and on in their wooden clogs. The mosquitoes sang until my tiny white cabin rang and resounded like the box of a violin, and, at last, a misty, pale-pink and pearl dawn relieved me.

It was a day of enchantment that followed, if I had been in a mood to let myself be enchanted. We floated over silver seas and between emerald islets. It was a daydream of delicate, exquisite colour, the most poetic of landscape panoramas. We slipped into the tiniest harbours and through the narrowest channels. It was Norway in miniature, the Lofotens through the other end of an opera glass; but, at thought of the Lofotens, a lump came in my throat and Vladimir's face swam before my eyes blinded with tears. Ah, Vladimir! We were happy then. We did not dream of this.

The sea broadened out to lakes, it narrowed to the merest canals, between steep shores terraced far up the hillside with green rice fields; and a row of pine trees was silhouetted on each of the sky-lines of

23

the hills, like the stiff mane of a Norwegian pony. Each toy town or village had its granite sea wall and mole, its lighthouse and harbour buoys—civilisation in miniature, compact, complete. White police stations showed in the thick of the grey-walled, black-roofed houses, and the gabled gateways and great sweeping roofs of temples, rose from dense groves of old pines and camphor trees. Heavens! how romantically, theatrically, impossibly picturesque it all was! Ideal Arcadia—dreamland—a world's treasury of scenery. And I looked on with dull eyes and a cool pulse, my eye mechanically registering, my brain automatically judging and awarding the degree of excellence to the scene from long habit. How different has been my attitude, how wild my enthusiasm in Norway, the Crimea, the Caucasus, and in dear Italy, where, with Vladimir, there was the advantage of seeing with four eyes instead of with two eyes.

We hardly stopped before these towns of Lilliput. The whistle shrieked, the engine puffed a great sigh and stopped, and passengers and cargo went over one side into *sampans* and came up the other. We whistled and went on, the *sampans* lurching in the sudden wake. It was all so admirably done, so quietly and promptly, with such exact cooperation, that it began to dawn upon me how the army of pigmies have come to humiliate the army of giants. In contrast with these tidy and remote little villages of fishermen and rice farmers of the Inland Sea, far from any foreign settlement, I recalled the muddy streets and tumbledown houses, the dirt, misery, and ignorance of our pigsties of Russian villages, even quite near to Petersburg and Moscow. Hardly any village in China is as filthy, the people as ignorant and in as low a condition as in that Tula village of Yasnaya Polyana beside the country home of our great reformer and humbug, Count L. Tolstoi.

I wonder why the procession of foreign visitors who go to Yasnaya Polyana, who lavish adulation and hysterical praises upon that crass socialist and mischief-maker of his day, never think to look around them and use their reasoning powers. Would it not be the logical thing for Yasnaya Polyana to be the model village of Russia? Something cleaner than Edam or Markem? A little of that magnificent humanitarianism and benevolence poured upon that insanitary village on his own estates would be more practical, it seems to me, than the thin treacle of it spread over the whole universe. Talk is cheap in Yasnaya Polyana, and the *Grand Poseur* plays his part magnificently.

Every visitor goes away completely hypnotised, especially the Americans with their frothing about equality and the universal brotherhood of man. Universal grandmother! All men are just as equal as all noses or mouths are equal. The world gets older but learns nothing; and it cherishes delusions, and the same ones, just as it did in the time of the Greek philosophers. Leo Tolstoi might well have lived in a tub, or carried a lantern by day, like the most sensational and theatrical of the ancients. He is only a past master of *la réclame*, of the art of advertising. The *moujik* blouse and those delightful tableaux of a real nobleman shoemaking and haymaking, make his books sell. That is all. And, under the masquerading blouse of the humanitarian is the fine and perfumed linen of the dandy. Leo Tolstoi, the Beau Brummel of his corps, in my father's day—the dandy in *domino* today.

July 28th.

Alas! I am dragging this, as that day dragged its hours along on that ideal summer sea. The vice-consul read, but I could not put my mind on print. I found myself at the foot of a page without having read it; my eye had mechanically traversed words while my mind was elsewhere—thinking, thinking, trying to picture precisely the situation that would meet my eye at the journey's end, for I could not bore my companion continually with my questions about Matsuyama.

At another time, what a voyage of delight that might have been! Yachting on the Greek coast does not give one so much of pure landscape beauty. In one broad stretch of waters, the little steamer, so like a yacht, coursed head on to a green mountain slope, that showed at last a green fold in its front. There opened a channel, as we turned a right angle, and we entered it, passing a quaint little combination of lighthouse and temple clamped to its perpendicular rock angles. We swept into a channel as narrow as a river, where the tide raced and eddied in rapids; we swung around more green headlands and sharp corners, and came to in the fairway between two little towns whose black-tiled roofs ran high up the hillside. Enormous temples spread their great masses of roof tiles amidst billows of densest foliage. And the activity of these little places!

Hundreds of picturesque junks and hundreds of schooner-rigged craft showed two stages in navigation, and flotillas of small steamers rested at buoys, while a dozen whistled and clanked their way in and out. It was diverting and so beautifully picturesque. Only then I remembered and thought of my camera deep down in one of my boxes. I had been too busy and indifferent to care to use it in Kobe, and it was packed with the film roll in it where Natalie and I had snapped the tableaux at our garden *fête* for the Red Cross at Tsarskoe Cercle. But at the mention of camera, the vice-consul started violently.

"My God, *Madame*, a thousand times. No! No! No! Do not ever think of a camera, much less dare to use it, in Japan. In this Inland Sea, all this beautiful landscape so ideal, these hills so green and smiling, all is fortified. It is crowded with forts and guns. All are concealed, hidden under these curtains of foliage, these vines and terraces, in fair mask of beauty, and they wish no one to know it. If the most innocent traveller points a photographic machine, they think him a spy who has some knowledge of their secrets. I warn you to never use your machine while you are here."

This idea of the horrors of war, or rather of the engines of war that produce the horror being concealed in the midst of all this peaceful, smiling beauty gave me a chill of disillusionment. I had been saying before that it was altogether too perfect to be real, too theatrical to be useful and economic in common life. Now it seemed to me that all was false, all illusion, all painted scenery; and the deceptive landscape palled upon me. I had no thought save how a sheet of flame and white smoke might puff from a green hillside and our tiny ship go to splinters in a second like poor Makaroff's.

We went on through islands and more islands, and at noon came upon an astonishing sight. In the midst of little villages, tiny steamers, and slow-sailing *junks*, we were suddenly introduced to a great harbour filled with foreign ships, and ringed with great factories, workshops, and chimneys. Ten, twenty, forty, fifty ships came in sight. The long black ships were smoking lightly from every funnel; cargo was going in and out; and flotillas of *bateaux mouche* flew over the water. It was busy, lively, inspiring. "But what is this? What new port do we find here? This is as great a port as Kobe," I said.

"It is Ujina. These are army transports taking supplies and troops, and guns too—as you can see—over to Manchuria. Even now, those cannon, which they are hoisting to that ship's side, may be going to be turned upon the brave men at Port Arthur."

I groaned, half sick at the thought, and then was drawn to watch men in white *kimonos* and pastry-cooks' caps creeping slowly down the side of a white hospital ship, the Red Cross painted on its funnel. "Are those? Are those—" I could not finish the question.

"No, no, *Madame*, they are only Japanese wounded. The launches are towing now a queue of hospital *sampans* away toward the city. They take their own wounded to the hospitals in Hiroshima, over there. The poor Russians are separated at the quarantine depot and sent to Matsuyama. The Japanese do it well, you see, which is merciful. They have imitated all the ways of Europe very cleverly."

On the shore there were sheds and sheds in interminable rows, and *coolies* ran like files of ants with bales and boxes on their shoulders to drop them in cargo lighters.

"Ammunition," said the vice-consul, pointing to a lighter filled with small square deal boxes. And the idea gave me a sickening chill. "Those rolls you know are rice, of course. And that is charcoal, so that camp fires shall not show smoke. And those are cavalry horses. The Cossack of Japan is none too well mounted, you see." And sorry beasts they were, tended by small jockeys in uniform.

At last, we were seeing real signs of war, for in Tokyo, not a uniform, not a sentry, not a sign of the army had been visible, any more than in democratic, peaceful America. In Kobe, the soldier was rarely seen. He most often went past on railway trains at long intervals, and the war had seemed to me so unreal, so imaginary and mythical, even here in Japan, that my mind was strained in trying to comprehend and realise things. But here on the Inland Sea war was real, visible, tangible. There were uniforms everywhere, and swarms of men in khaki, who were invisible against the long lines of unpainted warehouses and straw-covered stores. Soldiers stood and gaped at us from the landing stage, and *gendarmes*, with enormously long swords, paraded, keen-eyed, up and down the planking to see what they might discover, whom they might arrest.

A military officer came down the pier, everyone bowing low and saluting; his face set in an inscrutable smile, his salutes automatic, his breast covered with medals, a great sabre clanking beside him. "It is a riding general," said the courier wisely; and the cavalry leader, with his staff, disappeared in the little green velvet salon. "He goes to Matsuyama to look-see the Russian *horios*. Then he goes to Tairen soon, on that ship over there. Her name is *Tairen Maru* now, but she used to be Russia's ship *Catherine*."

"Yes," said the vice-consul drily. "It is a popular tour now to go sightseeing to Matsuyama, to regard there the *horios*, the prisoners. And the ship, you know it? You heard about it doubtless? It is the *Ekaterinoslav*." And there was our huge volunteer ship, painted over with huge, white Japanese ideographs! And called a *Maru*. Could anything cut one deeper than to see one's own ships in bondage? And the *horios!* the prisoners! Vladimir a *horio!* And the dragoons going over to look at the *horios,* as if they were in a zoo!

"Where is this Tairen? In Korea?" I asked.

"Tairen? Tairen? Why, it is only the Chinese Talien. It is De Witte's town, Dalny," said the vice-consul. "They have renamed it, too."

In a few minutes' steaming we entered another bay whose shores smoked with the chimneys of many red brick factories. Verily, this is a new Japan with a vengeance. "The Naval Station, the arsenal of Kure," said the vice-consul; and the clatter of ship-builders' hammers filled the air. All this activity, all this European method and progress reduced me to dumb wonder and despair. Who had ever dreamed there was such a Japan hidden away in the little crannies of the Inland Sea? Could the legation in Tokyo have known this and not warned them in Petersburg? What was Wogack doing? Surely, there was not such an Ujina and Kure here in those days when we used to laugh so at Japan playing soldier before our windows! How often did our visitors say when looking on: "Do the little monkeys think they are ever going to have a real war, that they need keep up this farce of being soldiers and drilling?"

And I can remember when an English military man said the Japanese were like the Ghoorkas in India, the best fighting material in the world, that D—— said that "the whole little Japanese army could not stand against one regiment of Cossacks, if they ever came over to Saghalien, with their grievances. They would sweep them off. Ride them down, like *that!*" and D—— brushed cigar ashes off a lacquer table top with a flip of his fingers. And now, what have our dreaded Cossacks done since the war began, but retire? Ride away, ride fast and far from these wicked little yellow mites! Brobdingnagians on horses fleeing from the Lilliputians on foot! Oh! shame on them!

CHAPTER 4

Matsuyama, the Pine-Clad Hill

Sunday, July 31st.

For all my life I shall remember the series of petty incidents that marked that last day of my long journey from Petersburg. We seemed to drag our way slowly across the last stretch of azure sea, so like a mountain-girt lake. In the end we came slowly toward the green Shikoku shore, where a round hill stood up from the rice plain, midway between the mountain wall and the sea. It was crowned with one, of those fantastic Japanese *châteaux*, all white walls and black gabled roofs, cutting across and piled one above another.

"Matsuyama!" said the vice-consul at its first appearance; and then I could not take my eyes from it—from the goal of my journey, which had reached more than half around the earth. For weeks and weeks only that name had been on my mind and in my thoughts, and at last it had become reality. I was overcome with emotion and excitement, with almost fear of what the crowning moment might reveal. If my gaze could only pierce through those faraway, fairy-like roofs and walls, and see Vladimir lying there, what ease, what respite from my long tension of anxiety!

"Perhaps he watches the steamer approach," I ventured to suggest.

"But, no, *Madame*, the poor sufferers, none of the Russians, are up there at the *château*. They are in barracks on the level ground, at the left, quite at the foot of the hill. You cannot see the city yet. It is a ring city, quite surrounding the *château*, and we must cross three or four miles of rice plain by railway train. Such a railway! The tiniest miniscule of a railway—a string of *netsukes* is the train. I might hang the locomotive on my watch chain—a *breloque* merely. So droll."

I was breathless with excitement, as we landed and walked up the bank to the station. I wanted to run, to fly to the prison, at once. The

29

THE HILL WAS CROWNED WITH ONE OF THOSE FANTASTIC JAPANESE CHÂTEAUX

miniature train puffed in, and a populace in blue and white garments dismounted. I looked at them, and they all looked at me, especially the boy-vendor of cigarettes, whose stolid, bovine stare in my face for full ten minutes irritated me beyond words. Then we took our places and the train ran slowly and smokily toward the *château* on the high hill.

★★★★★★

I shut my eyes, and held the side of the *jinrikisha* tightly, as we coursed through a few streets, past a field and some bare spaces, and stopped at an open gate, where sentries stood with muskets and bandoliers. This was the first real soldier of the victorious army on actual duty that I had seen. He was a hard-faced old peasant in a patched and faded khaki uniform. The vice-consul presented his card and my permit, spoke amiably in Japanese, and the sentry grunted, "Huh!" Another old trooper took the cards, fingered them, showed them to his mates at the guard-house door, and slowly took his bow-legged way across the bare earthen court to a row of wooden warehouses or barrack buildings. All was new and raw, and carpenters were at work on other new buildings, at which the vice-consul lifted his shoulders. "More barracks. More barracks. *Mon Dieu,* again more prisoners!"

It was a strange experience to me, this standing outside the gates, with rustics in the road, and uniformed rustics within the gate, staring at me stolidly, woodenly, like so many ruminant cattle—in the same Japan where every gate used to swing wide open for us, every head to bend low, politely, respectfully, when we touched the circle of the government.

"But is it possible that these people do not know that you are the vice-consul of France? Have you not been here before? And did we not telegraph the coming in advance?"

"Oh, yes. But be tranquil, *madame,* a little of patience. These are the conquerors, you know. And since the Oriental cannot impress us by making a grand tour of many apartments, we shall arrive at the sensation of awe by waiting in humility at the outer entrance."

The bow-legged peasant in uniform returned towards the gate, stopped at a distance, and beckoned to us with his fingers to advance—quite as you summon a porter at a railway station. I was fortified then for anything that might happen in this changed Japan, my heart beating to suffocation, and my face burning with colour. We went along an endless covered *piazza* to the door of the chancery, a bare room, where clerks without coats wrote at many wooden tables, and the air was that of a furnace between thin wooden walls scorching in the

31

afternoon sun. A young Japanese ran forward, with head erect, in a bold, familiar manner, and took the vice-consul by the hand, to my utter amazement, and began stuttering a jargon of bad French. The vice-consul presented him.

"Ah, the companion of one of the prisoners!" said the youth, who it seems is the official interpreter, thrusting his hand out from where he stood a few paces from me. The tactful Frenchman moved forward, seized the hand, and effusively shook it a second time, and the blood that had been beating in my face so fiercely, ebbed back and back, and a chill struck my heart.

"She must have a permit, of course," said this recently uniformed *soshi*, staring at me with a *sangfroid* that far passed the plane of equality.

"She has one, which the guardian at the gate has brought here," said my French ally. "It is from the Minister of War, and I have yesterday telegraphed explanations to the commandant, and asked that, under the extreme circumstances, he will permit her to visit her husband immediately upon her arrival. Has he not informed the hospital?"

"Ah! perhaps. Yes, truly, he has. It is here," said the young autocrat, picking up the most prominent written sheet on his table, and with it my permit sent in from the gate. "She may go now," said the lordly one, and he almost waved us from his presence, but not before the vice-consul had recovered my official papers.

"Have the goodness, please, to send someone to *M. le Colonel* to announce that *Madame* has arrived at Matsuyama and will soon come to him. It is not good for him to have too strong a shock," said my brave man of France.

While a messenger in mule slippers went ahead, we followed slowly, my considerate Frenchman stopping now and then for a few moments, for I was gasping rather than breathing, a mist filled my eyes, and stumbling, I put out my other hand to steady myself against the walls and posts. I saw dimly white-robed hospital patients standing here and there, saluting; I toiled up a little slope of floor, the vice-consul lifted a white sheet of a curtain, released his arm, and dropped the white cloth between us.

A muffled, crying sob: "Sophia! Sophia!" and I flung myself by the wooden hospital cot I had come so far to reach. A head, shapeless with a swathing of white bandages, lay there; and from it looked the dear, dark eyes, but—shadowed with such depths of unutterable sadness, of woe unspeakable, the mute record of pain endured, and of a noble soul's humiliation, an agony more excruciating than any mere physical nerve vibrations.

Tuesday, August 2nd.

The vice-consul remained two days making his parochial calls, as he termed it, and making my position for me with the Japanese authorities. "It is beyond all your experiences, of course," he said, "but it is better that I present you formally at headquarters and have a precise understanding of the limits to which you must constrain yourself. Let it be written down now, how often you may visit the barracks, at what hours, and how long you may remain; whether you can visit other prisoners in the city; if you can go beyond certain limits in your promenades on foot and in *jinrikisha*; and the same privilege for your maid. Also, let it be understood that you will wish to come to Kobe to replenish stores for your household and for yourself. You will need a distraction, if you are long restrained to this hot little town, and the recovery of *M. le Colonel* you see is distant."

The military commandant, with whom I should have most relations, was after the German mode. He had the recurved *mustachios* of the *Kaiser*, guttural *ja's* and *ach's* dotted his remarks, and when anyone rapped at the door, he said "*Ho!*" in a way that should have brought a parade ground to salute and attention. It was agreed that I should visit the barracks from two until six o'clock each day, or Anna could go in my place for one hour. I could have wept with joy at this merciful dispensation, so far beyond all that I had expected.

The commandant gave me the addresses and prices of four houses, which I might rent. I had perfect liberty to move about the town; and apparently, the only restriction put upon me was that all my letters, correspondence, and telegrams must suffer the same censorship as if I were a prisoner of war. It was so liberal, just, and reasonable that I was not a little bewildered to find that nothing else was required. I was as free as any tourist or resident had been in the old passport days in the interior—as free, in fact, as in Russia. I could at any time obtain permits to visit the prisoners at the town hall and other places of detention on the two visitors' days of each week.

I was at the gate of the barracks enclosure at the stroke of two o'clock. The heat was intense, the sun glaring down on the treeless spaces that had been cultivated fields before the rows of wooden barracks had been erected. I dreaded the familiar contempt of the young jackanapes in the chancery, but he was humility and courtesy itself,

33

really Japanese after all; and he presented me to the chief-surgeon, a serious kindly man in spectacles, who was of the manner of old Japan, the exquisitely polite and refined Japan of the upper classes, of the court circle I used to know. I sat for a few minutes in his room while tea was brought and the courtesies passed between us, and then he went with me to Vladimir's ward. It was a comfort to have Vladimir in charge of such a man as this.

"The *Herr Colonel* is my most interesting case," said the chief surgeon, with a smile at this very professional view. "I shall expect him to improve rapidly now that you have arrived to care for him. Have you had any nurse's training?" I told him and Vladimir, in German, of all the serious work we had done in the Red Cross in Russia, for our soldiers at the front; of our lectures and practice classes, where we learned to bandage and to do regular hospital work.

"Yes, yes," he said, "our Japanese ladies are doing the same in Tokyo. Our empress spends several hours every day in nurse's dress, rolling bandages. She has sent several thousand rolls to be divided between the army and navy, and our grateful patients do really make miraculous progress when their wounds are dressed with Imperial bandages. We have to mark them to be washed and used, over and over again. So much can the mind cure."

I met all Vladimir's immediate confreres, and fellow sufferers, and the head nurse and an interpreter conducted me through the other wards, where there were Russians of every province, every arm of the service, every degree of rank, all suffering from grievous wounds, all bearing their pain so bravely. Poor fellows! Poor fellows! And you never even saw Bezobrazoff probably, nor heard of his wretched old timber claims! Yet, for that, you lie here and suffer, and go through life maimed! For Holy Russia's sake? No. For Bezobrazoff's schemes? Yes. And Alexeieff's. May the Japanese soon capture him!

It seems strange that in such a few days I should settle down to a routine of living as natural to me as if all my life I had known Matsuyama and the road around the moat to the barracks. My furniture soon found place in my little Japanese house, which looked upon the loveliest little *jardinette* I ever saw. There was a better house to be had, but it was far from the barracks, in the so-called court quarter of the town, where the old *daimio* had dwelt, and it had a yard just four feet wide and twenty feet long. Into that ribbon of land, however, were condensed all the features of a park-thickets, hedges, a pond, a rocky hillside, a bending pine and a pebbly beach. I have a clipped camellia hedge twenty feet high that shuts out other roofs and chimney tops, and above the shining camellia wall rises the pine-clad hill, with the fantastic castle gables running along its sky-line.

My four lower rooms bound two sides of the garden, the camellia hedge a third side, and the fourth is an arrangement of foliage with the thatched roof protecting the picturesque stone well-curb admirably placed for effect. The kitchen, baths, and servants' rooms are between my living rooms and the street wall. I have six rooms on the ground floor and four rooms above—a spacious mansion, as Japanese homes go. All my upper-floor rooms can be thrown into one, by removing the sliding *fusuma*, and if the papered lattices, or *shoji*, are removed I have an open pavilion, all three sides balconied to the air and only one solid back wall remaining. It is the most ideal of summer villas; but, if Vladimir were only here in the quiet and privacy of this *maisonette* and the landscape garden!

We cleared out all of the soft straw mats that hold so much dust, dampness, and fleas, and cannot be walked on with our rough foreign shoes, and laid down instead the fine straw matting that is made for the European market, all through these Inland Sea provinces. Beside the wicker furniture and beds that we brought from Kobe, Anna found other chairs here, and a clever carpenter has made her a deep, luxurious sofa, over whose back and seat of laced ropes she has fastened soft mattresses. She has found the most artistic blue and white printed cottons for covering her cushions and chairs; and every day on my return, I am led with pride to some new creation. The courier, who has proved himself an universal genius, has worked with a zeal equal to Anna's to equip us for comfortable European living, and quotes M—— and his hotel as the standard and paragon he must satisfy. In Kobe, we rummaged some really good old bits out of the trash the curio shops are now crammed with, and, quick to note my special passion for painted wood doors and golden *fusuma*, the courier has sent his scouts out through the province to find more treasures.

My little home is indeed charming, but who sees it? Who knows it, but myself and Anna? Vladimir asks daily about my *maison bijou*, and is amused by Anna's makeshifts and inventions. He warns me not to make myself too comfortable, not to settle down too entirely, or I may have to stay forever in Matsuyama.

One of the American ladies told me about the camellia hedge's blooming, and I wished that I might see it in December covered with huge pink blossoms. Vladimir's eyes flashed merrily as he regarded me and said: "Have a care! Have a care! Strike a piece of wood, quickly, or you will have the luck to see it in December. God forbid! Never camellia Japonica for me any more—never—never. You may wait here until December to see your *tsubaki* hedge bloom, but not I—not I. I hope to be well out of this, and have this flash-in-the-pan campaign over by that time. July! August! September! October! November! December! Six months? No! No! I could not support life that long here—impossible. Kuropatkin will have gotten on his feet by that time, and straightened things out. The campaign cannot last that long."

CHAPTER 5

The Barracks Hospital

August 5th.

Vladimir's eyes wore slowly away some of their sadness, and at times, when the early morning dressing of his wounds had been less painful than usual, a gaiety bubbled up from his heart, wit flashed with its old brilliancy, and humour played merrily upon even his own sad state.

"Ah! Sophia! Sophia! *Madame la prisonnière! L'Accusée de Quoi!* How can you lose the count of my mortal wounds? Can you not address your whole mind to it and remember that I am wounded forty-two times! Three perforations, a simple and a compound fracture, and a bone shattering; a scapula, a tibia, a cranial grafting; also a torn ligament, six cicatrices, ten cuts, twelve stabs, some slicings and contusions, and last, the right knee-cap, which is my X, the unknown quantity. I am 'Exhibit A, *Hors Concours*,' for any museum or college of surgery. The whole faculty could hold clinics over me, each specialist in turn. No need for chart, manikin, or cadaver. You should call the roll and check me off, all my casualties and deficiencies; put down a bamboo counter for every item of my disasters, as the *coolies* keep tally of their rice bags on the wharves. Hold up your left hand, Madame She-Who-Forgets, and count me over again on your fingers—carefully. Good! Well done! Repeat the enumeration once again from the beginning! Ah! Now backwards! The knee-cap, which is X, say it—say it—say it—Ah! *Bien!* you may yet win a prize." And with such nonsense, he cheered the hours.

"Sophia! Old Paul says he suffers from seven mortal diseases. Each one would kill him at once, if the lot of them did not quarrel among themselves as to which should have him first. So, at last, I am more than his rival !"

Several times I asked him how, where, he received all these terrible wounds, and he turned my questions. He would only say that it was near Haicheng.

"Ah, after a time, Sophia. After a time. Ah, God, do not make me think of it. It was too terrible. Paul there may tell you. Ask him. Ask Akimoff to bring his violin in here and let us have some music. Sing *Ave Maria*. He will accompany you. Oh! what ages since I have heard your voice." And so he continued to put me off, to turn the subject; and each day I hurriedly left the barracks at the last moment of grace, ignorant still of how it had happened.

"I will tell you, *Madame*," said Akimoff, when I went with him to inspect the kitchens. "It was at a conference at headquarters, and a little reconnaissance was wanted to develop the enemy's position. 'We must know if they are bearing down this valley road with this hill as objective,' said Mistschenko. 'Send some Cossacks off at once,' said the chief; and at once they began considering who should lead the scouting party. 'One daredevil young lieutenant will do,' says Kuropatkin, and Mistschenko names two to be summoned. But, at the end of an hour, the orderly returned to say that one of them could not be found at all. He had last gone down to the grand duke's headquarters, where there were always gay times at night, as at a cabaret or *Bal Bullier*, and from which they dare not summon him; and the other lieutenant was sick in his tent and could not stand on his feet. 'Ah! pigs! swine! Drunk, both of them. Vodka and champagne will lose us the whole campaign, if I cannot find a way to stop this thing soon. Whom can we send? Who knows what a map looks like or calls for, and knows enough to bring back the right news?'

"'Let me go, your Excellency,' said Von Theill. 'I used to be good at this sort of thing in Ferghana, you well know. Let me have an adventure again, for the fun of it, I beg. Paul Lessar and I were talking over our young adventures together only last month. Let me renew my youth.'

"'You! A staff colonel! A legal councillor and diplomatic secretary. You! lead a little band of Cossacks to reconnoitre a hillside at night! Oh! impossible! Wake up the other lieutenants; it is duty for them. Wake them all up, and I will take my choice. It will be good discipline for them.'

"'But, I beg of you, let me do it, let me do it,' the colonel had urged. 'I know the map. I understand exactly what you seek to know. Get me a lieutenant's coat, and I am off in ten minutes. I'll take the pickets whose horses are ready'; and, truly, with his pockets crammed with biscuits, he was off for the twenty-mile ride down the road. I did not see him again until we encountered at Matsuyama. One wounded Cossack, found the next day, told that the colonel had found the map wholly at fault; had ridden on and on until long after sunrise, before coming in touch with the enemy's scouts. Then turning, he rode his tired horses straight into an ambush of Japanese. They said he fought bravely, was wounded and unhorsed; but, bringing down a Kakamaki with every charge in his revolvers, he kept his surrounders at bay with his sword, until it was struck from his hand by the swing of a musket. Another blow left him senseless.

"When he first came to the hospital here, he used to wake up in the night screaming, having dreamed the scene over again, and seen the faces of the Japanese as they surrounded him, lunging with their bayonets and yelling like fiends. He said those faces would never be blotted out. Always he could see them, like the fiendish faces of some frightful Japanese masks he had once seen. If he had not resisted, you see; if he had surrendered when he saw it was all up, it would have been much better. As it was, they had to hack and batter him to pieces to capture him at all. It was magnificent, though. No quarter, no surrender—and he did not yield his sword. Oh! but Kuropatkin was in a fury when the word came back. He could not blame Mistschenko and himself enough for letting the colonel undertake such a mad enterprise, so out of all rank and order. They dreaded, too, what l'État Major and all Petersburg would say. Did they tell you in Petersburg how the commander himself was reprimanded for it?"

But no, there was nothing to ask but how to get to Matsuyama. To flee from Petersburg to Matsuyama direct was all that I had thought of in Russia, and the general staff were too cut up with the reprimand from Tsarskoe itself to dwell on the thing. Count Keller told Akimoff that he would rather have lost a regiment, than have had the thing happen.

All our wounded Russians, when captured and taken down to the Japanese hospital at Dalny, were there arrayed in clean white Japanese *kimonos*. These they wear still in the hospital wards, day and night. It is a dress well suited to this hot weather, but it is more or less becoming to some of our stalwart officers. Usually less so. Their arms and their ankles stick out too far, despite the extra sizes provided for the *horios*, and it is very much more an undress than *pajamas*. I feel embarrassed when I enter the ward, but we are in the closest intimacy and informality here, and I suppose I shall become used to it. The officers parade up and down the corridor upon which their alcoves of rooms open with perfect ease and *sangfroid*, as much at home as in top-boots and long-skirted coats. Here they live, two to each alcove, free to wander in and out and visit each other and go to adjoining wards, when they are able to walk. It is not my idea of a prison at all. Surely there is the fullest liberty within the barracks. There are no fetters, no restrictions. Everything is plain to a degree; simple, hygienic, and clean; and when I consider and sum up all these things, I wonder if there is anything at all to complain of. The prisoners' lot could not well be a happier one, and I, for one, would less willingly be a prisoner-of-war in some places I can think of in Russia.

CHAPTER 6

The Red Cross of Japan

August 6th.

The little Red Cross nurses in the hospital are a daily wonder to me, their ability a revelation and a surprise. Long ago, I used to meet Japanese great ladies of the court circles in Tokyo, who spoke only Japanese, and very few words even in that language. A visit was chiefly an affair of who could make the most bows in ten minutes. The Japanese ladies, then in their first foreign clothes, were automatons only, wooden, stolid, impassive. *Harem* visits in Cospoli are a wild excitement, intellectual feasts, beside the miserable quarter-hours of my official visits in Tokyo. And official dinners! Ah, me! My pantomime partners and the dumb great ladies at the funereal dinners at the ministries! Only one thing ever saved the day, or the night, and that was that the menus and the wines were always irreproachable; the Japanese having a most exaggerated regard for the obligations of hospitality and a jealous sensitiveness lest they fall below the highest European standards at a feast. They could command food and wine in the open market, but wit and liveliness, gaiety and "go" cannot be commanded anywhere when the chairs are filled with people chosen only by rank. I have suffered also in Rome.

Repression and self-effacement have been ground into the women of the race for such uncounted generations, that it will take several generations of education to give them any social emancipation and courage. Even the Protestant missionaries in Matsuyama, English and Americans, who called on me as soon as I arrived, say that the war has already worked wonders for Japanese women; that the active work of the Red Cross has called out the women of all classes from their homes; that the men have had to confer with and work with them on a plane of equality, and in such public works the superior brains

41

and ability of the women have often been conspicuous. It has been a wholesome experience for the men of Japan, and in this Red Cross Society of a million members, some of the old traditions are receiving hard blows. Under the news laws, a few Japanese women control their own great fortunes and administer great estates, and their cooperation and leadership in Red Cross work are eagerly sought.

The thousands of trained nurses of the Red Cross are for the time a part of the military establishment, they have military rank and discipline, and through that nearly enjoy equality with the men workers; the surgeons must rely upon, confer with, and work with them on new lines, regarding them as human beings possessed of individual souls. Much enlightenment in this regard has come to Japanese men through the war, but it will take some generations for them to acquire the instinctive deference to women, the sense of chivalry which prompts European men to show consideration to women because they are women. *Bushido* is a fine moral creed and cult for the warrior, but women have no part in *Bushido*, and romantic love has no place in the Japanese school of chivalry.

The Red Cross nurses had three years of hard training in the schools for nurses before they received diplomas, and had good hospital practice before they came here. These at the barracks hospital are the cheeriest, most capable little things I know. They never seem tired, although they never rest. They are never cross or impatient, but always smiling, exquisitely polite. Even when bandaging, they make little ducks with their heads in lieu of bows, and say their regretful *Gomen nasai* (I beg your pardon) whenever the patient groans. In their immaculate white dresses, caps, and stockinged feet, they are refreshment to the eye on these hot days. They are like children beside the huge Cossacks they care for—very precocious children, when one observes their skill and courage in the operating room. They seem to humour and charm their patients with indulgence, yet they are martinets in their precise obedience to surgeon's orders. The patient is never crossed, yet he always obeys too. It is the old, old story of the hypnotic East. The big Cossacks cry bitterly when their nurses are changed.

Vladimir insists that only the wise, kind, cheerful chief nurse of the hospital-ship kept life, or hope of life in him, during the agonising days on the Yellow Sea. His nurse here is a little mite of a thing with rosy cheeks and soft sympathetic black eyes. *Nesan*, some of the officers, who had known Japanese tea houses, called her, and she is known now by no other name. I find that her name is O'Shige San; that she came from Meguro near Tokyo, and received her nurse's diploma from the hands of the empress herself at the Red Cross hospital in Tokyo. I find Japanese words and phrases coming back to me after all these years, as I try to talk with her. I shall begin studying Japanese at once again, as it will be helpful, and the lessons will fill the long morning hours, when I cannot be with Vladimir.

I wanted to do something for O'Shige San, but of course I could not make her a money present, and as the nurses wear their white uniform in the hospital, and a black dress, bonnet, and military coat when travelling, there is no use to give her the pretty *obis* and *kimonos* that one usually presents in Japan. Vladimir suggests that I make a contribution to the Red Cross Society and to the Volunteer Nurses' Society, composed of Japanese ladies of position, who take hospital training and relieve the overworked Red Cross nurses. These volunteers wear the prescribed dress and do all of a nurse's daily duties, roll bandages and arrange supplies, meet hospital trains and ships.

I made an appointment to call upon the governor's wife, and gave her the five hundred *roubles* for the Red Cross, and five hundred for the Volunteer Nurses, as a little thank-offering from a grateful Russian. She was very quiet and formally correct, and with exquisite courtesy accepted and thanked me, through the interpreter. She was the aristocrat, the *grande dame*, to her delicate finger-tips. She had soft, kind eyes, and in her calm was not so wooden as those of her class whom I used to meet; but there was a chasm between us. She, the real woman, whom I would like to know, was far-away, unattainable, close shut in the conventions as in her cool, dove-coloured silk *kimono*.

Then the governor himself came into the interview, and the atmosphere became more sympathetic to me. He had been in Russia years ago, and had kept up his study of Russian ever since. He was sorry that he did not feel at liberty to go oftener to the hospital and the places of detention, as he should greatly enjoy the society of so many cultivated foreigners at this remote post of duty, I easily understood, that in time of war the civil officials must refrain from embarrassing or interfering with the military in any way. He could further anyone else doing things for the Russians, but he must avoid for himself any direct attentions beyond the severest lines of etiquette. He begged me to come to him or send at once, if any need or want arose; and to feel quite safe and sure that he had me in the especial care and keeping of his officials.

He assured me that my little paper and bamboo house was guarded night and day beyond all chance of harm or intrusion; and he only advised that during the next week, when the town would be full of country people saying farewell to the departing regiments, I should not go about the streets any more than necessary. He would be distressed if any ignorant rustic should offer rudeness to me in his prefecture. "I think all the Matsuyama people know you, and admire so much your coming this long way to care for your wounded husband; but the country people are very ignorant, and might be impolite."

A few days later, ladies from the two societies came to see me, and after the first salutations and the first sip of tea, there was life enough in them. They had accepted a portion of my fund as a subscription for life membership in both societies. They accepted the rest as a gift, and they brought me the beautifully written certificates and the badges to wear. They were more animated and alert than any Japanese ladies I had met before; and I found that they were the wives of Japanese officers who had gone to the front, wives of local officials, and wives of rich merchants and landowners, all leading spirits and active workers in their missions of mercy. One of them was the daughter of the old *daimio*. Her, they mentioned in awestruck tones, but I could not distinguish her from the half-dozen prim little women in shadow-, and cloud-, and mist-coloured silk and crape *kimonos*, who sat on the edges of my foreign chairs, with hands and fingers in the precise pose of Japanese good form.

They made cordial and sympathetic speeches, full of nice feeling to me the stranger, who was to be as a guest and sister to each one. They were nice; they were true gentlewomen; they were sincere, and I liked them. Every week, they leave their beautiful homes and picture gardens, and go to look upon wounds and agonised faces at the hospitals all day long; bandaging, dressing, feeding, and tending their own Japanese soldiers, and also our poor Russians. I felt drawn to them at once, as I never did to the great ladies in Tokyo, and I am sure we shall be real friends—especially one little grey wren of a woman, whose gentle eyes and smile made hers the most attractive Japanese face I have ever seen. She noted my garden row of blooming plants and dwarf pines, bought from the grizzled old gardener who waits for me at the gate every afternoon when I come home, and she begged me to come to her garden—to come at six o'clock any morning and see her *asagaos* (*convolvuli*). This is surely the land of early rising.

I went to the hospital the next day, wearing all of my new decorations with my Russian Red Cross badges; and, from the first sentry at the gate to Vladimir, the row of buttons and medals across my white dress front created a grand sensation.

I waited for Vladimir to say something; and in silence I watched the humour rise and twinkle in his eyes. The fun bubbled and bubbled, and finally flashed out, as he smiled broadly and asked, "For the love of the Lord, Sophia, where did you get all those orders? Have you been to the little shop in the Palais Royal? And what are they? For merit, for deeds of valour, for good conduct, for standing around while an ambassador signed his name, or a grand duchess descended from a railway carriage, or for good roubles laid in the Japanese palm? I am not a shadow beside you in my gala uniform. You are, as the English officers say, decked out like a Christmas tree. Would you like Akimoff's St. George, or Drachenberg's St. Anne to help out?"

And he called them all in to see me, the *chevalier* of the Red Cross! The commandant of Volunteer Nurses! He bade them go tell little Sienkiewicz to come and see me wearing full dress and ordinary decorations, grand cordons and small buttons all at once, at the same time, side by side; for Sienkiewicz would rise from his cot, plaster-bound, bandaged, with his leg in splints, as he was, with the horror of it, they knew. The son is the father all over again, only more so; and splits the hairs of court etiquette and regulations here in prison, as if he were the old count safely at peace in the bureau of decorations in Petersburg.

With all the fun they made of me, and the amusement it furnished them to see a loyal Russian wearing the Japanese Imperial Chrysanthemums and Phoenix over my heart, Vladimir was pleased with what I had done.

I fear I did look like those wrinkled old sentries, second-reserve men, who wear all their China War, Boxer Expedition, valour and sharpshooter medals as they stand sullenly guarding prisoners here, instead of winning more medals in Manchuria. Poor veterans! We do not see here the fine flower, or even the average of the active army of Japan, which is doing such inexplicable things in the field. If all their officers and men in Manchuria were as these we come in contact with in Matsuyama, our Russian troops could tell a better tale.

No ambitious soldier can be satisfied to stay back here and protect the enemy. Oh, no! Unfortunately, we see most the petty Japan of the petty officials, the surly Japan of the disappointed old third-reservists. The *preux chevaliers*, the true followers of *Bushido*, the knightly creed

45

of Japan, are busy elsewhere, over in Manchuria—all save the surgeon-in-chief. He is mercifully left with us, as type and living example of Japan's best.

CHAPTER 7

The Doyo

Wednesday, August 10th.

It has been for years my role to act as special advocate, defender, and expounder of the Japanese, with Vladimir often taking sides against me and finding a certain delight in teasing and goading me on to the most extreme and extravagant statements, in my zeal and partisanship. How often have I stopped breathless, with crimson cheeks and moist forehead, after a bout with my fun-loving tormentor or the dear circle in Rome, on the everlasting topic of Japan! I have declared the Japanese to be the people of the future; Japanese art, Asia's last and best gift to the world's civilisation. But after Alexeieff assumed his calamitous viceroyship, and relations became tense between Russia and Japan, the subject was taboo for me, and I had to sit still and silent while the most abominable slanders and misconceptions were bandied about me. There were many awkward moments for me in Petersburg, when some malicious or tactless woman, like Sophia A——, for instance, said: "But of course, Sophia Ivanovna does not agree with us. She has always loved and praised the Japanese, and thinks them the only perfect people on earth. Is it not so?"

"I knew many good people in Japan, when I lived there, but it was many years ago. I cannot say that I know any of these Komuras, and Katsuras and Kurinos, who have made so much trouble with Russian affairs; and it may be that Japan has entirely changed now, with all the new ways they have adopted. They are much like Europeans today, I hear." This was as much as I could say in reply. I wanted to say: "They are not savages, believe me. They have religions of their own; there are many Christians; they possess a unique, special, and high civilisation of their own, and if they borrowed, they did not borrow nor copy their philosophy, their jurisprudence, and their arts from Greece or Rome as North Europe did. Read their book *Bushido*, for the code of the samurai, and you will see that our army is meeting an honourable foe, an enemy which demands great generalship to defeat."

Deep down in their inscrutable hearts, the Japanese soldiers feel themselves consecrated as to a religious cause, when they go to war for their emperor, who is to them still a sacred being, the Sun God, divinely descended to earth. I know how high is the principle and how unselfish the abandon with which Vladimir went to this war; and I know how differently, from what other motives other officers went to Manchuria. And the rank and file? Have the *mujiks* in our wheat fields the same enlightenment, the same comprehensions of any such warrior's creed as this *Bushido*, which the toilers in the rice fields and the *jinrikisha coolies* know, and can expound to one?"

Now Vladimir begs me to talk more about Japan, to explain *Bushido* and other things to Akimoff and D——, who have the strangest notions. Despite the fury of those first weeks in Petersburg, and the exciting weeks in Manchuria, Vladimir can still see with clear impartial discerning eyes the real, true Japan that surrounds him in this far province. He realises that they are people, human beings, although he and the other Russian sufferers saw little of Japan as they were carried off and on hospital ships on stretchers, and through the streets. But, from that bird's-eye glimpse and their acquaintance with the doctors, nurses, and attendants, the hot-heads know it all—the country, the people, the national character and ideals, social institutions and home life—all—everything.

And there is no use to contradict them. They cannot be misinformed. They know things by their own second sight and intuitions, evidently. Dr. Rein, the German savant, is a babe and a tyro beside them; and Lafcadio Hearn, the one true expounder of this human mystery, Japan, is a visionary, they say. These swashbuckling young Cossacks are convinced of the inherent savagery and cruelty of the Japanese people. They cannot distinguish between them and the Chinese, and several times they have recounted things the Chinese did during the Boxer Rebellion, as things that happened in Japan: "Well," say they, "may be the Chinese did do it that particular time, but the Japanese will do it, too. They are not a bit different. The same race, the same race! One wears a pigtail and the other does not. That is all."

It is useless to try to do anything with such wrong-headed people, but Vladimir begs me to be patient with them a little longer and try to convince them that all Japan is not waiting to torture and slaughter

48

them, and that their lives do not hang by a slender thread. They really believe that the continual presence of an Italian gunboat in the Straits of Shimonoseki is the only guarantee of their lives being spared. These tell me, that in the event of an uprising, that Italian gunboat will come and in the name of all Europe demand the Russian prisoners and take them in safe keeping. I know the size of Italian gunboats in the Pacific, and I laugh, remembering those fleets of huge ships at Ujina and Kure—also our converted volunteer ships in Japanese hands.

"Why should the Japanese rise and slaughter these unarmed prisoners in Matsuyama?" I ask.

"Oh! You see, when the turn comes and we are winning all the victories, then the Japanese will be crazed by their continual defeats and make a savage onslaught on any Russian they can see—kill every European on their islands."

I laughed at the absurd notions, and Akimoff was almost offended, and said I laughed at the idea of a Russian victory!

"*Mon Dieu!* She is right. I laugh, too, at the idea of those asses, those fools, those imbeciles, at Liaoyang ever crying *Pobieda! Pobieda!* (Victory! Victory!)" cried an irate old officer.

Soon after I arrived we learned of the raids of the Vladivostok ships down to the mouth of Tokyo Bay, where they sank and captured merchant ships at their will. All the Japanese warships were ranged in front of Port Arthur, and the coasts of Japan lay at our mercy.

"More's the pity," Hansen says, "that they did not sail in and destroy the railway wherever it came near the shores, drop a shell into the shrines of Ise, and sow the mouth of Tokyo Bay so full of mines that no ships would dare sail there while the war lasted." He thinks of nothing but the loss of Makaroff and the *Petropavlovsk*, poor man, and they begin to think that his mind is affected, unhinged first by the shock and horror of that experience, and then by the night of horror when he floated in a typhoon sea, when the junk by which he was escaping with despatches from Port Arthur to Chefoo was blown up by a mine just as a Japanese torpedo boat overhauled it.

When he heard that Skrydloff's ships had been ravaging the coast and preparing to land and effect the rescue of these Matsuyama prisoners, he lay awake all night. When he dozed by day, he begged the others to wake him if the welcome sound of Skrydloff's guns were heard. "More likely the shrieks of the mob coming to murder us before Skrydloff's men can reach us. But we will make a fight for our lives then," he says grimly.

49

Now Hansen has settled into a gloomy, sombre mood, lying for hours with his face covered, making no sound or answer. "God grant he does not go insane here," sighs Vladimir. "There is enough without that. This *doyo*, the very hottest part of summer, is when most people do lose their reason."

The sun burns by day and the nights are breathless. Only the thick, thatched roofs save the thin wooden barracks from being so many ovens, and the merciful darkness comes as early as in the tropics. This is the weather that is good for the rice crop, and if the fateful hundredth day passes without typhoon, the kernels of grain will be formed and will stand any further storms. The promise is for the greatest rice crop ever known, something to surpass the great crop of last year which the peasants said was a sign from the gods to go to war. I suppose a great crop this year will mean to continue the war. And we in Russia? What crops are they gathering there? What signs from the gods for us?

Sunday, August 14th.

Last night there was a *Banzai*, that is an illumination of the houses with strings of lanterns, and a lantern procession to celebrate the naval victory they claim was won just outside Shimonoseki. The *major-domo* of my household says the Japanese sunk the *Rurik*, and captured all the crew. I do not believe it.

It was a beautiful sight, and Anna and I went to the upper rooms, when the shouting told that the procession was near our gate. We looked out through the gap in the house roofs to the long line of the moat reflecting the rows of red lanterns that hung along the eaves and doubling every lantern that moved along the highway.

But what sorrow the gay sight drove to my heart! How the shrill, ecstatic cries of *Banzai! Banzai! Banzai!* always three times in succession, made me wail with misery, with anguish for my country's disaster; made me realise that the day of victory and peace is yet further removed.

It was my one wish that Vladimir and the poor sufferers in the hospital would not hear all the chorus of rejoicing voices and the discordant blare of fifes and drums; but it seems that the procession did march entirely around the barracks compound. The prisoners heard and knew that it signified fresh sorrows for Russia.

Today, every patient is worse, fevers are higher, wounds inflamed, and nerves worn by a sleepless night. With Vladimir, every shattered nerve is on edge; each sound and jar is pain; his head burns, and the wounds throb through their bandages.

"And I lie here, a helpless hulk of flesh! the wreck of a man, who must listen to jeers at Russia's defeats!" he exclaims, with tears burning in his eyes. "Ah! why have I lived for this? Why do I wish to live?"

Hansen roamed the ward all night, raging like an angry wolf, grinding his teeth, tossing his arms, and making efforts to break away and grapple with the celebrants outside. Today, he lies scowling on his cot, his face covered with a fan half the time, although it is a day of great heat. It seemed to me that I could not refrain from going to protest to the surgeons against such inhumanity to helpless, wounded, suffering men, as was committed last night; but Vladimir, moaning and beating with his fingers on my hand, as waves of pain swept through him, besought me not to speak of it.

"No, no, Sophia. It is better to endure. Perhaps you will want to protest later on for something else. Keep peace, keep friends. The surgeons and nurses like you, you know. They will not, if you see things, or say things. That was a touch of their *Bushido* last night. Show your *Bushido*, and do not refer to it."

But I left with sorrow and walked home in depression from the gate where Anna was waiting to walk with me. "Watanabe wishes to go the first of September," she told me. "He says the tourists will be coming then, and he wishes to get a travel engagement."

"But what shall we do without him?" I cried almost in fright, for it seemed that disasters were heaping upon me; that more and worse would follow. "How shall we get on without our courier as interpreter? How shall we manage with the police visits and all.? No, no. He cannot go."

"But, *Madame*, we shall manage perfectly without him. The butler and the cook are both very discontented that he stays. He really absorbs much of the profits which would come to them. I do not like him. He is too much the spy. I fear he may like to make sensations, since it is so dull here for him. *Madame* knows the Japanese language now."

He brought me a Karatsu tea bowl as a farewell present, and when I added it to my shelf of tea bowls, and sighed to think it might be the last of the same *Tien hai* quality, he assured me that his friend, the curio dealer, would continue to bring to me any choice pottery pieces, and that he would soon have some from Tosa and Bungo provinces. I expressed fear that the many officers now here might prove rivals, and Watanabe struck an attitude and said scornfully: "Oh! these officers here do not know, unless you educate them yourself. They are just like tourists. We can sell them anything, if we make it a big price and tell them it came from old *daimio's* go-down; or from someone whose only son is killed in war; or some rich man who wants to buy war bonds. They don't know anything about the real articles of Japan, those other *horios*."

I would like to tell that to Vladimir's visitors from the Kokaido; who, having been in Nagasaki once or twice on ships, know all of Japanese art and preach Japanese art, *de haut en bas*, to us at the barracks.

Before Watanabe left, he had the pleasure of ushering in and serving tea to the governor and his wife. During the visit, the dignitary expressed regret for the procession that passed by the barracks and jeered outside the Kokaido. "It shall not happen again," he said. "The chief surgeon is quite angry that the city people should be so unkind to his sick foreigners. You will hear it here at your house, of course, when there is a *Banzai*, but the wounded soldiers shall not be wakened and made unhappy again. The common people do not always think, you know. You must excuse them, that they seem so impolite. You will tell me also if anyone is impolite here at your house, or in the street. We want to do every kindness to you in Matsuyama."

Somehow, something, homesickness, over-sensitive nerves or morbidity, made this bit of chivalry and sympathy so touching to me, that I could not keep back the tears in telling the governor how kind he was, and also the chief-surgeon, and all with whom I had anything to do in Matsuyama. "It is so far beyond any kindness I had ever dreamed of. I only wish my friends in Russia could know all the consideration and courtesy shown me here."

"Yes," said the governor, sighing, "I dare say the people in Russia have a very wrong idea of us in every way. Because we are not of their skin and their religion, they think we are all uncivilised and barbarous as the Turcoman tribes. Perhaps the war will have one good result in making the two nations acquainted."

How I admired those two! Aristocrats to the finger-tips, cultivated, courteous, refined, with a dignity of manner incomparable. While I puffed and fanned, in the thinnest of lingerie blouses, the Japanese *grande dame* sat cool and calm in a grey silk *kimono*, girt around the body with double folds of a heavy brocaded satin *obi*. She was a harmony of soft silver grey and sheeny dove colours. There was a glint of gold in the stiff fabric of her *obi*, a tiny gold clasp on the cord that

52

bound the *obi* in place. A single amber shell pin was thrust in her hair, and the head and neck, perfect in their lines, in the massing and relief of black and ivory, stood out from the surplice folds of the *kimono* like a superb etching. As a work of art, she was perfection, a restful, perfectly composed and balanced study; the tones and values true. I gazed at her enchanted, and thought how different this *grande dame* before me from the vulgar travesty of the Japanese woman that parades our stage. Think of those plays we saw in London! the *Madame Butterfly*, and *The Darling of the Gods!* What a million miles between this *daimio's* daughter and that giggling *hoyden* with frizzled hair and cabbage bunches of flowers over each ear! No, Europe does not understand Japan. Despite all these years of travel and photography, Europe does not yet know what a Japanese lady looks like, how she dresses, nor least of all how exquisitely smooth and simple is her *coiffure*.

Chapter 8

The "Rurik's" Men

Tuesday, August 16th.

Another disaster! The saints seem arrayed against us. Stackelberg's corps has been defeated, routed, driven back from its march south to relieve Port Arthur! The prisoners arrived this morning with a budget of news. The relief of Port Arthur would be a step towards our relief, and now our hopes are set back many weeks.

However, I am here with Vladimir now. He lives. He can speak. I can do for him, and be with him; and I find that I have so much to be thankful for in these instances that I do not fret myself about rescue. I shall be glad when it comes, and oh! Vladimir, too. If he is only able to move about and walk, and able to go to Kobe, and on board a mail steamer, when the relief comes. *When* it comes! Yes. When?

It is true. There *was* a naval battle. The *Rurik* was sunk, and the officers have all arrived here. None would believe the accounts read in the Japanese papers, but the English newspapers from Kobe tell it, and Russia's sorrow is complete. "Plenty *horios* come today," said the maid when she ushered in my Japanese teacher in the morning. "Will missis go with Red Cross ladies to Takahama today? All ladies go eleven o'clock train to see prisoners." But I could not think of such a thing, as a sightseeing trip. It seemed to shock and offend me greatly, that the Japanese ladies were going down to the steamer landing to watch and to look at our poor wounded Russians until I remembered what service these Red Cross members render.

As I passed the operating room on my way to my own ward in the afternoon, they were taking away two litters. One face looked familiar, possibly only the fair-haired, Courland type, and when the little sister of charity smiled her cheerful greeting and said: "*Rurik sans,*" the lump in my throat made me look away. In Vladimir's ward, all was excitement over the arrivals and their sad news. The vice-commander of the unhappy *Rurik* was in Akimoff's room, where the others had gathered, and we could hear the slow, sad monotone of a sick man's voice, as someone related a long, long story which no one interrupted.

"How I wish I could hear them," said poor Vladimir. "Go, Sophia, and ask them to let you listen for me. They will, they will. They say Von Woerffel was on the *Rurik*, and badly wounded. Ask them. They put him on a cork mattress and threw him over, and so he was saved. Those Japanese picked up every man from the *Rurik*, the whole six hundred of them. Of course, we prisoners are their assets, their gold reserve, their pawns and chips in the game. We are as good for exchange and quotations as bonds or gold. Oh! God! to think that I—I, myself—my own poor body has its daily market value in this stock-gamble of nations! Bid, Sophia, bid! Make your game, gentlemen! Make your game! What am I worth? What do you give, give, give?"

"Von Woerffel! Impossible!" I said. "He is still in Petersburg, Vladimir, or at Cronstadt, rather. I saw him the very day I left. He could not have joined the fleet at Vladivostok in this time, surely. He was complaining that his admiral would not let him go to the Pacific. But, Vladimir," I cried, jumping to my feet. "He is here now. I saw him. It was he, of course. They were taking him from the operating room. I saw the side-face only, in bandages. Oh! to think that I have passed him by!"

Poor Von Woerffel lay in the next ward, his face whiter than the bandages, whiter than the pillows. How changed from the alert and trim young fellow in spotless uniform, who had talked with me on the Quai des Anglais such a few weeks ago! He was amazed at the idea of my going to Japan, and at my courage in taking the long journey into the enemy's country. How gaily he had said: "*Au revoir*, I hope to meet you in Japan. The Vladivostok fleet will not let our brave officers linger in sea-coast prisons. We will make a sortie while those poor rats sit in their trap in Port Arthur and do nothing. We will come to your rescue. *La Revanche* is for us."

And now we meet in Matsuyama! What irony of fate! What sarcasm in prophecy! What sorrow and humiliation!

"Mikail Ivanovitch, are you sleeping?" I asked quietly, and he opened his eyes, stared a full minute, shut them, and again looked at me, without a word. "How is it that you are here? Sophia von Theill! Sophia von Theill! But why are you dressed like these Japanese women? Yes, you were leaving for Japan when I saw you on the quay. And

I too have come to Japan. Direct to Japan! From Petersburg to Matsuyama in twenty-seven days! I only had two days in Vladivostok, and then in two days more, we—we—oh—our ship was sinking—and we were all made prisoners; it was better than drowning—perhaps. And I am here, you see. But Vladimir? How do you find him?"

"Ah! a wreck. So maimed, so crippled, I cannot hope hardly that he will ever be himself again. You will find some old acquaintances here. Others, like yourself, came from Petersburg to Matsuyama direct—straight to the arms of the enemy. There are even some traitor Poles and some political exiles who were permitted to volunteer for Siberian regiments, who have intentionally surrendered to the Japanese. One even surrendered to Japanese hospital nurses! to stretcher-bearers! When they showed him there was no one with hands free to accept his sword even, he took a bearer's place in carrying the stretcher and let the hospital *coolie* have the sword. Paul Akimoff was in the stretcher, half dead from a wound, but not too dead to see and hear that. Akimoff lives to give that miscreant his dues, as much as for the great revenge—revenge for being a prisoner of war.

"Yes. The army and navy are full of traitors. I had no idea what the army was like until I came across Siberia. I may have seen four officers on the way to the front who were not drunk, but not more than four. It is one long champagne and vodka carouse from the Urals to the Amur. All are quarrelling and trying to displace and circumvent one another, when they get half sober. None of them will work together. Each balks and undoes the other's work. Each one is struggling for promotion, decorations, or the commander's favour—or the viceroy's, which seems more important. The real war is at headquarters. The Japanese cannot undo us as quickly as this dual authority will, if Nicholas does not soon put an end to it, and send one or the other home. Vladivostok and the fleet are ringing with the scandalous conduct of the army. No discipline, no order—a pack of drunken officers, who do not know their duties, or anything else.

"It made me sick to reach Vladivostok and hear of the glorious cruise Skrydloff's fleet had made down the Japanese coast. That was before my arrival. They sank everything that came along, even one British ship that may make us a war with England yet. The ships went near enough to see the smoke and the lights of Tokyo, and if they had had time they would have come around here and carried off the prisoners. I hoped I was going to be in for a trip of that kind, when we put out of Vladivostok and headed south; but instead, we ran alongside the whole Japanese fleet and their infernal gunnery rained shells on the poor *Rurik*, until it was all up with us. The roar of the Japanese shells drove the breath and life out of me; and every roar meant the wreck of some part of the ship, the slaughtering of more men on deck. Ugh! I stepped over blood and corpses, and stepped on blood and corpses; wiped my face when it was spattered with flesh and blood of my nearest comrades; and threw overboard, once, a mangled arm that minute torn from a sailor's body, the fingers moving as it fell to the water.

"Oh! We tried to run for the Korean coast and beach the ship. We could not. The engines were injured, and the last one beat, beat, beat, so slowly—stopped—the pumps stopped—and then, but for some one rolling me over on a mattress and lashing me fast, I should not be here. Here! Here! In a Japanese prison! I don't know that it is so much to be alive after all. Better those who died in the fight; who do not know how it feels to be a prisoner. A prisoner! A captive behind Japanese bayonets.

"The *Rurik* had come down to meet the Port Arthur fleet, which had been ordered to break out and run for Vladivostok. Our *flotte peureuse* lived up to its record, and ran. It was too hot; the sun was in his eyes; an admiral had forgotten his toilet vinegar, or something equally momentous; so, as soon as that demon of a Togo came at him, they cut and ran for the home harbour, like a pack of children playing at war. Now they are all safe, if not too comfortable, under the guns of Viterbo's forts again—all except the few ships that got away to Kiochao and Shanghai. They blame Alexeieff for everything. He and Starke had let things run to such a pass that Makaroff said it would need a year for him to make it a fighting fleet. It was good for a gala parade, and birthday salutes only. Bah! Better that we had never tried to be a naval power and to have fleets than have these fiascos. War is an entertaining spectacle—if one remains the passive spectator."

CHAPTER 9

The Czarevitch

Wednesday, August 17th.

Today we Russians are rejoicing over good news. The chief-surgeon made the rounds to announce it and see the beneficial effects. It is our *Banzai*.

I knew it myself last evening, when the Japanese *amah* ran into the garden with a pink *gogai* slip and told me: "*Rossia—Kogo San-Akambo—Kodomo—Banzai!*" (Russian empress, a child, a boy. Hurrah!) I could hardly believe it at first. Could the gracious *Czaritsa* really have attained her dearest wish? Has the long-prayed-for *Czarevitch* really come? Can we be sure that there is no mistake? Or only another girl?

How different is the whole future of Russia! I lose myself in thinking and in picturing the dismay of certain personages at Tsarskoe; the grand *bouleversement* that must ensue; the grand rearrangement of personal values! I see the rueful faces of Marie Feodorovna's following; the discomfiture of the clique of Mikail Alexandrovitch; the dismay of Vladimir Alexandrovitch! I laugh, and throw my arms unconsciously, as the Japanese do when they shout *Banzai*! Ah! *Banzai!* indeed. Christ and the saints have been merciful at last. They have given Russia its dearest wish. They have answered many millions of prayers. We are lifted out of our darkest despair.

But how, how did *they* let it happen? By what miracle did the newborn one live? What spared him from those merciless fingers? But he lives! Our *Czarevitch*! Our little Alexis Nicholaivitch! And the gracious *Czaritsa* must be almost dead with joy. May the saints protect her!

Von Woerffel's rage and fury keep him in high fever and retard his recovery. Akimoff says he talks calmly and dispassionately of the fiasco in my presence; but if so, I am glad not to have seen him when his wrath was at its height. He denounces the whole "Port Arthur gang," rakes over the viceroy, the grand duke and the Admiralty, the Cronstadt and the Black Sea fleets. All of them have just such commanders, he says, timorous, cowardly, fussy, old landlubbers and grannies, who jump if a gun pops, who have no notion of working, of suffering personal discomfort, or ever fighting—fighting to cripple and sink the enemy; fighting to win. Their only use is for naval reviews and parades, in a calm sea, on a sunny day, the imperial yacht or a grand duke looking on, crosses and ribands coming down in showers.

"Bah! When there are any trial trips, any manoeuvres or cruises to make, then the Finnish and Courland officers, who made the navy in the old Alexander's time, and who never get any promotion—then these officers from the Baltic provinces are made use of. "That's all we are good for," said Von Woerffel bitterly—"the crosses, the compliments, the court banquets are for the Alexeieffs and the Admiralty gang. You mark me, not a ship will do anything at Port Arthur from now on, except it has a Lutheran—a Finnish, or a Baltic-province commander. The line of greatest efficiency is a religious and a geographic one; just as the line of promotion and favouritism is also."

Nicholas de Lieven had the luck to get down to Saigon with his gunboat the *Diana*. He must disarm and stay there until the end of the war; but then Saigon is like a home in friendly feeling. It is the same as a Russian port, and he is not badly off. Another gunboat tried to go clear around all the Japanese islands to Vladivostok, but the Japanese chased her and they only managed to reach the Saghalien coast, run the ship ashore, and make their escape. Funnily enough, the Japanese papers go into ecstasies over this performance of the *Novik*; and my Japanese teacher was all animation when I next saw him, his mask of a face alive and twitching, the statuesque manner all off.

"What brave little ship of yours the *Novik*," he said. "We admire it much, but we are glad that you have no more like it. Very glad."

Monday, August 22nd.

The little social amenities and small courtesies of life still go on. The military commander makes stated visits to the wounded officers at the barracks, and to the others at the town hall or *Kokaido*, and at the house opposite, where the *Rurik's* officers are quartered. The officers have a certain amount of liberty; a surprising amount, it seems to me. Twice a week they, in turn, go out to Dogo Hot Springs in the suburbs and enjoy the mineral baths, and they can go about town shopping with a soldier as escort. They are not half as badly off, not a tenth as much imprisoned in the real sense of the word, as we imagined in Russia. I am surprised, shocked, I might almost say, any time I meet them, at the little shops in the city. The sergeants who go about with them too seem so much more amiable and polite than the upstart interpreters.

These interpreters are the cause and the source of all trouble and misunderstanding. No one here, any more than in Europe, would dream of studying Russian as an accomplishment, or a necessary part of a liberal education, any more than we should have dreamed of studying Japanese. So, when the war broke out, there we were, both sides at the mercy of a few trained official interpreters and a horde of dispossessed barbers, small curio dealers, photographers, and houseboys from Siberian towns and Manchurian garrisons. The two most difficult languages of the two hemispheres came together with woeful results, as we see daily.

One of the imperial princes of Japan sent an equerry down the Inland Sea to visit all the military hospitals and convey his kind inquiries to the wounded. With fine courtesy, they made no distinction between the two peoples, and the little man went through every ward of the prisoners' hospital, and into each Russian officer's room. I missed the event, but I had a dozen accounts of it, and Akimoff's was most amusing. The equerry was serious and courtly, and seemed most kindly, but his message from his imperial master was translated to Akimoff's astonished ears:

"His Imperial Highness sends his compliments to you brave men, who have been wounded in the field of battle. You have served your country well and his Highness honours you. He regrets that you must now suffer from the heat of our Japanese summers, but *if you will behave yourselves it will soon be cooler!*"

Bon Dieu! Did the conventionalities and banalities go further! I had to laugh myself, when Akimoff detailed it with profound bows. All this was stammered out to him by the interpreter in very bad Russian, in the nursery idioms and phrases we use to small children when they are naughty. A prince's compliments in *mujik's* language!

We have so many kindly little attentions from the common people, that Vladimir begins to admit much that I claim for the high soul of the race. Every few nights, a rain of cigarettes, plums, fans, and little trifles come over the fence of the Kokaido and the Dairinji. There are officers downstairs at the Kokaido, and two hundred of rank and file upstairs, and at the Dairinji there are only soldiers. This rain of *manna*, of course, pleased the Cossacks, but neither they nor the officers could understand it. I spoke of it to one of the American missionaries with whom I walked from the photograph shop to the post office, and she laughed greatly. "Oh, that is the Japanese way of sympathising with the poor *horios*. The Red Cross can give such things openly, when the prisoners are arriving at Takahama or passing through a railroad station in train; but here of course there is a difference.

My cook told me with glee as a great secret that she had been over with her friends last night to throw some cigarettes over the fence for the poor *horios*. They are so sorry for them. You might think these poor, hardworking people would envy the *horios* their lives of ease, and compare their present tasks with the prisoners' leisure. But this is the Japanese way. Altruism in an object lesson. The European philosophers ought to see this situation. I hope that someone showers mysterious gifts on the Japanese prisoners in Russia. Do you fear the Yellow Peril, Madame von Theill, when such incidents can happen down in the remotest provinces, where we are so little Europeanised? I will challenge you to give me an incident comparable to this on either side during the Franco-Prussian war."

"Yes. That is something to think about," said Vladimir as he lay still, immovable, ready for me to read to him some ever-charming chapter of Pierre Loti's *Ramuntcho*.

Thursday, September 1st.

Loris K—— arrived this week with Boris Tikhon, that soldier of fortune, revolutionist, and stormy petrel, who is always everywhere when things are seething; in the Balkans; flying from the Boxers; tramping Afghanistan in disguise; and even coming down through India in turban and gown. The agitator has been shut up in Port Arthur these last months, and has been defying General Stoessel, who refused him privileges as a war correspondent. Stoessel said that he was a reserve officer and must go on duty; and Boris said the War Office had given him a special standing and exemption, and that the viceroy knew and approved it. As Stoessel still tried to force him to duty, Boris slipped out through the Japanese lines last month, went to the viceroy at Liaoyang, and brought back to Port Arthur a special order defining his status, as officer on leave and civil detail or something.

Stoessel was furious, of course, so Boris kept out of his sight until last week, when Stoessel again ordered him to take duty or leave. It seems that the real siege is on now, and it is no longer possible to pass the land lines; so Boris started off with Loris K——, who was going to Chefoo in a *junk*, carrying naval despatches. They were becalmed and delayed in a fog, which cleared and showed them three Japanese torpedo boats in sight. They tied stones to the despatches and threw them overboard, and as the Japanese were watching through glasses and saw both foreigners drop white things into the water, both were called despatch bearers, and Boris could not convince them of his civil and non-combatant quality. He also had uniform in his portmanteaus, so here he is with Loris, who loathes him.

As a naval messenger, they imprison him; as a war correspondent, they do not quarter him with the other officers, but in a little chalet in a garden at the back of a building, where seventy Cossacks are kept. "My bodyguard," says Boris magnificently. "An ideal retreat for an anchorite or a literary man," he further said. "I shall prepare now the conferences I shall deliver before scientific societies when I return to Russia. I shall give addresses also in Vienna. I am now free to carry out my idea of writing a great historical novel, a romance of war and battle."

"Umph!" groaned Vladimir, "that is continuing the occupation of war correspondent, it seems to me. A romance of war and battle! That's all they have written to Russian and French journals so far. Maybe not such pure fiction, such wonderful creative work and feats of imagination as the English papers put out. Ah! Bah! Why were we ever drawn into this war, anyhow? How Paul Lessar fought to prevent it! It will kill him before the winter begins. He has fought against it these two years, but Alexeieff would have it. All these humiliating disasters are upon us, solely that Vladimir Alexandrovitch, and the viceroy, that Bezobrazoff creature, and the harpy crowd might get dividends on their Yalu stock. Poor Paul! Poor Paul!"

CHAPTER 10

My Japanese Home

Friday, September 2nd.

I am getting along famously with my Japanese. All that I ever knew of the language has come back to me, and with daily lessons I seem to grasp it quickly. I understand the servants, and can make the servants understand me. I can speak to the surly old sentries at the gates, to the little Red Cross nurses, and to the underlings at the hospital; and yesterday was flattered indeed, when they asked me to come to the operating room and interpret for the surgeon in charge. The doctor was profuse in thanks, escorted me back to Vladimir's room, and thanked *him* and praised *him* for my help. As if that were not Japanese surely! The Oriental view of me, as Vladimir's piece of property. It was a tonic for Vladimir though, to see me thus patronised and put in the Japanese woman's place.

I had not noticed until then, how I am appealed to every now and then at the barracks to straighten out some tangle of language; to tell the nurses what it is the sick one wants, and to explain things to the sick ones and make them reasonable. Already, I have been able to smooth over many difficulties, and twice, the offensive young interpreter in the chancery, the one who was so forward the day of my arrival, has appealed to me to know how I should put such and such a Russian sentence into Japanese. Each time he was blankly surprised at my rendering and dotted it down in characters; and I am sure that they were sentences from prisoners' letters. I hope my translation proved the harmlessness of the phrases and helped to speed the letters on the long way—forty days to Russia, by the way of Suez and Odessa!

Watanabe told me that this barracks interpreter, the most obnoxious young cub I have ever met in Japan, and of a type which is new to me at this visit—is a *soshi*, or lawless student agitator, who got away ten years ago without passport to Vladivostok, and from being a house-boy advanced to owning a barber shop. He picked up Russian, and while holding his officer patrons by the nose and ear as he shaved them, picked up all manner of military gossip and secrets, stole maps and papers from engineer headquarters, and got away with his information a month before war broke. Because of this service, the Japanese pardoned his past, and he was taken on as interpreter.

His case is typical, and here are our poor officers, who write an academic Russian, with their letters subject to misinterpretation by these vicious little uneducated barbers and *soshi*, who never studied a Russian grammar or used a dictionary. They have picked up the gabble and *patois* of East Siberia, and what they cannot understand they suspect. I myself have been startled at the translations they have made to the surgeons on their rounds. Several of our officers are now beginning the study of Japanese in self-defence, and I can believe that the Cossacks of the rank and file are served in most reckless fashion. "Translation is treachery," is the truest of axioms.

I find my small household running smoothly without the ubiquitous Watanabe. My Japanese serve us to a marvel and give me a comfortable *ménage*. If Vladimir could be with me here, to enjoy the toy house, and the doll's garden, and the little pleasures of living, how happy I should be! I have the stage setting of Arcadia, but did ever anyone enjoy Arcadia alone?

The flower peddlers and the gardeners have found me out, as they did in Tokyo; and my garden now is perilously near to being overcrowded with pots of charming things. My *ipomoeas* are my greatest distraction, and all my little household are as keen as I for the heavenly "dawn-flowers," or Japanese *asagao*. But all to ourselves! Vladimir cannot see them. I cannot show them to him to my sorrow, and if I were to attempt to carry a few beheaded blossoms to him in a dark box, as the Japanese connoisseurs send them to flower shows and around town to rival growers, it would be a day's work to get the permits for such a suspicious proceeding. So, we enjoy our sunrise flower shows, and I exclaim over and rave to Anna, at each day's novelty in blooms.

Each evening, when I am cooled and rested, before my solitary dinner, I watch my evening primrose open; and where my dining-room and drawing-room *engawa* (verandah) meet, I have a dozen pots of trellised moon-flowers or night-blooming *ipomoeas*, long trumpets of buds all day that open at dusk into spreading white corollas as large as my hand. They hang motionless in the warm, still, night air, flowers of enchantment, and they are so placed, that when the moon rose last week, the white light of heaven fell full upon the mysterious blossoms. I lie luxurious in my long chair, and look approvingly on my little drawing room with its soft grey walls, and its dark brown ceiling, a glint of light irradiating the gold screens in background. I look approvingly upon my enchanted garden, my tiny paradise, my miniature Arcadia. And Vladimir! No further away from me than Villa Lante is from the Garibaldi statue! Vladimir lying on a high, wooden cot in a room of bare pine boards, his one window looking upon a little court of bare earth, and the rough walls of the next barrack! And what has he done? What crime has he committed to be treated so?—to be punished, to be restrained of his liberty, poor helpless wreck of a man that he now is—what has he done?

He has served his *Czar* and Russia. That is all.

But bitter reveries lead to nothing, and I try continually to lose myself in my immediate surroundings, my daily work and occupations, and not to look forward. For, cut off from and buried from all our own world, separated from each other for all but a few hours of the day, what can we base our hopes and plans upon? What have we to live for? What is there in life for us?

But, we are together. Mercifully, the Japanese permit this. Think, if I were not allowed to come here, not to see him during all his time of suffering! He would die surely. He would have died long ago!

If Vladimir only recovers! If, now that the hideous cuts and wounds are healed, the bruised and broken ligaments, the stiffened joints and muscles could perform their work; if the shattered nerves would recover tone and the fever cease recurring, what more could I ask for? But the weak digestion, the little food we can persuade him to take, will not fortify the weak body. Each day, when I go to his little room and see him still lying there, the arms inert, only a thin, white, bloodless finger moving, the head fixed and immovable on the pillow, the great eyes in the bleached and sunken face flashing a vivid speech to me, as they follow every movement in the room, I feel a heart-sinking! Shall I never find him sitting up, even standing, or moving about the room and the ward, like others who have been brought in since my arrival?

Of course, the victories will all be ours, as soon as the cold weather comes, for the cold of Siberia and Manchuria is the same, and of course the Japanese troops cannot endure that. These little rice-fed manikins in cotton clothes will be in sad plight when the north winds begin to blow. It is all very well for them, now that Manchuria is a blazing furnace deluged with typhoon rainstorms. They are used to this. Our soldiers will thrive on the hoarfrosts and snowstorms, huge, fur-clad, meat-eating creatures that they are.

Watanabe set such a current of curio dealers in my direction that my little house is getting more attractive each day, and each day I wish more and more that Vladimir could see it. It is a solitary pleasure. The Japanese ladies who called, never noticed my Sotatsu screens, a tangle of flowers on gold-leaf grounds. The high military officer, who has twice called, accompanied by his Japanese-Russian interpreter, and has then talked bad German with me—save when we all three talked Japanese together—paid no heed to my precious flower picture in the deep recess. Young Japan, who studies in Europe, is a graceless wight on the subject of his national art. He knows more of Von Moltke and Meckel, than of Korin or Sotatsu.

It was a shabby little schoolmaster, in pathetic black broadcloth clothes, who made a ceremonial call on me, after my contributions to the Red Cross Society, who most appreciated my treasures. He drew in his breath, looked incredulous, and really did go down on his knees to my precious pictures—signed with that awe-compelling red circle and the dagger-stroke of Korin—to study the signature with microscopic closeness, to scrutinise the silk, its edges, and each detail of the mounting. All in silence.

CHAPTER 11

After Liaoyang's Battle

Sunday, September 4th.

Liaoyang, the headquarters, is abandoned, and Kuropatkin's whole army has retreated to Mukden!—from the strong place he has been fortifying for six months! All are depressed, and suffering in mind, and O'Shige San told me on my arrival that all the big children were *ydkamashi* (bothersome) today. Every wound is inflamed, every temperature is higher, every ragged nerve is straining. I have hardly known how to be cheerful before Vladimir's mournful eyes, nor how to keep him occupied with other subjects, so that he may not talk of this Liaoyang.

Vladimir sighs, shuts his lips tightly, and pitifully appeals to me: "How could he abandon such a place? It is fortified by nature, and they were building forts and forts all around the circle of hills, when I first arrived there from Petersburg. I saw them twice again, the most splendid defences. It was impregnable by July. I would have held it then with 50,000 men for six months. Only a long siege could have taken it, if there had been any spirit or sense in the army. How could they, how dare they abandon it and all the stores that were accumulating there?"

Loris tells us the news, and all that he has to tell inflames the wrath of Staff-Colonel Grievsky, an old comrade of Vladimir's, a huge blond man from Kiev, whose hands and feet—in fact, his arms and legs—stick far out from the largest-sized Red Cross *kimono* they can find for him.

"Remembering me in this," says Grievsky, thrusting out his bare wrists and looking down at the long display of ankles, "will Sophia Ivanovna ever speak to me when we meet again on God's earth, or in heaven, or in Russia, which is quite the same affair?"

As for the white pastry cook caps which the Red Cross provides, our officers will not wear them at all. I suggest that they save their Red Cross gowns and caps for future use at fancy dress balls, and they scorn the suggestion. "Never! Never! Never!" they say.

I urge these idle disconsolates to form a Matsuyama club, and all dine together in Petersburg once a year to celebrate the triumphant peace; and they say: "No! No! No!" They do not wish to remember, only to forget, to blot out the memory of these humiliating days. When the peace comes, they want to see all Matsuyama razed as flat as the Taku forts, and the *château* tumbled into the sea—its name taboo.

Grievsky rages and thunders at the Russian enemies of Russia, as a rest from reviling America and England. The perfidy of England is an old story, but the defection of America rankles with all of us. Grievsky has thirsted to meet an American and upbraid him with his country's baseness.

He does not count the Protestant missionaries, who live here, and who are so good and kind to our sick ones, as enemies of Russia, nor blame them for being Americans at all. These religious ones, these American popes, are subjects of the Kingdom of Heaven, he says. They are like people without an earthly country. They have put nationality behind them in their vocation, he says; and he puts a thousand questions to the Americans about their government, their parliament, their elections. He startles them too by telling them that we Russians all regard their Commodore Perry as an interloper, a meddler. Commodore Perry should not have rushed in and opened up Japan as he did. It was for Russia to have done that. We had already begun. We had it in train at the very time. *Trop de zèle.*

Loris and Grievsky are of one mind on Russia's national policy. Both have always been violently opposed to the whole Manchurian adventure. Russia's true interests are in Persia and the Persian Gulf, they say; and all this digression to the frozen end of far Asia, all this Manchurian madness, has been time, money, and opportunity thrown away. Beginning with Mouravieff, they curse with fine frenzy all who have ever had anything to do with far Siberian affairs—De Witte, Hilkoff, Alexeieff, and Bezobrazoff. They detail, and relate, and repeat all that they know to their detriment; and all Trans-Baikalia, the Amur, and Ussuri are the damned provinces.

"Had Trans-Caspia continued to occupy Russian statesmen, had they remembered Peter the Great's admonition, we should long ago have had railways into Persia, across Persia to the Gulf, and Russian naval stations there, face to face with India. And then," says Loris, "Russia's 'great idea' would be realised. But—we have no statesmen any more—only court favourites and speculators. Since Alexander the Liberator's death, everything has gone worse; mediocrity on top, ability below, or—in Kavkaz and Siberia. Our brains are in exile. Petersburg is a madhouse where the lunatics themselves are in charge. And Nicholas! Well—Nicholas is blind. Poor fellow! He indeed rides in a perambulator still, with Marie Feodorovna pushing him."

I remember, too, when Vladimir finally quitted the diplomatic service, or went on a long *congé*, he said: "I have no pride in serving the Russian Government any more. The government is a self-willed, selfish woman-usurper, and a wolf pack of Grand Dukes. We are little better off than the! Chinese with their Empress Dowager. Nicholas and Kwangsu are autocrats in name only. *L'État* just now is Marie Feodorovna, and I cannot be loyal to her. That is not being loyal to Russia. If a *Czar* should rule again, I would serve; if enemies rose, if war came, I would defend my country."

Grievsky almost weeps, as he declares Persia is slipping from our grasp, and Tibet already seized by the English, while we are occupied with this miserable colonial war.

"Now the chance of Persia is going; for, with Russia's longest arm busy with this colonial war in Manchuria, England will intrigue against us in Afghanistan and confront us in Persia. Lord Curzon is plotting, plotting all the time against us; and it will take years for us to recover our lost ground. Ah! Ah! Marie Feodorovna and her circle! Alexeieff and that creature Bezobrazoff! They are Russia's worst enemies. They are the traitors. They have thrown us into, this foolish war with Japan—and all about that cursed Manchuria for which no Russian cares—*that,*" snapping his fingers like the crack of a whip. "Ah! Ah!" and he ground his teeth with rage, "This will cost us Persia and all our chance at India. What do we want with Manchuria? You and I even? Did you ever hear any one cry for it in Russia? Was it not always a huge sort of joke? Military duty there a little better than the Caucasus—until that Peking affair, when they all got so much loot. Ah! that was a chance!

"And we! *We!* We endure heat, thirst, and privations in Manchurian camps and com fields. We are wounded, mangled, crippled, made captives, and dragged to Japanese prisons. And why? For what? Because Bezobrazoff has promised to Serge and Vladimir and Alexis, and Marie Feodorovna, and Alexeieff too, great money from their timber lands on the Yalu River. And what need could there be for this timber? What market for it, if there were not Port Arthur and Dalny. Who wants Dalny? Who made Dalny? Who else but De Witte, to make trade and give excuse for that damned railway? And who wants Port Arthur? Only Alexeieff to make himself Viceroy of the Far East and to kill De Witte's free city and trade port in the next bay. Ah-h-h! villains, thieves, scoundrels!

"And who wanted this war? Who made it? What for? Alexeieff and his officers, who wanted promotions, decorations, contracts, loot of any kind! And his *Novo Krai!* The censor would not have let it live in Petersburg. But Alexeieff was censor. He was editor; he was all in all. Every day he threw down the gauge to Japan and courted war. Did not Paul Lessar warn him? Did he not implore and implore Alexeieff to keep the pledges and evacuate Manchuria? 'Not now, not forcibly, defiantly,' he said. 'Do not rouse the world. Slowly, inevitably, in time, we shall of course get Manchuria,' said Paul; 'but do not let us get all the powers down on us for broken faith and broken pledges.' He begged, he wrote, he telegraphed, he sent couriers, urging Alexeieff not to put off or refuse evacuation; not to reoccupy places like Mukden and thereby rebuff America. He begged him, too, to stop the *Novo Krai's* recklessness, to be more cautious since all the East knew it to be his mouthpiece. And then Alexeieff himself wrote that thing in the *Novo Krai*, the '*J'y suis et j'y reste*' article, and marked it, and sent it to Paul Lessar, as answer. Poor Paul! Poor Paul! To live for this! to die by inches seeing it!

"Ah! Scoundrels! Scoundrels! I wish all that Yalu and Port Arthur crowd were here. Here! Here! As I am here," he fairly roared, pounding his hand on the table. "They deserve it. Not I. Not I. Not your husband, either, *Madame*. We are the victims, the sport of their ventures of greed. Yes, greed."

Poor Grievsky! Such a frank, sunny, happy temperament, if it were not clouded by his sufferings of body and mind, his humiliation, and his fretting at this inactivity, when there is hard fighting and hard work for good Russians to do. Vladimir says that no one so loves a good fight for the sheer love of fighting as Grievsky. The bang of shot and clash of steel and smell of powder are more than food and drink to him. They are the wine of life, intoxicants. Grievsky in battle or skirmish is a very god of war and giant of battles, electrified, intensified, his face illumined with exaltation, his voice a clarion that inspires the men. They were together years ago in Ferghana—Vladimir, Grievsky, and dear old Paul Lessar. There they knew Kuropatkin too. In these despairing times, it is a pleasure for Vladimir and Grievsky to turn from the present and live over the old, triumphant, Turcoman days. They had only victories there and—all the world was young then. Grievsky stayed on in Turkestan, and in Ferghana; he built more railways and more forts, and laid out lines of canals; surveyed with the Pamir Boundary Commission, and, as he said, acted as guide and host for exiled Grand Dukes, explorers, scientists, and butterfly-catchers from all countries. We laugh at his accounts of the explorers who came to him wanting to explore Tibet.

"Ah, *Gott!* I was only a forwarding agent, an innkeeper for the explorers. I ran an excursion bureau there in Ferghana.

"It would have paid even to have built a railway to Lhassa, solely to accommodate the many gentlemen-explorers, the discoverers of an unknown country. I was 'Thos. Cooks & Sons, Limited,' for the 'Roof of the World.' There were all kinds, even women—all nations. They all wanted to go to Lhassa. Every fool was sure he would succeed, where other fools had failed. I got them their caravan leaders, and their servants, their animals, their stores, and I started them off. Oh! Speed to the parting guest! as you English say. They never got to Lhassa, of course, although it was a dull season in Samarcand and Kashgar when I did not have two or more Lhassa excursions on my hands. And most of them returned to my sheltering arms! Poor fluttering birds of search!

"They had excuses, they had Tibetan teapots and turquoises, trumpets of thigh bones, and skull drums, and—much experience. And Lord! What it must have cost them to go on their cold picnics! *Roubles*, and *roubles*, and *roubles!* Think of shivering in a tent with a cup of tea and tallow at your own command and at your own expense, when there is champagne in Paris for half the price! Ah! there are so many kinds of madmen running loose nowadays! We saw all these madmen off with a last dinner, and they returned, hairy and hungry, dazed at the sight of a civilised table again. And God! *How* they could drink the champagne after a little of the Pamirs and Lop Nor!

"There were all kinds—Germans in spectacles, with their specimen boxes hung all around them; and Frenchmen—let me not speak disrespectfully of our flat-chested, but richly-investing allies—and Englishmen! Englishmen! *and* Englishmen! until I thought I should go mad; and they, those Johnnies Bulls! they all came with letters to me! To me! As if it were a deliberate joke. Bah! Those fellows in Petersburg did it on purpose. Those British spies told me that Prof. This and Dr. That, in Petersburg, had told them that I knew it all, and they sat and admired me, and opened their ears, all the valves in their ears, to hear what I should say. Curse their souls!

"I knew then they were only spies. And I! Even I, ran with Mr. George Curzon! *My Lord* Curzon he is now. He, who would keep us out of Persia, and drive us out of all Trans-Caspia—If he could. He, who will not hesitate to undermine us in every way, now that Kuropatkin is tied up, hand and foot, in this accursed Manchurian mess. Lord Curzon! The Viceroy of India! Who could think it then." The pale, little university student, who was writing in the *London Times*, and wanted to find the source of the Oxus, *and* the course of the Pamirs, and the lord devil knows what not. Ah! Spy! Spy! I could wring his miserable neck, if I could but see him now. Would I lend him my horses, my maps, my everything again? A Viceroy of India in disguise! And I his tool, his fool! Ah! Ah! Grievsky you deserve all this—this, the convict dress, the sentry at the door, the high fence! And Mr. George Curzon should come, and see, to make the comedy complete!"

Lord Curzon and Commodore Perry his equal abominations.

CHAPTER 12

The September Moon

Thursday, September 15th.

The chief-surgeon has said, that in time they hope to let me re-move Vladimir to my house, and continue his nursing there. He must give his parole that he will keep the same hours and restrictions as the other officers in detention at the town hall. I shall be his jailer, and responsible to the Japanese Government for him. I nearly fainted with joy when I heard it, and Vladimir gave a great sigh of relief.

"I shall see that garden then. And we shall live, Sophia. It will be a home. I shall never complain then. How pleasant it will be to leave all this, the bare walls, the sounding floors, the noisy, grumbling men; to go to the clean, quiet, little Japanese house and live stocking-footed—to watch the goldfish, and the birds, and the 'morning face' flowers. I feel better now."

The surgeon said: "I am recommending that he be isolated from the ward. He must have quiet, and be free from fretting and excitement. They talk too much, all these friends of his. As soon as his wounds are healed, and he is out of his plaster casings, we can turn him over to you as his skilled *masseuse*. I have two cases now that I shall ask you to help the nurses with. In that way you will learn the treatment, and I can advise to the commander that we give the honourable colonel to treatment in a private ward, to make the room which we shall soon need at the barracks.

"We are short of nurses, and short of interpreters for all the sick ones who will arrive here this week, and if you will be so good as to go with the Red Cross ladies to Takahama to receive transports, you can help us very much. And afterwards, if you are not too fatigued, we may wish you to interpret a little for us at the barracks here. There are so many wounded coming, and the doctors and nurses are not speaking your language enough yet. You are much cleverer, Madame von Theill, in learning the Japanese than our people are in learning Russian. However have you done it. We have never known a foreigner to speak like you in only a month."

To have Vladimir all to myself again, and nurse him back to health quietly in my own little villa! To be alone by ourselves! To speak without being overheard! To have absolute quiet around us! What joy that will be! And to be allowed to help with our wounded Russians is a privilege indeed. How glad I am that I have taken Vladimir's advice and never asked for anything, nor complained of anything! Now that I have not proved a nuisance, they will let me be a helper. How truly good and kind the Japanese are—as individuals! But the people and their government are always two different things. Look at us! See Russia!

The season seems going rapidly now, and with the changes in the face of nature, I feel that time is hastening as I want it to. The lake of emerald-green rice, that rippled in the warm breeze that day I rode up from Takahama on the toy train, is now a lake of golden yellow grain.

Loris, who knows a little of peasant life and the growing of crops in all countries, has always some new fact in agriculture to communicate to Beletsky when he comes to see him, and Beletsky longs for the time when he can ride out and see the Japanese at work in the fields, caressing and tending each rice stalk individually.

"We have no idea of work in Russia," says Loris, "of work as a fine art, of work lavished on the crops and the land for love of it. Our peasants plough, and plant, and reap mechanically, with their muscles only, with no more mind, feeling, comprehension, or soul than the horses that pull the huge American machines through our wheat fields. The Japanese lavish more work on a single crop, they do more working of the soil, more weeding and tending, more trimming and straightening to one grain crop than our peasants give to ten crops. They pet their sheaves of rice like children. They coax them, talk to them, pray to the gods for them, and bring charms from the temple to protect them; and carry the very first ripe ears to the temple as offerings. It is no wonder that the seed grain responds with its best.

"It is the sight of a life to watch these Japanese in the fields. Work, work, work! Wade in the mud, grub among the roots, all day, every day. I only wish I could have watched the whole thing; seen the rice sown in the seed beds and then transplanted, but it was yellowing when I arrived. And the harvest! What a sight! All these dull blue figures among the yellow stubble! And then the dooryard scenes, as they beat and winnow the grain in full view, in the open sunshine! Bronze men and bronze women, with the sunshine on their fine bronze bodies. Ah! it is superb. Consider Millet's draped peasants in their turnip fields! Bah!

"And we never understood, we never knew about these Japanese in Russia. The Japanese make their war over there in Manchuria Just as they work these rice fields, thoroughly, intently, intelligently, with loving devotion all the time. Our *mujiks* might as well lay down their rifles now and go home. They will never conquer these people. Victory is not with us. Man to man, officer to officer, peasant to peasant, we are no match for them. These are the people of the twentieth century, and we are of the eighteenth only. Ah! Curse the luck!"

★★★★★★

The dear little volunteer nurse, who attracted me so when the committee of ladies came to thank me at my house, is at the barracks on duty each alternate week, and often comes to speak to me, to inquire for Vladimir and to bring him a flower. Her husband is a son of the new *daimio*, and is an officer at the front in Manchuria. The other night we both stopped to admire a rosy young moon balancing on the ridge of the eastern hills. "Next week there is the moon-viewing night. You will come with me to see?" and I gladly assented.

The next day she told me much about this great September moon; told me as much as my limited and practical vocabulary could let me know of poetic things. It is the moon of moons, the best loved moon of all the year, and the poet's moon in Japan. I have watched my great white moon flowers in the moonlight for several nights; and later, from my balcony, have pushed the *amados* wider, to see the picturesque castle and the black pine trees swimming in silver air against a dark azure sky. But for this fifteenth night of the September moon, when the great disc is completely round, all Matsuyama gathers on the castle hill, or on the far hill across the railway track, to watch the moon rise behind the Dogo hills.

After dark she rumbled in under my gateway and carried me off with her. Anna's bewildered face gave me the sense of being off on an adventure, and my spirits took on such a leap of elation, as the *kurumas* sped through the streets and around two long sides of the moat, that I had forgotten all worry and trials as we ran through a long street of shops and came to the foot of the abrupt castle hill, darkly clothed with its ancient pines. We went up a stone staircase and steep paths

75

through the trees, then up more staircases and tree-shaded paths, with the *kurumaya's* lanterns bobbing beside and before us like big glow-worms in the warm darkness. The moist fragrance of the pines, the soft voice of my little Red Cross sister, and the respectfully hushed voices of our attendants, all fell upon me with charm unspeakable, and I was consciously happy.

We came out on the broad terrace that I have often looked up to wonderingly, and then we looked out, from high in air, over the city of dotted lights, and over the dark plain with shadowy hills beyond. Scores of people were sitting there on cushions and red blankets. A perambulating restaurateur had brought up his twin boxes, and from those magic treasuries had distributed tea trays for all the company, and the moon-worshippers were amusing themselves with doll wafers and fairy cups of tea and other aesthetic imitations of real food, as it seems to us bulk-consuming, barbarian peoples.

Towards Dogo, the mountain rim was more sharply cut against the dusky, violet-indigo sky, patterned with faint constellations. Over there, the moon was getting ready to rise; and when we had recovered breath and fanned ourselves cool, we went through a medieval gate-way, climbed some broad stone steps, between the black walls of the old castle's barracks, turned a court and another gate, and came out on a long terrace—a hanging garden.

There was a company of quiet Japanese people there, grave old men and quiet, shadowy women in dark *kimonos*, and they gave me, one by one, ceremonious greetings. They were cordial and kindly be-yond believing. Each one, during the evening, came and made some second little speech of greeting; inquired for Vladimir and the sick ones at the barracks; wished for their recovery and comfort, and told me some other pretty, picturesque thing about the moon-viewing custom. It took me all evening to put things together, and make out that I was the guest of Matsuyama's highest circle; that my little Red Cross colleague was a true daughter of a *daimio* in the highest sense, since she stays here to work for Iyo soldiers' families, while her hus-band is at the front; and that nearly all the company was composed of the kinfolk of the two *daimio* families, who ruled this rich province before the Restoration.

It was a "black" Vatican company, a gathering of the *ancienne no-blesse* of the Faubourg St. Germain, there on the Iyo heights, and the *daimios'* old poetry-teacher, in his Chinese-cut coat of dark gauze, his mitre cap, with long white beard and staff, looked like Jurojin himself.

76

He only needed the spotted deer to complete the picture of the God of Wisdom, Learning, and Longevity come to life.

We moved slowly along the high terrace. A wall on one side, starry space on the other; and the lights of the town glimmered as if they were but stars reflected in the dark pool of the rice plain far below us.

We were somewhere above my own house, my tiny garden of camellia hedges, of moon flowers and *asagaos*; and by the outlines of the hills, I knew that a turn to the right would bring me over the barracks where Vladimir lay—Vladimir suffering in the stuffy alcove of his ward, with lights and voices, noise and confusion around his tired head and bruised nerves, and I here, high in the cool starlight with poets! My heart sank with a guilty feeling, with a remorse for my being up there to enjoy freely the fragrant darkness, with the cool shadow and silence of the castle walls and embankments beside me, in a company of soft-voiced poets. And they were Japanese poets! Ah! Japanese! Japanese! My enemies! Vladimir's assailants, and Vladimir's enemies! Was it right for me to be there with them? Could it ever seem right for him to be there at the barracks, beaten, bruised, maimed, perhaps crippled for life, by these same people? Perhaps Colonel Takasu, himself, had captured him; perhaps Iyo soldiers had clubbed him to unconsciousness, when he would not yield and surrender. Maybe Colonel Takasu was the officer whom he had resisted in arrest, for which they threatened Vladimir with a court-martial and the death penalty over there in Manchuria.

But these wild notions left when we entered another deep gateway, and came into the courtyard of the citadel itself, and I could see straight above me the fantastic gables, set one astride the ridge line of the other, that I had so often admired from below. Then we went into the dark and echoing interior, to vast halls and galleries, half seen in the lantern light by which we climbed steep stairs to the first room of the great tower open on all four sides to the night sky. We climbed to a second storey where the east-facing windows were pushed wide, and we sat on cushions on the floor, and watched the outlines of the hills grow sharper and clearer against a dusky blue, silver-lighted sky.

An electric flash came as the great yellow-white disc of the September moon first showed on the mountain's edge, and quickly the whole round splendour rose, poised on the fantastic peak, and soared up into the shadowy azure, the bluish, grape-coloured sky. "Ah! Ah!" sighed my companions around me softly, with intense joy in the beauty and the sentiment of the scene; and I found myself swept with them upon the same high, exquisite plane of feeling and emotion. There was grave silence, the tap-tap of a tiny pipe, lighted without sound against the burning coal buried in the *hibachi's* ashes, the only break in the harmony of stillness.

The great moon, not cold and silvery white like our frosty Russian moon, glowed golden and refulgent, glorious as the moon of Italy in mid-air, and sent down a mellowed daylight, first upon Dogo's clustered houses and tree masses, and then on the level of the golden rice plain, distinctly yellow in the moonlight, cut with dark lines and divided by the broad white Dogo road. It was enchantment—a midsummer night's dream—old Japan—ideal, poetic Japan—and I a Philistine snatched up to this height by Heaven's favour, for my soul's expanding to this rare night's opportunity. I sat thrilled through and was soon choking with an unreasonable melancholy and emotion; and, as from a trance, I came down from the heights of the soul, and found myself weeping in a company of Vladimir's enemies—and he, stricken and suffering, somewhere in the long buildings showing dimly in the night-azure, Cazin landscape immediately below us.

CHAPTER 13

The Liaoyang Men

September 28th.

Another day, I did my day's work in the Red Cross tents at Takaha-ma, and from noon until four o'clock saw the wounded from Liaoyang brought ashore, fed, bandaged, and ministered to, until they were put in the little train. They were pitiful in their weakness and dejection; many of the rank and file not yet convinced that the evil little pigmies would not cut them in strips and torture them. The officers, poor fellows, were stung with chagrin, with humiliation unspeakable; and to many wounded pride was as acute a suffering as the shooting pains and throbs of agony in their wounded bodies. Hopeless, despondent, heart-sick, and suffering, they lay with their eyes closed, not caring to see the beautiful green hills and blue water around them, after the hideous bare hills and muddy shores of Manchuria. It was a pleasure to speak to these inert ones, and see the faces waken at sound of the Russian language. "Ah! God! to hear my own tongue again, after these days and days! Is this really Japan? You *are* a Russian woman! Where did you come from? Are you, too, prisoner?"

And when I told them about myself, they marvelled greatly. They could hardly believe that the Japanese let me stay here and tend my wounded husband daily, or that I was safe. "Yes! they have certainly surprised me, for they were kind to us all the time. We have been treated as their own wounded; and when we have groaned in the railway carriage coming down to Dalny, they have said, truly, that our own wounded Russians were no better off among our own people. Ah! that railway ride was hardest! How I wished they had bayoneted me on the field where they found me, as our Cossacks do. I expected that. I did not expect them to pick me up, and carry me to the surgeon, and dress my wounds; feed and fan me, put a cigarette in my mouth and light it for me. Then a French-speaking interpreter came and asked me if I would like to go to the expense of a telegram to my family, lest they be alarmed from the Russian report of missing. It was all very strange, very surprising to me. And that they let *you* stay here is more surprising still. I don't understand *these* Japanese at all. I never heard of such Japanese before I *came here*."

He wanted to talk more and all the time, but I told the ladies a little of what he had said, and they eagerly took my place, to do more for him, to heap surprises upon him.

It was too late that day for me to go to the barracks when I got back, but Anna had gone, and looked after Vladimir. The first of the new arrivals had reached their wards before she left. "No sleep tonight, *barina*," said Anna. "They are all wild to hear the newcomers. And I do not think it is good news, because they are very still, and listen quietly to what the sick man says."

It could not indeed be good news. It was the same sickening recital of stupidity, and blundering, and hesitation—of reinforcements not ready in time; of peevish, pettish officers abandoning strong places to spite and pay back the commander, and thus precipitating failure, ultimate flight. They had so nearly caused the capture, the inglorious surrender of the commander and his staff, that some of the wounded were only assured of Kuropatkin's safety, after they reached this hospital.

The sick man told how the commissariat failed them and how they picked the millet heads, and ate raw grain for the two days of fighting. He held trenches on a hill that commanded the key to the Russian defence and the whole position. That night they were to crawl down for water, but the whole company crawled down and away; scattered and refused to return; and daybreak saw the Japanese safely in occupation, without firing a shot. "I raved, I stormed, I cursed, I beat them, but it was only '*Niet! Niet!*' I could not drive them, they were too ready to turn on me. Ah! if it were not for this getting killed, how our Russians would fight!

"I sat down and wept, and only my servant, dragging me by main force, could make me realise that the Japanese were upon us. Upon us! They were all around us; and they bagged the last of my mutinous men, who ran into the arms of a flanking party that came out of the *kaoliang*, as if out of dense woods. So, here I am—a flesh wound in the arm and a bullet through the leg—wounds that will heal in a fortnight. But I am to stay here, in prison, until the end of the war. Stay

"I Did Not Expect Them to Feed and Fan Me, Put a Cigarette in My Mouth and Light it for Me."

here until Kuropatkin retreats to Lake Baikal! Ah-h! It is too much."

"But," we all said, "we keep our courage up by counting on a speedy rescue by the Vladivostok fleet. Skrydloff's next raid will be down this west coast. We can only dream of our release, and of Russian victories on Japanese soil—a Russian occupation of Tokyo! The loot of Tokyo, a richer prize than the loot of Peking. We will get it."

"Never! Never! By all the saints, never! There will be a Japanese occupation of Petersburg first. We can no more win a war against these cursedly clever generals, these intelligent armies, against these hardworking, incessantly-studying, scientific soldiers, than the Turcomans, with their flint-locks, could win against Skobeleff and his machine guns. Only a miracle can save us now. Skobeleff on his white horse, or Alexander Nevski will have to appear and head our columns to carry our flag back even to Liaoyang or the coal mines. What have we done but retreat! withdraw and run! Run! and run faster still, ever since that day on the Yalu River? It has been one long story of stupidity, inefficiency, unpreparedness, shameful failure and defeat. The Japanese have landed armies where they chose, and gone along quite as they pleased; pushing our headquarters ahead of them—from Yinkow to Haicheng, to Liaoyang, to Mukden! And how soon will we be driven out of that, and Harbin too?

"And our generals shrug their shoulders, and say they are unprepared! *Ach Gott!* Unprepared! What have we ever done in Russia but prepare? I have studied, and drilled, and practised, and prepared for war all my life. What is the standing army, the conscription for, if it is not preparation for war? We were prepared on paper. Oh! yes! And have we not been getting prepared for this war every minute since the siege of Tien Tsin? Of what did all the casernes, and canteens, and messes, and clubs talk in Peking, that winter after the siege, but of the coming war between Russia and Japan? Everyone in Port Arthur knew it. The Viceroy knew it. He counted on it. He told again and again how long it would last. He disclosed his plans confidentially every midnight.

"And then Kuropatkin came out; and he looked over the forts in Manchuria, and he listened to Alexeieff, to that sailor on horseback, who knew no more about the Japanese army establishment than he does of the Patagonian army, if there is one. Kuropatkin was slow, and he wanted to be sure; and he asked to see the forts at Port Arthur, and they brought him maps, maps, maps. 'No,' said he. 'Come let us take a walk,' and that hot May day, he made them all climb to the Chinese wall, and walk over all that rough ground toward the west. While the engineers perspired and explained to Kuropatkin, the Viceroy was down in the cool palace. 'And now,' said Kuropatkin, 'where is the fort "K"?'

"'At your very feet, your Excellency. Where you stand is the site, and these are the plans—a lunette—a—'

"'Damnation,' says his Excellency, the Minister of War, 'show me no plans, no paper forts. Where are the guns.? Eight-centimetre guns.? They left Kronstadt months ago.'

"'They are in the storehouses, below there, your Excellency.'

"'Very well,' he roared. 'When they are mounted here, we will call it a fort and talk of a campaign. You must be ready to defend before you attack. The war, when it comes, will not all be a quick descent upon Nagasaki and a gay march over to Tokyo. I miss my prophecy, if those little yellow devils do not make us a siege of Port Arthur that will come near to Sebastopol's siege.'

"'Pouf! your Excellency. We shall wait until winter before starting the campaign. Then we can impose our will on the Japanese, and they can never come here. The north wind will fight for us.' And Kuropatkin sneered, looked at the vice-admiral, and walked down to the road. '*Quelles bêtises! Bêtes! Imbéciles!*' I heard him say.

"And now! What have we? The viceroy and the commander at daggers' drawn, and each general the fighting foe of the other; each willing to see the enemy triumph rather than his rival score a success. The viceroy and the commander wisely keep their headquarters on railway trains—yes, actually, with steam up all the time. Even a locomotive at both ends of his train, and balloons fastened to the car roofs by this time, as the Japanese cartoons show. They both keep advancing to the north, pressing on Harbin, just ahead of the Japanese. It is retreat, retreat, retreat; sending the colours, and the artillery, and the supplies on to the north, and then racing after them. *Sauve qui peut.* 'Give me time,' says the commander, and they give it to him. 'Soon we shall be winning great victories,' said the braggarts in Liaoyang cafes in May; and now, it is September. 'The Imperial Navy has sunk more of its own than of the enemy's ships. And the Imperial Army! Not a victory yet!"

With all that I myself helped to send out from Russia, I am distressed by the stories of hospital mismanagement. Liaoyang hospitals were unprepared for the wounded that came to them from Haicheng. There were no lamps, no candles, no ice. The Red Cross sister herself went into the city and bought lemons, and found the Red Cross stamps on the boxes—a gift sent out from Odessa!

With thirty grand dukes, the only member of the Imperial family at the front is Boris! Boris Vladimirovitch! Boris! with a vaudeville company of blondes to see the fun and the excitement of a campaign, to watch a *battue* of men instead of a *battue* of partridges!

CHAPTER 14

The Shaho Men

Wednesday, October 12th.

Another battle is on, and we do not dare to hope. The last prisoners brought in—picked up while reconnoitring near the coal mines at Liaoyang—have told us more of the terrible losses at Liaoyang, of the mad panic of flight, and the latest quarrels of the generals. Each general accuses the other of disobeying orders, of delaying reinforcements, of deliberately abandoning posts to ruin another's plans; and each vows vengeance. All have appealed to Petersburg, and Petersburg bestows—not ribbons and crosses and orders—but blows and curses. Poor Nicholas weeps, they say, and is so melancholy and depressed, that only the little *Czarevitch* can make him smile. It is a dull, unhappy court. "Cannot my generals even win one battle?" cries poor Nicholas in despair.

After Makaroff's death, Vladimir was called over to Peking at Paul's request, to inform him about the situation. They had their days unbroken and lived over again their time in the deserts and the Pamirs. Both felt that it was a farewell visit. "I shall die of chagrin and humiliation," Paul wrote in May, after Zassalitch's disgraceful failure on the Yalu River. "This war of Alexeieff's has nearly killed me. I have not 'long to live,'" were his farewell words to Vladimir in Peking. We too well know that each battle is another deathblow, each defeat brings death nearer to "Iron Wrist," as they called him in the Khanates. "How I wanted to see Vassili Verestchagin!" Paul said. "I wanted him to come here and paint these Manchus and their palaces. There is nothing so gorgeous in the rest of the world. The old empress, a tigress enthroned, is the greatest sovereign of twenty centuries. Europe has no match for her. If she were a man, I could make her out. I can only threaten and frighten, and they tell me she does fear me. If it were not for the for-

85

eign women who have her ear, I could do more. I could do more."

Poor Paul! How earnestly he wished America had never been discovered; his American confrere in Peking continually undid him. The Americans were of course hand in glove with the Japanese, and their ladies had an *entrée* at the palace that our Russian women could not obtain. Poor Paul! Poor Paul! Although prostrate and handicapped, without social aids, he is a match for the whole *corps diplomatique*—and Vladimir had the hint from him that the Chinese would soon be brought into the *mêlée*, and then it would become an international affair, and Japan would be put in her place by a coalition of continental powers.

Sunday, October 16th.

The most glorious weather has come to us with the rice harvest; and the clear dry sunshine, the fields of yellow stubble, and the vivid patches of red lilies have made me think again and again of Italy. I am homesick for the villa on the Roman hillside. If I could only some morning step out on the terrace and turn the telescope on the forum, and see how Boni's new excavations were going on! or look over on the Pincian, or to the Medici terrace and see who was taking a morning ride, that would be joy! When I remember that splendid Roman outlook of ours—out over the great city valley from the heights—I feel smothered and oppressed living and moving about on the flat, flat level of a rice plain.

The Japanese are making more temples ready, and have begun building a great barracks of officers' quarters to make room for all the new prisoners that are coming, and to prepare for the fall of Port Arthur! They speak of it as if it were as certain an event in the near future as Christmas Day; but all who come to us as prisoners tell that the fortress is stronger than any one in Europe imagines. It has food for two years and a half, and ammunition for two years. The storehouses are overflowing, supplies stand in miles of goods trains on sidings there, and are heaped in mountains on shore. The building of fortifications has gone on night and day, and the commander cannot complain of forts on paper any more.

The forts are almost touching on the hills surrounding the city, and an army can no more force an entrance between the forts, than a fleet can get in between the forts and mines of the harbour. The Japanese tried to take by assault all summer; but now they are discouraged, and only keep up the appearance of attacks, and "save face," while the real fighting is further north—with our "General *Rückwärts!*"

Women and children are still living at Port Arthur in safety. A shell hits the town now and then, but so far there is no panic. When the coldest weather comes, the Japanese will have to retire to warm barracks somewhere, and their fleet will run for the milder weather of Nagasaki, They, of course, cannot stand our Siberian winters; and Port Arthur can then lay in more provisions and send away the sick and the women and children. Port Arthur's assured safety is our great comfort in these days, our one cheerful subject of talk. That and the little *Czarevitch.*

Sunday, October 23rd.

The ten days' battle of the Shaho has ended. Kuropatkin has retreated, of course, and all my sick ones are worse. One or two are really becoming affected in mind. Our Slav temperament is prone to melancholy and dementia, and men like Grievsky, who are either at the height of joy or in deep despondency, do not bear up well under long-continued sorrow. Bismarck knew us when he said the Russians were feminine in character, too volatile, sentimental, and emotional. We are not the race for cold reason and pure logic. Grievsky and the others here argue, argue, argue by the hour, enthusiastically, excitedly, and then with frenzy, each in the support of his own opinions, blind and deaf to another's opinions, facts, or reasoning.

Abstract discussions occupy their time, and from the frothings of these cleverest men, one gets an idea of what a Russian parliament would be like, if a benevolent *Czar* ever carried out the Liberator's intention. It took the Japanese a dozen years to learn the ways of constitutional government, and to arrive at a tolerable imitation of British parliamentary ways. We Russians are a different people; slower to assimilate ways so foreign to all the genius of our race. No, the parliament, the deliberative assemblage, is not for us. An exciting debate would send all our parliamentary leaders into hysterics and dementia; a division would mean duels, assassinations, civil war—even barricades and street fighting.

Tuesday, October 25th.

With the arrival of the wounded from Liaoyang, I took regular all-day work at the hospital, for a fortnight; going at eight o'clock in the morning, donning my nurse's cap and costume, and assisting and interpreting in the operating room or in the wards, as needed. I always had my fixed hours with Vladimir, and often I was so weary that I dropped off into little naps while I waited for our afternoon cup of tea. With such grand rounds of the barracks establishment, I always came to Vladimir full of the day's news, news from the Russian camps and Petersburg.

A Buriat Mongol was operated on today—a gunshot wound and some sword cuts on the right arm. The bone had been splintered and taken out and a metal substitute inserted. It is wonderful what these Japanese surgeons can do; and I am not yet used to the interest they show in the suffering Russians. "*Do good to them that hate you*" has its illustration here, for the surgeon-in-chief laboured over this Cossack of the ranks, as if he were a Japanese officer of the highest class. I fed some buckwheat gruel—the Japanese know it and make it well—to the poor fellow, after he was brought out to the air, and he told me his regiment, and that he had been servant to an officer, who came out from Petersburg to command his troop.

The officer was Lyov Siemenoff, our young guardsman, military *attaché* of the embassy in Rome, my special pride and pet for three winters. He was such a splendidly handsome chap, so typically Russian, yet so free from the vices of his fellow guardsmen. He was daft on archaeology and coins; and he and Vladimir had rapturous times together hanging upon Boni's words and workmen; and never missing a Sunday evening at St. Catharina, with Donna Emilia and her archaeologists.

Somewhere, in that awful millet field by the Shaho, Siemenoff was cut off from the rest of his troopers, and came out from the tall millet into the arms of the Japanese. He was wounded, and fell forward, his horse was shot and came down with him. "*Barina*," the Cossack said, "those little Japanese devils were thick like midges—everywhere—everywhere—in the air, and they cut me down. When I knew myself again, it was dark; they had me stretched on a table and were cutting and trimming around my leg, and then I slept some more and woke up in a railway train. I never saw my master again. I suppose they left him dead there where he fell. Dead! dead! But when I am out again, I shall go and search for him and bury him. I shall know the place. I could easily find it, even if the crops were all cut."

Lyov was the sort that Russia needs, and can so poorly spare. There are so few like him. Vladimir had known his family. The mother was a great beauty. The father went out on active service with Skobeleff under General Kauffmann; and then afterwards went to the Balkans with Gourko, and was killed at Gorui-Durbrik. When Lyov was in Rome, we always had the fiction of hunting a nice English "Meess" for him; and many a bouquet of young beauties have I gathered at my table and for little dances, under the plea of marrying Lyov off well.

"You see," he said, "the one path to success nowadays is to have an English or an American wife. The English I know a little more about; but America is too far off, and we hear such strange stories. So, I think, if it is the same to you, Sophia Ivanovna, I will forego the American beauty and her greater *chicness*, and continue to seek out my adorable 'Meess.'" Then, of course, he fell madly, frantically, Slavically in love with an American who would not love him, and next with an English girl from Canada, which is America. A goddess of beauty she was, with a manner and style not one of our grand duchesses could equal. She ordered men about, and they obeyed, not meekly, but eagerly, frantically. Even Englishmen fetched and carried, and waited on her. "I think she hypnotises me," one heavy Briton said. "I shall not be surprised any time to find myself tying her adorable shoe laces, blacking her smart little boots, even."

The divine *mademoiselle*, "*la belle Canadienne*," for a time seemed to listen to Lyov; and then, all of a sudden Lyov was plunged in melancholy, left Rome, and went back to the *Garde à Cheval*. We were soon startled with the announcement of her marriage in London, to Count Foresta, an Italian, who was all well enough perhaps as a *parti*—a good title and estates, mediaeval castle, and all that—but a poor second, as man for man, to Lyov Siemenoff. And now, Lyov is dead! Killed in battle, like his father before him. The Forestas were living on one of their estates near Siena, awaiting an heir, when the *conte* came down to Rome for the cavalry rides, and, in doing some of those mad Italian rides down steep banks, was killed.

CHAPTER 15

In Kaki Time

Thursday, October 27th.

All the kaki trees are hung now with their gorgeous, golden fruits, and they add the last touch to the mellowing landscape of ripe autumn. While nature sings this rich melody, and all the earth looks peace, our wounded continue to arrive in heart-breaking numbers. We continue to hear news from our own people, news direct from headquarters, and also the last news that had come out to Manchuria from Petersburg.

Vladimir shows a real improvement now that there is an end to the suffocating heat and dampness. He sits up a few hours each day, one arm free from plaster casings and resting on a pillow. Poor, feeble, shrivelled, dead-looking arm that it is, with the puckered scars, and stretches of hideous, thin skin that has so newly formed and healed. The other arm is in plaster for another week, the knee is rigid, immovable; but I am now such a skilful *masseuse* that a Stockholm institute would give me a degree. I rub and rub, and work the poor paralysed muscles and broken nerves by the hour, and now I regularly attend on Vladimir as professional *masseuse*, after the surgeon sees him in the morning, and again for a last hour, before I leave in the afternoon. In this way, my whole day goes by, passed in the barracks; and I have no need for lessons or any devices for passing the time.

I have little time for my garden, or hardly for curio buying any more. I see Madame Takasu and the American sister of charity only when they are on duty in their week's turns at the hospital, bandaging, feeding, changing, and bathing the patients, and tidying the wards. It is always a wonder to me how these two quiet, delicate women, with no previous training or experience, can rise to the emergency of these war times, and stand up under this heavy hospital work. But then, I never could have supposed that I myself could endure such things, could even look upon such raw and gaping wounds as I have washed, and helped to dress and bandage. Here, I wash a *mujik's* face, as naturally, without thought of the strangeness of the proceeding, as if it were the face of one of my little nephews. Yesterday, it was a poor Siberian Cossack, with a face and a shock of hair like any wild animal, whom I made ready for the surgeon. A piece of shell had struck his back; had gouged a hole as large and deep as a wash-basin, down to the very bone, and his sufferings were acute. He moaned and looked at me, with the piteous eyes of a dumb beast.

Human life seems so cheap, when one considers the thousands who lay dead on the Liaoyang plain, and the tens of thousands who marched away, that one wonders if it is worthwhile, if it is merciful, to rescue such a wrecked and battered piece of humanity, who never can be useful, strong, or sound again. And then I think of Vladimir and of the man he calls the "*Grand Prix*," the hospital patient who is beyond all rivalry in the number of his personal casualties—that sailor from the *Varyag*, who had one hundred and forty-two wounds in his body! That many splinters and bits of shell, some as fine as bird shot, had been driven into him. They picked the pieces out one by one, cured him, and sent him off.

With these disasters in Manchuria it is now plain that we shall spend the winter here. I shall see my camellia hedge in bloom after all. I have lived on from day to day in such absorption in the one thing—Vladimir's progress—that I have forgotten all outside affairs. I had talked vaguely of going to Kobe for stores, for necessaries for myself and Vladimir, but finally felt I could not leave him for even three days. Anna went with the returning French Consul, bought everything, and returned in the charge of one of the professional guides, with such a mountain of boxes that we were put to it for a place to stow them at first. Everyone wanted shopping done in Kobe, and Anna had shirts, *pajamas*, overcoats, dressing gowns, smoking jackets, and such things made to the trunk full. Vladimir is cheered, I am sure, by his quilted gown, and his fur slippers, and new bamboo lounging chair, and he wears now the look of respectable invalidism. I affect to shake him that he does not hurry faster to get well, that I may have him under my own roof for the Christmas.

And that roof! Alack and alas! What a time I have had with it! Anna brought down stoves from Kobe; iron ones made in America, and the imitation of them made in Tokyo, and also stove-pipes for all.

91

I thought I had only to employ the workmen and show them where to put them. But, ah me! there was the landlord to reckon with! I had said nothing about putting up foreign stoves when I leased the house in July! *Bon Dieu!* who could think of stoves then! The landlord was sure it would set his house afire to put stoves in, and that it would dry and shrink the exquisite woodwork, until there would be cracks and draughts everywhere. For my own comfort, he begged me not to use foreign stoves. Finally, through, the help of the Protestant missionaries, who had stoves and yet never burned the houses down, I won over the old obstructionist—at an increased rental, of course, to cover fire risks.

Two of the suspected sick officers are now very plainly on the verge of insanity, if not wholly in that condition. One lies on his cot with the blanket drawn over his face, and refuses to speak or eat. I have been called twice to help coax and humour him into taking his food, and after a childlike acquiescence, he covers his face again, and lies silent by the hour. At night, he mutters under his blanket, or parades the ward, lifting the curtains and walking into each room to count the people there. Vladimir has had two terrible shocks by waking in the darkness to feel a presence in the room, and to know by whispered mutterings that it was the lunatic at large in the night. We spoke to one of the young doctors about it, but he only giggled, thought it was funny, and said he would ask the chief-surgeon to have these dangerous men isolated, or at least locked up at night.

The other man has the uneasy excitement and the glittering eyes of one who might become dangerous at any moment; and I am thoroughly unhappy at having Vladimir, weak as he is, in such surroundings. It does not promise a nerve cure, and fate could not have done anything worse than to send those two unguarded lunatics into his ward! Ah! if I could only take him to my little house! If I could only take him away, away, far from Japan—over to America—anywhere—where I could keep him away from this atmosphere of war—these sights and perpetual reminders of battles and, worse yet, of defeats! Why not release this poor battered wreck of a man now, as much as the seventy aged and crippled Russians they turned over to the French Consul a few weeks ago? He can never fight or harm them again. He is a non-combatant hereafter.

Sunday, October 30th.
Today it is admitted that the Japanese have again captured the

mountain that looks down upon Port Arthur. The slaughter has been awful; worse, Loris says, than when It was captured and recaptured by the two forces in September—when one side of the hill was blue with the bodies of dead Russians, the other side brown with the dead Japanese. They seem to love to talk of these things of horror there in the hospital; to dilate on trenches heaped with dead, and fields soaked with blood; and Vladimir is fed on horrors every hour that I am not with him.

Why will they not let me take him out to my house? We will not run away. The police may watch us. We could not possibly get off this island of Shikoku, if both were agile and active. Their caution is absurd. If it were not for Vladimir imploring, and the consul's advising me not to do anything just yet, I should talk seriously with the chief-surgeon and see, if by appeal to Tokyo and a little legation help, we could not get something granted in such an exceptional case. It is so hard to wait and wait, and see Vladimir grow worse, or arrested in his recovery. He will never be able to leave the barracks, if he is to be kept there in a ward of restless, nervous men forever arguing and talking and harping on their woes.

On these perfect autumn days it means much for the officers in town to forego their long walk and come here to the hospital to see the sick on the two days of the week when general visitors are allowed. These are sad travesties of our "at home" days at Petersburg, for in their Red Cross gowns and makeshift uniforms, the ward has rather the look of a fancy dress ball, but it is a comfort for us of common woes to sit around a *samovar* and maintain some semblance of our social traditions.

I must say that this year's experience has Russified me beyond all measure, and intensified my patriotism, my loyalty, and all my race instincts on the Muscovite side. As with all whom I know of mixed parentage, my Russian traits, Russian leanings are strongest. The Russian blood dominates. No war of England's, not that unhappy Boer war, has touched more than the edge of my nature; while this war, from the first shot at Port Arthur, has fired and roused to life everything in me. It was instinct for both Vladimir and me to instantly rush to Petersburg when Russia was attacked—Vladimir to volunteer, to push for, to insist upon active service, and I to see what I could do for the cause, for the wounded, for the soldiers' families.

In Petersburg, they continually taunted me with being English in my sympathies, with being pro-Japanese; and there were many, many unpleasant incidents. Here, when Vladimir and I argue for moderation, for patience on the part of the reckless officers who want to quarrel with their guards and interpreters, and threaten to escape; when we try to explain things or put them in another light, to prove to them how really kind and considerate the Japanese are to us, how generous are the intentions of the regulations that petty officials distort by their cramped mental vision—then these brother *horios* upbraid us.

"You take the side of the enemy, Sophia Ivanovna. But you and Vladimir are not true Russians—you are foreigners. You have lived all your lives outside Russia. Your country is the Riviera, or England—you are subjects of Albert of Monaco, or Edward VII. No, not quite that. Vladimir has served his country well, and you—yes, you too. Ah, I take it back. I prostrate myself in penitence, and we all know that you, Sophia Ivanovna, have saved us from many follies and disasters here."

Grievsky is now in high spirits and thinks he reads in all the Japanese faces a depression at their failure to reduce Port Arthur—a realisation of the impossibility of that attempt.

"Viterbo and Kondrachenko! Those are our only generals now. They have planned, they have made the fortifications at Port Arthur. They have made it the strongest fortress in the world. I was Kondrachenko's senior. Now he outranks me—he must be a general now. Every month in that siege counts for a year's service, and soon even my own nephew will outrank me! *Ach Gott!* What fighting is there there, now! And I, no part! I am fast aging towards my retiring pension here. In prison! Here! Here! On a little island in Japan! Japan! Japan! What was it ever to me? Have I ever wished for it? Even to see it? What craziness this whole Manchurian adventure! De Witte and his cursed railroads! Alexeieff and his cursed empire of the Far East! Bezobrazoff and his cursed intrigues and Korean forests! For them, for their schemes, I am here, here, here!" And down comes that terrible hand.

Monday, October 31st.

Esper Petroff appeared yesterday, and in a dazed way greeted us all. "I came to see you, to find you and Vladimir, but I cannot believe yet that it is really you. It is too strange. I have been dazed. I have doubted half my senses ever since I started for Manchuria. I continually wonder if I am awake. It has been such a procession of undreamed of and impossible things, ever since I began my 'military promenade' across Asia. I waved my hand and said, 'To Japan!' when I left. And it was true—I came—to Japan direct—by express. I only stopped long enough to report at headquarters, and be assigned to Orloff's command. And then, I walked straight to the arms of the Japanese.

"I saw Anna Pashkoff, as I came through. She is doing great work, good work, taking the sick as they come from Harbin, and she is enlarging her kitchen and hospital all the time. No one else can get lumber, workmen, supplies—but she does. She rages, storms, commands; she scolds the generals, and swears at the colonels, telegraphs to Alexeieff, to Petersburg, and to Tsarskoe Selo, if she doesn't get what she wants. She is the viceroy, the Autocrat of Trans-Baikalia.— Magnificent! She went down on the train with us to Mukden to get some general orders issued by the commander.

"Mukden is a strange headquarters. All this war is strange, anyhow. It is not like the Balkan campaign. There is no imperial camp at Mukden, with the sovereign driving to the field every day, and lunching in sight of the operations. Ah! those were days at Plevna! We have no Skobeleff now, either. There are none like him now—only such generals as he fought against in Ferghana—the thieves and speculators of the supply department. Skobeleff fought that crowd to the finish in Ferghana, and they fought and finished him afterwards in Russia. They are ruling again now, with no Skobeleff to oppose them.

"They saw to it that he never got a promotion, a command, nor a chance again for years. It was only chance, an accident, that put him in the front line at Plevna. After that affair, Alexander Nicholaivitch saw that the clique of army thieves did not run Skobeleff to the rear. These Japanese generals are something like Skobeleff. Their army is all a 'Sixteenth Division.' Oh! don't speak of it.

"Now, Skobeleff in a new white uniform on his white horse was a picture for any soldier to worship and go wild over. He fired the imagination. He appeared from the smoke of a battery, all shining white, like an apparition, like a vision of St. George or St. Alexander Nevsky. Now, there is no powder smoke. No Skobeleff. No heroic figures such as there used to be. The generals do not have *al fresco* luncheons with their staff on the hillside, and do not watch the attack with field glasses, as if they were at the opera. Oh, no! They hide in bomb-proofs and galleries, and listen to telephones to know what is going on. The romance, the picturesqueness, all the theatrical pageantry of war is gone. It ended in '78. Skobeleff was the last general worth putting in a picture. We have a fat admiral holding a telephone receiver, to personify the 'Soul of War' and the 'Spirit of Battle' now. Ugh!

"This war ends everything that could bewitch the imagination.

95

It is all mathematics and mechanics now; plain killing, slaughter by equation and cube roots, by high angle and logarithms. Nevermore will our troops march to battle in parade position, with bands playing, the priest leading, carrying the crucifix to bring blessings on our cause. The last of that was with Zassalitch on the Yalu. No, no! *Without* Zassalitch. He was in a cart driving frantically away from the Yalu. He is a specimen of our generals.

"Now, I suppose, we will have to turn to and study, and work and drill, and pass examinations like those cursed Germans. The Germans! The Germany! They are at the bottom of all our troubles in this war; even if they did not encourage the Japanese, like the English; nor put up the money for it, like the Americans. I always expected us to go to war with Germany next. No one ever thought of Japan. Skobeleff always said there would be a war with Germany, greater than our Turkish war, or the Franco-Prussian. He said war was inevitable between the Slav and the Teuton. One or the other, Pan-Slavism or Pan-Teutonism, would rule the continent.

"And German officers have been boasting all these years that they had conquered Austria and France, and that Russia would come next. Bah! Pan-Slavism dragged us into the Turkish war, and what did we gain? Some promotions—yes; but death, cripples, taxes; and then England cheated us out of Constantinople. Yes, and Bismarck helped her do it; and now, the *Kaiser* continually gets the ear of Nicholas, and what happens? No good, I can tell you. William of Hohenzollern hates us, as he hates the French. Only he is afraid of us. No, I don't know that he is, since our army and our navy are both the laughing-stock of all the world. It is that French alliance that the *Kaiser* hates so. That alliance has been our greatest calamity."

"Oh, no!" I burst in on this sad philippic.

"Yes, it has. Without the frantic adoration of that most enlightened people of Western Europe, we Russians would not have been so complacent at the ignorance and backwardness of our people. That French courtship set the autocracy the more firmly in their pleased self-sufficiency. It put back progress, really. It showed Russia she had nothing to fear from the powers or public opinion of Europe. And then the French money! The millions and millions of *francs!* Where are they? One loan is borrowed; and then another loan is needed to pay the interest due. *Haut finance* that, surely! Oh! great is De Witte, and Wishnegradski before him! What can he show for the French millions?

"Of a truth there would never have been this war if it had not been for those French loans. And if anything happened, and the French wanted their money back, I suppose we would be like Turkey, with an international board to manage our finances. I suppose that is what is ahead of Russia, after this year's downfall and disgrace. And yet, see what a proud place we held a year ago! The foremost power in Europe! The greatest military power. And now? Under the chief command of a thick-waisted, short-winded admiral-viceroy we have lost, lost, lost-r-every battle, every engagement and skirmish, all the affairs of outposts. Never a victory. Only *General Rückwärts! General Rückwärts* in command. And Russia! Great Russia!—has come to this!"

Silence fell. No one spoke; and after a few puffs, Esper began again: "I suppose we will re-form the army after this. We will have to. Then, belonging to the Guards or any of the crack corps and standing well socially in Petersburg, will not stand with the examining boards. Those of us who are blockheads will be weeded out and set to guarding wells and canals in Trans-Caspia. I don't know that they will change much in regard to the men, the rank and file—except to give the poor beggars better food or more pay. They will do very well as they are—*Kanonen-futter, Kanonen- futter.* I don't take all this sentimentalism about the man who carries the rifle. There's socialism in it; and all these great ladies of the Red Cross washing the *mujik's* wounds and binding up his broken leg, is rot.

"A soldier is just a soldier, a machine to load, aim, and fire; to shoot and get shot. I don't think of him as a man; of each unit in a long line of thousands in the same uniforms as a man, a human being, a person like myself, my relatives, my friends, my brother officers in front of these lines. No, all this 'brotherhood of man' sentimentality is rubbish. A soldier is a munition of war merely, like the cannons, the rifles, the ammunition, the horses. So many thousands of each article go to make an army. It is quite the same which is the first on the list.

"You do not think of each individual unit as a man, a brother, an immortal soul, when you see a company of these cursed little khaki-clad monkeys drilling around here, do you? I think not. Oh! that I might never see khaki colour again! All Manchuria is khaki colour— dead, dull, dusty brown. And I suppose we, too, will soon be in khaki, like the English, and like the American *attachés* we had with us. Khaki! Khaki! all the time at the headquarters mess. And all the Japanese a wriggling mass of khaki, like a ripe millet field moving. The Japanese soldiers are all khaki colour, except their eyes and teeth. I looked at

Kuroki well, when he rode by to inspect the prisoners. Well, he was all khaki; all of him, clothes, boots, and even his horse. It made me bilious, jaundiced. Ugh! All the earth, the stubble, the standing crops, the dead millet stalks, the mud houses, the Chinese peasants in them, and also the bare hills. Oh! everything was khaki colour; and when it subsided, we Russians were khaki colour, too—faces, clothes, hair, caps—all coated an inch thick with the infernal yellow-brown dust.

"That khaki reminds me too much of the English at Peking, in 1900; and of those outrageous Americans, who just smiled at us whenever we tried to go a little ahead of them on the march to Peking. They are too smart, those Americans. I wish Germany would thrash them well and take the blague out of them. I would like to see the English and the Americans fight a war *à l'outrance*. Then there would be peace in the world, and freedom for the other nations of the earth. Those two stand in the way of everything. It is these two, and their 'open-door' nonsense about China, that brought on this war, anyhow. They put Japan up to fighting, and they will profit by it more than Japan, their little cats-paw."

Tuesday, November 1st.

That silly boy M—— has tried to escape again, and only wandered about for the night in a paddy field over the hills. Of course, there is no disguise for a tall foreigner here; the country people would not hide a *horio* in their houses for any sum of money; and if he had reached the bay and found a boat, where could he row to." where get food or water? It is such childish foolishness to try to escape; but M—— said he could not stand the confinement and monotony; anything was better for a change. He had been deprived of liberty and confined to his own temple and graveyard compound for a previous attempt to escape. Now he is condemned to six months' imprisonment; and he is taken to a veritable prison, a place for locking up criminals, and is put in a cell, with none of his own people to speak to. Vladimir says it is unaccountable that the Japanese did not shoot him at this second attempt. In any other army, it is the rule.

CHAPTER 16

"La Veuve Anglaise"

Wednesday, November 2nd.

Yesterday we had a charming visitor—the English widow, who has given her services to the Japanese Red Cross Society in Tokyo. And then too came Mme. H——, sister of the bachelor British envoy, who, having rolled bandages with the court ladies in Tokyo and visited the hospitals there, was interested to see the Red Cross work in the provinces. She was like an apparition from another world, as she came into our ward in her mourning robes, with the white halo, the white collar-band and cuffs, as immaculate as if in London that minute. My eyes rested upon her, fascinated, and then the chief-surgeon passed her over to me. The soft English voice was music to my ears; the very sight of her was refreshment after my long routine of unbroken days among nurses, doctors, kimono-clad patients, and others in parts of their uniforms.

Grievsky ruffled like a porcupine when he saw her, was stiff, stolid, and barely courteous, I afterwards told him. "But oh! Those English!" he exclaimed. "Must they follow me, haunt me even here? *Ach Gott!* All their tourists in pith helmets, with red guidebooks, will come next. Sightseeing! My God! The eight remarkable views of Iyo province! And we, the *horios*, are one of them. All of them, I might think, the way some of these old *Kakamakis* on the roads stare at me—stare at me with their back teeth! their palates! their vocal chords! Ah, me! I have come to this—to be a curiosity! An animal in a cage! A monkey at the zoo! A Russian bear in captivity!" And the usual bang on the table concluded the monologue.

Our English visitor left her niece at Hiroshima. And her niece is the Countess Foresta! The *contessa* has married, buried husband and child and mother since I saw her, and is now travelling with an aunt in

Japan. The *contessa* had a sad headache from going so rapidly through six miles of hospital wards at Hiroshima the day before, and had remained there, as her aunt had to leave at daylight on the precise day as prearranged by the Japanese officials who accompanied her to Matsuyama. I begged her to remain another day and to telegraph for her niece. I offered my house, and the chief-surgeon urged her to accept.

I must have come in like a whirlwind in my great excitement, for Vladimir turned in surprise. I sat down weakly, in an access of fear lest Vladimir should denounce me for what I had done, the complications I had deliberately pulled down out of a clear sky.

"Oh! Sophia! Sophia! why will you meddle with such things! Am not I, and my forty-two wounds, and three broken bones, enough, without your dragging two broken hearts into the scene? You have begun it! Now what will be the end? Can you foresee it? Those two may only denounce you, when you have brought them together. Let well enough alone. Don't try to control fate, to direct destiny. You have how many guest-rooms in your spacious villa? And what will you do when you get *la belle* here?"

"Do?" I cried. "Heavens, but you are dense! Is it so long since you were young, Vladimir? Do? What did you do, that summer you met me again at Yalta? Did you need phrase-books to carry on conversations? If I remember, you"—and Vladimir pulled me down and gave me a lover's long kiss. "Yes, that is just what you did. That is what I expect Lyov to do, precisely. And then, all will be settled."

Friday, November 4th.

I went to the station to meet the *contessa*. I think we were both impressed with the strangeness of our meeting in this way and here—*la belle* having run through the whole gamut of a woman's soul-existence since I had seen her. She had lost husband, child, and only parent, within the brief time—a whole chapter of tragedies. Sorrow has chastened and softened her beauty, given it an appealing, a more human quality.

After the banalities of formality, she indicated her maid and guide; and we walked on through the sunset light through the temple grounds—past Dairinji, and into the narrow street that leads to the moat. With the side of my eye, I took in the supple, graceful figure in severe black, that walked with me, and—worldling that I am—it was with the joy of long deprivation that I noted the perfect tailoring, the touches of modernity in the simple costume. It was my own world, my own kind again; after this queer life here in a far province, seeing no foreign women for days on end, save Anna in her cotton frocks.

"Ah," cried *la belle*, as we came out of the little street of book and paper shops to the corner of the moat, with the *château* high above us, just showing its black gables against the rose and gold sky. "This is the ideal. This is my castle in Japan, that I have read and dreamed of. I must go up there. None of their other *shiro's* and *gosho's* come up to this for placing. And what a dream of a trip it is over here from Ujina! I sat in the pilot-house all the way. I could not lose a minute of it. Switzerland! Italy! Japan! I am torn to tell you which one is the most beautiful country on earth. Just now, it is this! It is this! It is this! And so strange! So different from all the other countries! I always wanted to come here. I had my mind quite made up to coming to Japan one winter in Rome."

We had a dear little dinner quite by ourselves, we three; *la belle* in a severe white gown, that made her more than ever a goddess of beauty. Such lines! Such pure and perfect contours! Such fine and delicate colour! Certainly one of the most beautiful countenances I have ever looked upon—a sculptor's model, as she sat. I have not looked on her like since she vanished from me in Rome; and I have seen so little of beauty in these last months, that I could not keep my eyes from her face—nor any more my mind from Lyov.

It was arranged for them to see the sights, and on the following day to visit the hospitals and *Ide-bude-machi,* where the young naval officers have a charming *quartette.* The Queen of Greece sent the piano, the violins came from the Grand Duchess Serge's funds, and those clever boys have had Japanese make other instruments for them. They play well, and we urge them to go on tour when they return to Europe. "The Prison Orchestra!" Consider the furore! Tickets, fifty *roubles* at least.

A Prisoners' Orchestra

CHAPTER 17

"La Belle Canadienne"

Saturday, November 5th.

I hardly dared to go near Lyov, nor yet to stay away. I felt guilty. I had excruciating dread lest he find me out, lest my face declare my embarrassment when I looked in on him, as I passed to Vladimir's ward.

"Oh! Yes. Thank you; a thousand times. Better, I suppose. I really don't know though, that it makes me glad. What for? What for? Except that I appreciate the past. A sound body and whole bones! What blessings!" he sighed. "Do you know, Sophia Ivanovna, I had a curious dream last night? We were all in Rome again, dining with you. We drank *Aste spumante* with the fragrance of peaches; I can faintly taste, remember tasting it, yet. We were all there—the Canadian beauty—Contessa Foresta, too.

"Well, something happened, a fire, an explosion, or Boni's excavations, or a campanile collapsed with us; but anyhow, I lay among great stones that weighed on me. One where there is the break in my leg, and another on this slashed arm. I could not move. You and Vladimir were there; but Vladimir was under great weights too, and you were trying to help him out. *La belle* came to me, and said: 'Come!' I struggled. I could not move. I told her to see how I was weighed down. 'Come!' she said, in that grand manner of hers; and suddenly, I felt myself rise and move! move out, move past all these wards, the operating room, and the chancery. We passed the guardhouse, we went past the sentries, and out, out!

"*Ach Gott!* it was too real. I have lived it over, thought it over, remembered it all distinctly, a hundred times since I woke. I see her now, the very curve of that perfect chin, the gold lights in her hair. Ah me! Sophia, I do not want to live. What can I live for, hope for now?

Where shall I go when this is all ended? In what corner of Europe drag out my maimed life? I, a cripple!"

★★★★★★

"Oh, Sophia! Sophia! See what you have done !" said Vladimir. "You have loosed the fates, and now you cannot control them. Here's the fourth act of your drama coming on top of the first scene of the first act. Your little comedy, if it is one, and not a tragedy, does not develop artistically. They would never stage it at the Gymnase, nor the Odéon. Your events are moving too fast. How are you going to hold your players back, to check them up?"

"But she's not coming here today. They have only telegraphed for permits to visit the prisoners' quarters, so they cannot come till to-morrow; and they went this morning to Tobe, to visit the potteries. They can't come before tomorrow."

"Ah! That is better. You will have to think out a denouement—when one day has elapsed. It is your affair, not mine. I wash my hands, now, and go to my *fauteuil de balcon* to look on. But I shall criticise, remember—like a brute, like Sarcey and Scott rolled in one."

"But, shall I tell Lyov first that she is here—in Japan—in Mat-suyama—in my house—in this ward." or leave them to explain all themselves?"

"Oh, heavens! Sophia, don't ask me. Lead up to it a little, I beg you. Tell him that *la Veuve Anglaise* of yesterday is the *contessa's* aunt and sister of the British minister, who has just this summer come out to Japan. A fine time to change ministers! After the beginning of the war! But then, Sir John's a soldier, and better than the pale civilian with a liver, who has gone to Carlsbad. Sir John is a dozen of his predecessor at any game—picquet, cricket, and diplomacy. Anyhow, lead Lyov up to the possibilities. Let him plan it inside his own head, if you can. *Tiens!* but your drama grows interesting, now that you've called telepathy to your aid. Of course, the mystic air waves have carried signals of her presence, as our theosophical, hypnotical, mesmeric friends in Rome would say. This outdoes all the *séances* in the Barberini and at Monte Giordano. Lucky thing that Foresta broke his neck anyhow. It wouldn't do for the dramatic unities to have him around, alive, on the stage, now. He's better in background, in far perspective. It would take a whole act to put him out of the way."

I let Lyov tell me his dream once again; and then asked what he thought of *la Veuve Anglaise. Ah! bas!* he hadn't thought. He had not looked.

"But does she remind you of anyone?" I asked. "Is she like anyone you knew in Rome?"

"Oh, yes," she reminded him of her one hundred twin sisters, all replicas of the same conventional *veuve Anglaise—grand deuil* or *demi-deuil*, they were all *veuves* to him.

"But," I said, "she is the sister of the new British minister, you know, and he is the uncle of the Contessa Foresta. Now do you think anything at all?"

Lyov stared at me for a full minute. "By all the saints! Sophia Ivanovna!" he said, slowly, with difficulty. "I don't know what she looked like; whom she looked like. Not like *mia* Mira, as you know. For no one ever was as beautiful as she. But Sophia! That dream! It was a message from *mia* Mira last night. She must know that I am here. She will come and lead me out. I believe it. Has *la Veuve* gone? Will she come here again? Oh, ask her, and tell me everything about *la belle*—and—Foresta, too. Yes, I want to know. Is she happy? Will Foresta live forever, do you think? There are great epidemics and new diseases nowadays, you know. And Italy may go to war, too, some day. Ah! I shall mend."

******

My ladies came back charmed with their day's excursion, and loaded with vases and figurines of the soft ivory-white Tobe-yaki, that is so nearly the priceless old *blanc de Chine* that I have always loved the most. The *contessa* knows Oriental and shares my passion for *blanc de Chine*. And, by the way, if I live to be a hundred years old, *blanc de Chine* will never be the same again, and always must remind me of Matsuyama. For we eat and drink from Tobe-yaki plates and cups, and Tobe-yaki vases hold our flowers.

"Do you see this?" said the *contessa*. "Well, upon the advice of my superior guide, I have just paid an old sinner named Dorobu, in Kyoto,—never go to him by the way,—sixty-six *yens* for just such another trumpery little, white vase with lions' heads near the collar. The very twin, the very twin of this one. So, I demanded of *M. le Courier*, when I saw all these at Tobe, how it is? and if he doesn't think that precious bit of old *pai-tzu*, or *chien yao*, came from this same kiln at Tobe."

"What did he say?"

"Oh! what they always say when cornered: 'Very curious! Very curious.' And by the way, we had an addition to our party today. At the second station, a Japanese officer came in, bowed to us, and after a time spoke. He said he was from the headquarters office, and would go with us to Tobe, if we wished. If we wished! The idea! Of course, he was detailed for that very duty—to trail us, to listen, and question, and pump us, and to put it all down in those notebooks of theirs. I suppose it is necessary in time of war; as Aunt Ellen and I might liberate all these prisoners. Japan, without the *gendarmes*, and the policemen, and their notebooks, would be so much more charming. Except for the passport nuisance, it might as well be Russia here. They are mad on the subject of spies. Say: '*Rotan! Rotan!*' and they go off their heads at once. Even Uncle John advised me not to go near the prisoners here, and to always explain that I was English, even claim to be an American, rather than emphasise my Italian name. It seems that the Great Republic is most in favour now, in spite of the English Alliance; much to the disgust of mine uncle. It ruffles him.

"Our little officer, however, was very agreeable. He had a charming manner, and if he was a little slow with his English at first, he had a good day's practice lesson in colloquial. I was his *pedante*. I felt just like one of the *pedantes* walking their boy pupils around the Pincio. I made him talk to all the old peasants for me, and ask if they had sons at war, and we gave them money and—oh! one old woman, who was carrying a big bundle of staves along the road, said she had two *kodomos* at the war, and one of them had sent her a *yen*, and the government gave the son's wife two *yens* a month for the family of six! Think of it! She pays fifty *sens* a month for the rent of a house; *house* she called it, *o'uchi*. What could it be like for fifty *sens*? She earns twenty *sens* a day, carrying staves from the mountain down into the town, two round trips; four miles in the morning, and four in the afternoon. And this was her last trip down, poor thing. We put the little old brownie into my *kuruma*, bundle and all. You should have seen her face when the thing moved off! I gave her money to buy *katsuo-bushi*, rice, and some good strong *sake* for her honourable old health, and Aunt Ellen sent money for winter flannels for the son's children—four of them. Wouldn't you know *Madame la Tante* was English by that? Flannels! Oh! soup and flannels, to be sure, for the parish poor!

"Well, when we got to the station there was our old woman with all the family. The *o'uchi* was emptied out and drawn up on the platform in a bowing row; even the baby on her back bobbed its head, when mother and grandmother bobbed. All our beneficiaries of the day were bobbing there, too. And policeman and *gendarmes!*—a few—many hundreds of them, with those notebooks, of course. Being such distinguished visitors, with military escort and the whole police department all out in our honour, we tried to meet the situation. We managed to make up an even fifty *yens*, and asked the chief of police to give it to the most needy of the soldiers' families, as our appreciation of a day in Tobe.

"'To how many families?' asked the chief, while a sub took notes for him in a wretched little black book. 'We have twenty most needy families, eighty families in distress, and one hundred and eleven families insufficiently supplied in this district.'

"We assigned it to the twenty most needy, and I shall send eighty *yens* over for the families in distress. Although you see no beggars and no misery flaunted here, there must be great suffering among the reservists' families. This government relief of two *yens* a month is not enough to feed whole families, old women, young children and all. Oh! that this war were over! And I suppose you wish it more fervently than I, Madame von Theill? How happy if we were all in Rome again! At your villa as before."

"Yes. If we were only back in Rome again! Vladimir in an invalid chair on the sunny terrace, as he likes to picture himself, watching the forum through the telescope. If we only were! To see Vladimir, and Boni, and Lyov Siemenoff puttering over a box of green, copper scraps would give me all the joy in the world."

At the mention of Lyov's name, she lifted her eyes and looked clear through me and my bungling conspiracies.

"Is M. Siemenoff here in Matsuyama?" she put to me point-blank.

"His—servant was brought to the hospital some weeks ago," I weakly stammered.

"Where was his master then?" and the eyes, looking through my transparent answer, put me in the flutter that I had expected the mention of Lyov's name to produce in her. I blurted out all I knew, and submitted to her cross-questioning in penitence. A judge in court could not have been more calm and judicial than she.

"I shall stay here with my maid, if you will let me share your *ménage?*" said the impassive one; and at least seven scenes of my melodrama were swept away. They do things differently in this generation, I see. At least, the joke is on Vladimir for once.

CHAPTER 18

Lovers' Meeting

Sunday, November 6th.

Lieutenant Ito came to luncheon with us, and incidentally we explained to him that the *contessa* and I were old friends in Rome; that I lived in Rome always in the winter and went to England in the summer; that I had not been in Russia for five years, when the war broke out.

"*Naruhodo!*" (wonderful) said the lieutenant at that; and "*Naruhodo!*" he said again when the *contessa* told of Vladimir's occupations in archaeology. "Ah! he studies and learns something for the good of his country."

We repeated the Von Theill autobiography to make it quite clear, and then told him as distinctly that *la* Contessa Foresta, although a widow of an Italian officer, had been made a British subject again by the courts at Ottawa. All this for the benefit of the headquarters, where, of course, it was put in writing post-haste.

I looked in on Lyov, as I went by, and told him that *la Veuve* would come again, and that she could tell him about the widow of Count Foresta.

"Widow!" shouted Lyov, almost leaping from his bandages; and such a light flashed over his face, such a look came in his eyes, as it is not fit for any, but the one woman in all the world, to meet in man's eyes. It was the real Lyov again, the handsome young giant of the frank face and laughing eyes, that we had lost in Rome.

And Vladimir! Oh! man! man! what inconsistencies are thine! He knew the *contessa* would act in just that way. He knew it would come out, just as he said it would. Anyhow, the *affaire de coeur*, that seemed out of my hands already, was doing him good—a tonic that braced him visibly and took his mind off his woes and Russia's woes.

When the orderly told me the *Barina* were coming, I ran to Lyov to straighten his pillows and arrange my *mise en scène*. "The two English ladies are coming soon," I said.

"Two! Ah-h!" sighed Lyov slowly, luxuriously, closing his eyes. "I knew it."

Did he? Indeed! Really, he and Vladimir are too much.

While the officers greeted the great English *Kangofu*, I gave the *contessa* the routine account of the nurse's duties, how the watches were kept, the milk chilled, the water heated—and she looked at me. Looked through me again for a change, and looked protest at the idle delay.

The chief-surgeon lifted the curtain. "Captain Siemenoff, one of General Mistchenko's officers, severely wounded at the Shaho," he said, and as the *contessa* stepped in ahead of us, I started hastily for Vladimir's alcove as refuge, and almost ran into Grievsky. I presented him. He bent low over Madame H——'s hand, and Andrew Y—— shuffled his straw sandals together and paid his compliments. We all walked on together to Vladimir, whose face was blank inquiry, for no *contessa* appeared with us. I went back to tell that the *samovar* waited, and Lyov, looking at me with defiant impatience, said: "She does not want tea."

We laughed, the *contessa* bent and said something, and I pulled her away as the ferret-interpreter and a nurse passed by. In some way, I knew the affair was settled, and out of my hand. There was a sense of ownership, an air of proprietorship in the magnificent way in which Lyov put me aside and outside of it all, and my share in the affair was plainly over.

The *samovar* was hissing, the sun shone, the air of the little cubicle was full of chrysanthemum spice, and all was good cheer. Every man paid adoring court to the beautiful woman—the first they had seen for ages. And how old and yellow, faded and wrinkled, we others looked beside that piece of human perfection!

She carried a cup of tea to Lyov, waving aside all offers of assistance, and dumfounding me by the quiet matter of fact: "Two lumps, please, and a bit of lemon, he likes."

She came back for bread and butter; she came again for a second cup of tea. "The nurse says he is much better this afternoon," said the Goddess condescendingly, as if I were a stranger in the ward; and I retorted with the malice of the old cat I can be: "Oh, the nurse! I am glad you have a *duenna* in there." And was immediately sorry for what

I had said.

When our little tea-party broke up, the *contessa* was first to reach Lyov's curtain, and said: "Goodbye, Captain Siemenoff. I hope we have not excited or made you worse."

"Oh! quite to the contrary; you have made me well. Enter, I beg of you."

We all went in to see the artful beggar. The surgeon looked surprised at the change in his patient—at the smiling, radiant countenance, the strong cheerful voice.

"Why, the captain *san* is four weeks better than he was this morning!"

"I shall get up tomorrow morning; and if the honourable chief-surgeon permits the Contessa Foresta to give me the same tea tomorrow, I shall walk the next day; and carry my trunk to the Kokaido the third day."

"Ah! and me! Poor me! Me also!" cried Grievsky, "Will not the gracious *contessa* give me tea, too—now—tomorrow—oh! at any time? Oh! honourable doctor, please prescribe that same *tisane* for me. Tea *à l'Anglaise*. Everything *à l'Anglaise* for me. I also desire to go and live at the Kokaido, and wear real clothes again."

"Ah! Me! Me! Me!" cried Akimoff, waving his crutch above the floor. "*Eikoku, Ingirisu o'cha* (English, English tea). I will drink it too. Litres of it! Litres of it! If the Contessa Foresta herself prescribes it and gives it." The Japanese officers laughed gleefully at the mock comedy, and the *nesans* giggled sympathetically.

"I shall return," said the *contessa*, speaking directly to Lyov. And the others, all uncomprehending, capped it by wailing humorously: "Return—in the springtime? Oh no, *Madame la Contessa*, tomorrow, tomorrow. We beg you."

"Yes. Surely. Will the honourable doctor prescribe my *tisane* for all the patients, if they are really better in the morning?"

"*Saio de gozarimasu*," said the little doctor, helpless with laughter and under the spell of her beauty as much as we westerners.

CHAPTER 19

The Foreigner Kwannon

Monday, November 7th.

La Contessa and her aunt and I, and the faithful Lieutenant Ito, of course, went to Dogo and saw the sights—the hot springs, where Jingo Kogo stopped to bathe on her way to the conquest of Korea; and the rooms in the bathing pavilion occupied by the present crown prince of Japan, when he came to Iyo province a few seasons since. The bathing pool is the heart of the village, the market place and social exchange, as much as the forum of Augustus at Rome. It is never closed, and hums night and day with the companies of men, and of women and children, who boil in separate pools. There are pools of different degrees in their heat and sulphur strength, but only a Japanese could endure the hottest of all. There are parties of Russian officers at Dogo every day. The country people and the villagers receive them kindly and pleasantly, and no one looking on would think the *horio sans* (honourable prisoners) any different from other foreign tourists, who now and then visit this faraway province. The village children are always on the alert for the coming of the *Rokokos* (Russians), bob their little courtesies, and, just as surely, receive some present.

If we had been by ourselves, three ladies, they might have let us look in upon the tank, where the women and children chatter by the half-hour, up to their necks in hot water, but regulations do not permit mixed bathing, nor for a man to look in. Our little officer, too, was enough of Modern Japan to be consumed with a *mauvaise honte* over the naturalness and simplicity of the national bathing customs, and so distressed lest we should remark too much upon it, that we could only stop a moment to comment on the chirp and chatter from the community bath-tubs, and to note the thumps on the big barrel drum that warns them of the passing quarter-hours.

Tea houses surround this central bath-house, and they all possess stores of beautiful screens and pictures that are brought out to beautify the rooms of the convalescent Japanese officers, sent to these springs to recuperate—heroes to the worshipping Dogo people, who overwhelm them with gifts and attentions. In lesser degree, the convalescents of the rank and file receive the gratitude of their fellow subjects. They are quartered in the garden pavilions and tea houses of the public park, on the site of the old castle of the Hisamatsu family. The moats are dry, but their embankments and stone walls remain, and the glacis of the old fortress is a sloping lawn planted with young cherry and plum trees.

I must admit that a Japanese hospital is the cleanest, most spotless and immaculate place in all the world. For one thing, the soft matted floors are as clean as the white beds laid on the floor, and the Red Cross *kimonos* of white calico carry out the symphony in white. And the Japanese faces, yellow as they are, are always so shiningly clean. I wish our poor dirty Cossacks could be like them in this regard, but their heavy boots, coarse skins, and wild mops of hair on head and face, make them unattractive at best. And the white *kimono*, with their heavy leather boots, finishes any chance of their being objects of Russian pride. We are not a pretty people in masses; not an artistic race, not an aesthetic nation.

One pities, only pities the poor Cossacks that they do not possess that indefinable quality, charm; pities them that they cannot be cleaner and more civilised-looking; pities their ignorance, and that they are not even able to know how low in the scale of civilisation they are. *Ach Gott!* what years, what generations lie before poor, distracted, incompetent, ignorant, and uneducated, half-awakened Russia before its peasants and work people can be as clean and well educated as these average Japanese. Talk about the awakening of China! Let us wake up Russia first.

The Japanese invalids sat up on their *futons* and made nice bows when we were introduced, and I felt myself a museum specimen, when they explained me to the convalescent company. The surgeon told them that my master lay at the barracks hospital, wounded forty-two times; that I had come all the way from Russia to nurse him; and that as a thank-offering I had given a thousand *yens* to the Red Cross and to the Volunteer Nurses' Societies. Then, down on the mats went every black head, after a chorus of wondering "*So deska's*" (is that so?) and "*Naruhodo's!*" (wonderful), had interrupted the surgeon. Beginning with the first invalid on my right, each made some little expression in Japanese, that they were sorry the Japanese soldiers had hurt my husband and made me so much trouble; but that these accidents must happen in war; and that it was hard luck that the bravest men were always wounded first and most severely. They thanked me for my gifts to the Red Cross, and they thanked me, quite as much as they thanked the great English *Kangofu*, for coming to see them.

One man without arms had not been able to raise himself at all; so, while the others were distributing their picture books and gifts, I talked to him in Japanese, and told him more of his visitors. "Is that one a *Kangofu* too?" he asked, looking toward the *contessa*. "I wish she would stay here at Dogo. She looks like the *Kwannon* at my home temple. It is like hearing *Kwannon* talk. Maybe *Kwannon* can talk English, too."

We watched the young recruits doing calisthenics and vaulting on the castle drill ground near headquarters; and, saddest sight of all, saw the relatives of the soldiers waiting in the open pavilion of a visitors' shed. The reservists called in some weeks ago go to Manchuria this week; and for days the town has been full of country people, who have come in to see them off—pathetic old fathers and mothers, women with flocks of children, and always the baby on the back, sometimes borrowed, I am sure, to account for the universality of the fashion.

"*Okasama! Okasama! Anata Tobe sakujitsu?*" (Madam, madam! You were at Tobe day before yesterday?) said one to the *contessa*, and immediately the visitors' shed was in agitation. The whole countryside had evidently heard of the visit of the benevolent *Kangofu*, and they surrounded us, bowing and making nice polite speeches of praise for the kindness of the foreign ladies. "And are you English *Kangofu* also?" they asked me, noticing my Red Cross badge. I hesitated for a moment, before I electrified them with the announcement that I was a Russian *Kangofu*, Some started back in surprise and repulsion, and others came nearer to look their fill at such a living curio.

"Let me see! Let me have a look!" wailed a toothless old man, whose sight was dim, whose face was one mass of fine wrinkles. "I have never seen a Russian until today, and that was only a sailor. I want to see a Russian woman." After a long, slow scrutiny, "Old Age" turned away from me wearily. "Why, she is just like other foreign women, like the missionaries who come to our village every week. Not different. I thought the Russians were all very big and fierce, fierce as tigers, and had red hair. This one has the same high beak and the sharp eyes of a bird, like all the other foreign women. That is all." I sank far, far down, in even my own estimation, when the company of deep-voiced old women politely agreed with him in a chorus of "*Saio de gozarimasu!*"

We managed it very well at the barracks that afternoon. Madame H—— stayed at home to rest and receive some ladies of the Red Cross Society. The guide secured some charming dwarf trees, and those venerable pines, and cedars, and maples, as seen through the reverse of an opera glass, distracted even me from noticing how often and for how long the *contessa* was with Lyov. That was a triumph of Japan's floral art surely!

Ah! Japan! Japan! Why do you go to war, and slash, and shoot, and slaughter, and wallow in blood, when you can grow these adorable trees and do other things so much better?

Leave battle and murder to our Cossacks and to the Turcomans, who can do nothing else. It disconcerts me to find these Japanese supreme in the barbaric, murderous arts of war that require no civilisation. It shocks me to think of an artistic, flower-loving people going to war! To bloody, untidy, expensive war! It is incongruous.

★★★★★★

The *contessa* and Lieutenant Ito stayed as long as I did that afternoon, for we had music after the tea, and all who could walk, or limp, or be helped in, came to listen. Poor Lyov had to lie far away, to hear only and not see. For his benefit we went to his alcove, with Akimoff's violin, and sang the *Ave Maria* over again.

Later, the *contessa* and I walked far up the moat side to a curio shop, where I knew a tea bowl was waiting. We came home through the street of shops and we talked of—Japanese pottery! of Bizen and Seto! of Awata and Satsuma! of Karatsu and the rest! Was ever anything so banal!

There was a local *fête* going on at a temple, and a woman stood in the gateway holding a strip of cotton cloth with needles and black thread for the "*Sen nin Riki*" (one thousand people's strength). The *contessa* stopped and made a cross stitch and bit the thread, and then I stitched a knot on the bit of white cloth which the soldier-husband will wear to war—a girdle which will endue him with the strength of a thousand people, and by their thousand prayers carry him safely through all dangers. With every draft of troops that go to the war, many are provided with these magic belts.

★★★★★★

And now that my guests are gone, and life is running along in its same routine, I have a strange sensation of something come and gone; something missed from my life. I feel as if I had been in Rome, or as if suddenly snatched away from it. I indulge in daydreams, too. Lyov must have the permission of his commanding officer to marry—of the Japanese surgeon-in-chief, or Marshal Oyama, he insists with a grimace. I suggest the French ambassador, or a cable to Zakharoff in Petersburg. And then what about the religious service? How will they manage that." Lyov being orthodox and *la Contessa* officially Romanist since her Italian marriage, there are difficulties without end. It is not possible to arrange a marriage until the war has ended, and I do not think that Sir John will permit his beautiful niece to introduce herself to the affairs of the imprisoned enemies of his ally during this war.

Poor Lyov! What an eligible *parti* you were in Rome! And now what a detrimental! what a sad *mésalliance* for a young and beautiful woman to marry you! to marry a Russian! I dare say, Lord Salisbury, if he were alive, would lump us in as one of "the dying nations" now.

CHAPTER 20

In Kiku Time

Monday, November 28th.

I had word from the *contessa* that she had returned to Tokyo and had remained there, while Madame H—— had gone north to visit more hospitals. She had informed her uncle of meeting old friends, and has made him wish to do a tour of the Inland Sea also. Then the artful minx writes fully how she has met at Legation dinners the Minister of War, the Minister of Foreign Affairs, the famous chief of the general staff, etc., and how she has told them of the admirable arrangements she saw at Hiroshima and Matsuyama. She wrote:

"I quite delivered myself of a monologue on Matsuyama to the War Minister, and he agreed with me in my praises of the chief-surgeon, and could believe that his Russian patients grew fond of him. He was pleased, too, that the commandant has shown you such great kindness and consideration in your trying position, and he praises him to the skies."

I chuckled to myself, for the local military, of course, read this long before I did. When I took it to show to Vladimir, he shouted in his old joyous way: "Oh! this is rippin', as my English kinsfolk say. Trust the *contessa* to manage the whole affair now, Sophia. You may sit back and fold your hands; in other words, devote yourself to the affairs of your own heart—to your husband in the hand, while the *contessa* cages hers, who is still in the bush! What a loss to diplomacy that woman is!"

I had signs enough that the *contessa's* messages from Tokyo were read and approved by our guardians, and were doing good work for us all. The surgeons smiled in greeting, even the Prussianised commandant reined up beside my humble *jinrikisha* in the street, to pass the compliments of the day, and ask if my "*Herr Colonel*" was improving! Everything has seemed to go on so well and so smoothly. Vladimir has improved, and his spirits are so gay and the weather so glorious, so like our warm Roman autumn, that once or twice I have really asked myself if I had anything in the world to complain of.

Under my skilful massage, Lyov's shattered arms and knee have begun to feel a little life again. He begins to move, to bend and use them. Picture post cards come to him in showers. There is her big English handwriting on one side, and only her initials on the other; but that seems enough. Then she has written me:

I have definitely broken with Rome and begun Greek. Baptism soon.

Of course we understand, but however will they manage an orthodox marriage even then! And will Ah Shing or Ah Tom provide the trousseau for a woman whom Doucet has delighted to dress for these years? And Lyov, whose whole wardrobe is a Red Cross *kimono*—what will he do?

The spice of chrysanthemums is always in the air, and every day I take an armful to the barracks with me. I make Japanese floral arrangements, with Vladimir, Grievsky, and all the critics suggesting; and the little Red Cross sisters, the attendants, even the *coolies*, are eager to pose the stately flowers in ideal, naturalistic arrangements. The dullest-looking Cossack wakes a little to the beauty of flowers, and Lyov and Akimoff, who have most soul, are becoming apt pupils of the old teacher of flower arrangement who instructs us twice a week.

"*Ach Gott!*" said Grievsky, striking his forehead with despair. "To think of these monkeys knowing, inventing, evolving this finest of all fine arts, and poor old Europe never dreaming of any such things! Why, Paris knows no more about bouquet-making now than it did in Caesar's day; and yet these people have three wholly distinct and rival schools, each with thirty conventional, well-ordered, well-known ways of arranging each flower! Ah! What can we teach the Japanese? It is plain that I, that we, cannot teach them the art of war. And then they know all these other things beside! These arts are so fine, so refined, that the best of us—only us few—can barely comprehend! And think of our *coolies*, our peasants, the Russian *mujiks* spending an hour to pose three little yellow chrysanthemums in a fragile bamboo cup hanging on the wall! *Ach! Ach!* Let us not think of it.

"There are no masters of flower arrangement in our villages, nor yet in the provincial capitals. My head goes all *sakesama* (upside down) when I try to think out some of these things; racial traits, racial conundrums they are. They are too much for me. Oh! Damn Japan! I cannot understand it at all. Damn that American Commodore Perry who opened it all out."

And then Lyov: "Osip, I shall beat you, if you do not step more carefully. Every time you come in, you jar my flowers; and if you make them fall down with your galloping hoofs, I shall ask the Japanese to torture you." And Osip grins and lurches off on tiptoe, not sure whether his master is in earnest or in delirium.

The surgeons told us of an autumn salad of yellow chrysanthemum petals, which will secure long life, as the *kiku* is a longevity symbol.

Andrew Y——, *grand gourmet* that he is, pricked up his ears at this and went headlong to the execution of such a novelty. He served a *kiku* salad the next day, a loose heap of golden petals, shining with oil, salted, and just touched with a vinegar flavour, which went well with its natural spiciness. A portion was waiting when I arrived. "I present you with ten years more of life," said Andrew, bowing as he offered it, "for the Japanese say that any such wholly new sensation adds ten years to one's life."

"Ten years of Matsuyama?" I asked, and he made frantic byplay to toss the plate through the window.

I often find myself wondering how this life will seem to me in perspective, when I have lived some years longer and can then look back upon it. It will not be all sad retrospect, I am sure. My dearest ones, Vladimir, and Lyov, whom I consider one of my own kin, are safe with me here; I can look after them, see them, and do for them. I am sure that today I have much to be thankful for. It is dull, and sometimes irksome, this life at Matsuyama, but how easily it could be worse. How would it be with little Madame Takasu faring forth across all Siberia to find her wounded husband in a Russian hospital? Would that be possible for her?' I think not; and I should protest with horror at the idea of her, alone or with a maid, going straight into the heart of the enemy's country, as I have done. Could she live as safely and comfortably in any little Russian or Siberian town, as I live here? Would she find these perfectly clean, hard, white streets and country roads? these flower-peddlers and poetry-makers watching the moon rise over Siberian hills? Could she go safely about the streets alone all day and after sunset, as I go, and never meet anything but courtesy, kindness, and politeness from men, women, and children?

CHAPTER 21

A Happy New Year—For Japan

Sunday, December 25th.

Our Russian Christmas and the English Twelfth Night were to fall in the same week with the prolonged Japanese New Year festivities. My little household indulged in all the delightful Japanese symbolic decorations; and my doorway had its conventional pine, bamboo, and plum branches, bound with the twisted *shimenawa*, or sacred straw rope, to secure good luck and long life, and to avert evil. The servants had red rice and ceremonial dumplings, and each an extra month's wages and a new *kimono*, and it was a distinct pleasure to give to these who received it with such graceful courtesy.

My whole house was fragrant with the exquisite perfume of dwarf plum trees—veteran trees with mossy, lichen-covered trunks, and growing only a half-metre high. The cream-white flowers exhaled a fragrance that strangely touched and thrilled me. Was it memory, or was it the strange, indescribable charm of this most beloved of all Japanese tree blossoms? Sometimes, as the odour came to me, I seemed struggling from a dream. It was the Japan of long ago. It was Tokyo again, and I was in my drawing-room in the little No. 2 house, and saw the row of tiny plum trees, white ones and rose-pink ones, with down-falling blossoms, against the background of gold screens. The plum trees and the gold screens I have again, but in another, a changed Japan.

★★★★★★

We have really had a little of holiday spirit at the barracks, where Andrew Y——, as head cook, has planned a Christmas feast. It is part of the humour of this situation that Andrew Y——, once of the corps of pages with Vladimir, hussar officer in Alexander Nicholaivitch's time, should have charge of the hospital *kitchens!* That *flâneur* of the boulevards, that pink and pet of the Guards, now studies over menus and supplies, bringing the daily ration of officers and soldiers to the military requirements of so many ounces of this and that, and to the medical requirements of so much carbon, nitrogen, and proteids—so much starch and sugar, so much solid and so much liquid food. He puts his whole mind on it and works hard, and this stimulus of an interest has done him good. He walks now with difficulty, but he can get about, and he is full of projects for keeping the barracks warmer; for, although in sunny December we have blooming hedges and rose-bushes, and golden-fruited persimmon trees have but given way to golden-fruited orange trees, those thin wooden barracks are draughty and bitterly cold. It is rather a joke on us Russians to suffer with cold among the orange groves of Shikoku.

Tuesday, January 3rd.

All day Sunday, the Japanese new-style, official New Year's day, Matsuyama was in gala array, and I drove around the circle of the city in the morning to see the street decorations. The main street was a bower of bamboos and pines. All signs of trade were put away for the day, the little floor counters and show cases moved back; red blankets or precious old Sakai rugs spread on the floor, and the best screens opened out against the walls. Oh! that those gold-leaf screens had been for sale! But nothing was for sale that day. All stocks and commodities were pushed out of sight, and silk-clad companies sat in these golden bays, playing sober games of "go," or enjoying tea and ceremonial cakes. An exquisite flower arrangement was always set on a low stand before the screens, with a bowl or plaque for visitors' cards and souvenirs. Always there was a dwarf plum tree, with its fragrant cream-white or rose-coloured blossoms. Few people moved in the streets, save the rustling, silk-clad visitors, and girls and children, gay in scarlet and brilliantly-painted crapes, playing their New Year's game of battledore and shuttlecock.

"Port Arthur is still ours, ours! 1905 has come, and Kwangtung is still Russian territory!" said Grievsky. "It still affords a safe shelter to our brave fleet. You see! I told you so. A New Year has begun, and our flag is there, as it was last year, will be next year, and for all the years forever to come. Ah! I drink to our brave army! May the fleet, *that* fleet! *la flotte peureuse!*—come here—to Matsuyama! and rest in peace and quiet! *Dame!* but it would give me no heartbreaks to have Togo bag the whole lot, boats and boots, and bring them here—here, where there are men—men who want only the chance to fight for Russia. And *they* lie at anchor, under the guns of the forts! Ah! if I had one battery there! For just one hour! They would make a sortie then. They would move from their anchorage when I placed the sights. They could choose between my guns and Togo's guns. What is our navy for." What has Russia to show for the roubles she has spent for sea power? A flock of boats cowering in a land-locked harbour; a club full of champagne officers enjoying themselves on shore! Ah! let me ever meet one of them in Petersburg! I will pull his nose. I will challenge."

On Monday, I went early to the barracks to help in the operating room as relief nurse, and, on my way home for my *tiffin*, a fusillade came from the skies, the *pom! pom! pop!* of day fireworks overhead. More celebration of the New Year, I thought. The *coolie* stopped, turned a dazed face around to me, and said, grinning: "Ah! *Riojinkco! Riojinko!*" It was as if a shot had struck me. I felt collapsing with terror and fright. Instantly, people ran from their houses, and ran from the side streets to the broad road, recognising the prearranged signal that announced the fall of Port Arthur. They cried: "*Banzai!*" and ran to see the bulletin boards at the newspaper offices in the main street.

I met Madame Takasu, and she stopped her *kuruma* and stepped down to speak to me. Dear little woman! Even in that hour of her great rejoicing, she could feel for me. She put both her hands on mine, as she leaned over, the long ceremonial sleeves of her heliotrope crape coat sweeping my wheels recklessly: "It is your sorrow, I fear. Yes, it is true. Riojinko has fallen down to General Nogi. It was wise, we think, in General Stoessel to save lives and surrender. It could only have been for a few more days, at any rate—and many, many more deaths. It is very hard for you, and for the colonel *san*, I know. But, perhaps, it brings nearer that peace, and that home of yours. It is ordered that nothing be said at the hospital today. There will not be a *Banzai* tonight. It is not officially announced from Tokyo yet. I am so sorry to hurt you by being so happy; but now, no more of our Iyo soldiers shall die over there with General Nogi's sons. Port Arthur is restored to us."

CHAPTER 22

All is Lost—Even Honour

Thursday, January 5th.

Never had I entered the dreary hospital gates with such a heavy heart. I stopped to talk about nothing to Madame Takasu, who looked sympathy from her eyes, to ask Nesan about Lyov's gruel, and to ask the American sister about her home for factory girls, which she has just opened. All the delay did not pick up my spirits, as I dragged my way towards Vladimir, dreading the gloom that I should find there. How hard my life seemed! Vladimir and I tied to this rigid routine of life here in these unlovely surroundings, and our villa at Rome closed, echoing, empty! Sunshine and flowers on the terraces, and all our world driving past. All our world looking up at our walls and perhaps passing a question or remark about us; wondering where we are this winter; laughing at Russia's reverses.

Shall we ever really live again with our chosen friends around us, and come and go, hear music, read new books, and enjoy life's luxuries? Think of all that full, rich life in Rome! What a keen and lively pleasure it would be to dine again at that palace in Funari, or at Pamfili Doria, to sit under the Romano ceiling, and watch the Cellini gilt flagons and epergnes on the table! I am homesick in these holidays. Oh! so homesick for my home, my Rome.

They were not concerned about the fusillade of day fireworks in Vladimir's ward. They were not downcast, but in full, defiant, fighting mood.

"Pouf! Bah! *Madame*, you hear the bombs? Well, do not be disturbed," said Akimoff. "Believe it when you see the prisoners, when Kondrachenko comes and tells us himself. When Port Arthur does fall, there will be no surrenders, there will be no prisoners to come here. They will all be dead—dead every man of them. Not one living Russian will be left there to tell. The *Czar* has charged them. It is honour. As well surrender the Imperial regalia or the Iberian Virgin of Moscow. We have heard these day fireworks before. Come, let us practise our Mass again."

They convinced me, weathercock that I am, just as Madame Takasu and the rejoicing crowds in the streets had convinced me. I saw that it was all the exuberance of the Japanese New Year's spirit; that these men, in their heavy silk *hakama* and *haori*, rustling around to pay their New Year's visits, had had too much *saké*, and could believe anything; that the little butterflies of children, in their gay crape gowns, and the young girls in exquisite crape *kimonos*, playing a gentle battledore and shuttlecock bareheaded in the streets, said "*Banzai!*" as regularly as "*Omedeto!*" It was all a greeting of the season, and we had a cheery afternoon with our music.

There were more day fireworks the next morning, and the gardener brought me a little pink *gogai* that announced the birth of a third son to the crown prince of Japan. Three sons to insure this succession! What luck! Their own Gods surely love the Japanese. Three infant princes already, and not a useless girl-baby yet! And look at Russia with a nursery full of little girls, and the *Czarevitch* but a feeble infant! "Three good lucks!" said Kinsan, the little *amah*. "One piece good luck—New Years; Two piece good luck—Port Arthur; Three piece good luck—the baby! Oh *Banzai!*" she chirruped with a rising inflection, happy from her holiday hairdress to her new *kiri* clogs.

When the crossed flags were hung out at headquarters gates and at all the temples; when the red-rayed service flag flew triumphant from the tallest tower of the *château*, and a great bulletin was put out at headquarters, it was final. Port Arthur had surrendered! The treaty was signed at eight o'clock that night, just as the little prince was born. Will they call him Arthur, I wonder? They should.

The *coterie* in the hospital contradict all the news I bring, and doggedly maintain that it is impossible to reduce that fortress, all the forty fortresses that constitute Port Arthur. Yet it has surrendered; not to an army furiously storming and breaking through the defences, seizing the commands at their posts and the generals in the council chamber. It was not at any such last, desperate moment, that Stoessel betrayed his *Czar* and all Russia, and yielded up the fortress. The Japanese did not come to Stoessel. No. Stoessel sent the offer, and Stoessel and his staff rode to the Japanese headquarters the next day, and signed the humiliating capitulation. Who rode with that traitor that he did not shoot him in the back? And Stoessel gave his horse to General Nogi! Theatricals—heroics. It was not his horse to give. He had surrendered the fortress and all it contained. Why not have magnanimously made Nogi the personal present of a cannon, or a battleship? Bah!

With Port Arthur lost, why should the war go on? Let us go back to Europe. Let the Japanese have Manchuria. It may prove their undoing as it has been ours.

In every mind there is but one question. Why? Why? *Why* did they surrender, when there were food and clothing, guns and ammunition for a year, and more than fifty thousand men?

The lunatics are entirely insane, madmen now. This terrible news has been the last shock for tottering reason, and the surgeons have put them off by themselves, under guard. It was an unspeakable relief when they were gone from the ward, and Vladimir really gained. It must be a sorry night's rest indeed, when one is separated from a pair of lunatics by only a light curtain. The Japanese, who do not sleep or live with locked doors, cannot know how we Europeans feel. I never used to sleep soundly in the flimsy Japanese houses those summers at Hakone. I never got used to being at the mercy of the sliding panel. This life without privacy is different from real living. We Europeans must have locks and bolts, real doors on hinges. Screens and sliding partitions and paper walls give one too temporary, too insecure a feeling. They say it is because of our want of self-control, that we foreigners want to hide and lock. No wonder the Japanese have had to cultivate stoicism, self-control, and the immovable, unalterable countenance, to put the locks and bolts upon their faces and their own inner selves.

The last word is, that the *Kaiser* has decorated the two generals! Stoessel and Nogi. "The two heroes of Port Arthur!" Nogi, yes, perhaps; but Stoessel? No! No! Were he a hero, he would have died in the fort's defence. What a thing for that madman of Europe to do! As indecent as all his other exploits—rushing in where decency would hold back. Could he not wait, in common courtesy, for Stoessel's own sovereign to bestow the first reward—if Stoessel should even merit it?

CHAPTER 23

"Great Sovereign, Forgive!"

Thursday, January 13th.

Stoessel and his inglorious company have reached Nagasaki, to take the Messagerie steamer for Marseilles, and my obstinate Russians now abandon their pose and accept the sad truth. Port Arthur has fallen. The Russian flag has been drawn down from the strongest fortress in the world—the Cronstadt, the Ehrenbreitstein, the Gibraltar of the East. Esper is full of scorn at the details of Stoessel's theatricals when he reached Nagasaki and took farewell of his *confrères* for—three days! He addressed them, after the manner of Napoleon at Fontainebleau; embraced them, kissed them, and they all wept maudlin, senile tears together—to the amazement of the Japanese, who do not at all understand any such demonstrations and parades of emotion. Then Stoessel went down the gangway to his launch, and the gray-beards wept; and he went over to Inasa and occupied a house and garden, and they all came following after and occupied other houses and gardens.

The Nagasaki municipality voted a sum of money, for entertaining these foreign guests, and—how the God of War must laugh! The generals and the admiral will make their retreat at the old *château* of Nagoya until the end of the war. The lesser *horios* will be scattered the length of Japan, in all the old castle towns, where there are garrisons to guard them. We seem a small company here—50 officers and 1300 of the rank and file—in view of the army that is coming. And the viceroy said, before the war began, that his first move would be to land an army in Japan. The army is landing, but the Viceroy of the two-metre belt is not landing with it.

Up to this time, there have been only three thousand prisoners in all Japan. Now, from Port Arthur comes the incredible number of 42,421 prisoners! At least, that is the number of Russians the Japanese

125

say surrendered and were counted. It is staggering to think of. One only recalls Bazaine's army at Metz. A surrender that fitly matches this one. The numbers ring in my ears continually and dance in figures before my eyes. Grievsky snorts with wrath, calls the Japanese figures exaggeration and boasting, something to please the national megalomania; but he and Esper, for all that, run their finger down the printed lists in the Kobe paper and wrathfully comment and argue.

Stoessel sent word out again and again, at the last, that they were "but a handful"; and the Japanese believed there were but 6,000 effective soldiers for all the forts, since escaping torpedo boats had also given that word at Chefoo. All the world, as well as the *Czar*, had talked about a mere 'handful.' The Japanese were lost in admiration that these few thousand men could continue to withstand fatigue, exhaustion, and sleeplessness. The Japanese knew that there must be stores of provisions and ammunition remaining, because such things were rushed in by trainloads for months and months; but they knew also that the most frantic efforts were made at Shanghai in August, to get in medical supplies—anaesthetics, antiseptics, and bandages, which alone had been forgotten in the preparations for a long siege. There were champagne and vodka to last three years. Chloroform and bandages? *Niet! Niet!*

"Oh! this cursed prearrangement!" growled Grievsky, as he thrashed the side of his chair with the Kobe newspaper. "But see how they repelled the officiousness of their ally. Read that! I am glad the English got the rebuff. Bravo! for the Japanese! Yes, I—I—*I* say Bravo! for the Japanese! Read that, and see how those English at Wei-Hai-Wei loaded a ship with medicines and hospital supplies, and rushed over to Dalny as soon as they heard of Stoessel's surrender. And the Japanese said: 'Go away. You cannot come in here. We don't want you. We have medicines and supplies and stores of our own, all ready and waiting, to take in to the Port Arthur hospitals. It has all been prearranged.' Prearranged! Ah! The devil himself must put these ideas into their yellow heads so long beforehand. Prearranged! If the snub to the British had been prearranged, I could love them. Yes, love my enemy for slapping the British face. It was not humanity that took those English over with their accursed hospital ship. No, they wanted to get in there and see Port Arthur in its disorder; to gloat over the Russians in their disaster. They sneaked back to Chefoo, escorted by a torpedo boat, and they saw—probably the Golden Hill, through their binoculs! Good!"

Vladimir and Grievsky, and the older officers, who knew the Franco-Prussian war in all its details, in their cadet days, and also Plevna, are greatly concerned about these surrendered prisoners at Port Arthur. The Japanese cannot care for so many Europeans here in Japan, they say. It will be impossible to get foreign food for this army. The Russian prisoners now outnumber all the Europeans in all the treaty ports of Japan, put together; and the markets are strained as it is. If Germany could not decently care for the French prisoners in 1870, how are the Japanese going to care for these thousands of Russian prisoners? If, in the heart of Europe, the prisoners of war died of hunger and cold, and epidemics of smallpox and typhoid, at every place of internment in Germany, what must we look forward to here?

The Japanese had prearranged everything. Even the champagne for the treaty negotiators went ashore with the first landing-party in May—perhaps, too, the pair of chickens that gallant, old Nogi sent first-off to the supposedly starving Stoessel, only to have his messenger deafened with the crowing of Madame Stoessel's great flock of fowls raised for sale in the local market. The quarantine station in the straits of Shimonoseki was ordered enlarged at the instant the capitulation was signed. All, all was prearranged.

Lists of the spoils of war are published day by day, and we are the more dumfounded. How dare that Stoessel surrender our fortress? How could any man take to Chefoo for him, and telegraph to Europe, those whimpering messages that all were suffering hunger and blood-poisoning, and that only 4,000 men were effective for military service?

Esper and Loris, who knew Port Arthur in July, are consumed with a fury that is not good for either of them. It is hard to beat out and wear out such a rage, and passion, in the restraint and bounds of a prisoner's narrow quarters. "Ah! if I could get away. Go away, and walk *versts* and *versts* over the country alone, and curse and scream in the forest by myself, I could stand this better. But to be in paper walls, in sound of a sentry, in sight of people, other men, my enemies, and to maintain decent calmness and self-control! It is too much."

The Japanese official reports tabulate things with great minuteness. Every man, every ton of food, each piece of ammunition and piece of clothing, every gun, wagon, electric light and intrenching tool, is put down in plain figures. Every ship, regiment, and battery is given by name, with the numbers of officers and men surrendering; so many of this Siberian Rifles Regiment, so many of that; so many of Mixed Regiments, of Kwangtung Artillery, of *gendarmes* and volun-

127

teers. Even the 17,000 men in hospitals are put down in detail, and I read: "6,625 scurvy patients!" Scurvy, in a fortress provisioned for two years, without lime juice or onions! Scurvy! that Stoessel mysteriously called "blood-poisoning!" Twelve hundred and sixty-one officers have surrendered; or rather, Stoessel has surrendered them. And that fine old *samurai*, General Nogi, bade them retain their swords. There was *Bushido* in its finest flowering! It is solace when an officer has to yield, that he yields to one worthy of honour. I wish Nogi were our general! Grievsky holds daily court-martials and delivers fit sentences for Stoessel on earth, and provides hot fires eternal, in the world to come; throwing in duels and insults here, and picturesque arrangements of red coals and blue flames hereafter.

Even the Japanese despise Stoessel for his surrender, and smile scorn at the 664 officers, who have taken the oath and will return to Russia on parole. Stoessel heads the list of these cowards; and his tools, Reiss and Fock, also go with him. Share the fate of the men who fought for him and under him? Not Stoessel.

And then that nauseating message to the *Czar*:

"Great Sovereign, forgive. We have done all that was humanly possible. Judge us; but be merciful!"

He must have rehearsed that bit of rodomontade, ever since the place was cut off. He got his own Third Division sent up to Haicheng, and he meant to follow them, but they cut the railway and he had to stay. Smirnoff was the real commander of the fort, and he would never have surrendered. Loris calls him a fighter of the old school—grim, resolute, a good match for Nogi. The Japanese think that Stoessel should commit suicide. I think so too.

It does us all good to have Grievsky thunder and storm at Stoessel. While he was grinding his teeth and flinging his arms today, the Japanese interpreter, who stood blinking through his spectacles at this exhibition of force and passion, broke in: "We admire you that you think so, Colonel Grievsky. We do not admire General Stoessel, that he deserts his men in captivity," and Grievsky fell upon the astonished little man, embraced him, and kissed him loudly on either cheek. The shouts that followed were welcome relief to our tense nerves.

CHAPTER 24

"Kings In Exile"

Friday, January 13th.

The *contessa* was baptised a member of the Orthodox Church last week in Kioto. That was news for Lyov that roused him a bit from the awful depression and gloom that has weighed upon all during this dreary, cold fortnight.

Today—unlucky thirteenth day, by the new calendar, in the midst of our Russian New Year's rejoicings by another—the first of the Port Arthur captives are to arrive. I do not believe that, in their wildest dreams, the Japanese expected anything like this wholesale surrender at Port Arthur. Only Bazaine at Metz is any incident for comparison, and the dishonour is equal, if our numbers are short of the French army handed over by a feeble commander. Where will they ever put this Port Arthur army? How guard and feed? They have enlarged our hospital, ward by ward. Temples have been leased, and now they are building officers' quarters at Oguri, at the far end of town beyond the railway terminus.

Three thousand captives in all will come to Matsuyama, 210 but at first we heard that 3,000 sick and wounded were coming to the hospital alone, and Andrew Y—— went wild. "I cannot feed them. I cannot feed them. My kitchen will not boil and cook for that many more," cried the ex-marshal of the nobility, present *chef* of our barracks. "I resign. I must retire. I cannot cook for so many. It is impossible, impossible," he said, growing as excited over his cooking pots as Grievsky does over Stoessel's villainies.

We get some grim laughter out of the situation, but seriously, we do not see how the Japanese are going to provide foreign food, even plain bread and beef for all these additional ones. Our *mujiks* are big eaters. They eat much bread. They want soup and cabbages, and such strong food. They will eat Japan out in a month. The missionaries say that beef, chickens, potatoes, milk, eggs, and flour are all dearer here since the *horios* came; although everything went up once in price, the instant the war began. Shops of foreign goods have doubled in numbers since the New Year, and all Nagasaki, which has been in depression since the loss of the large Russian trade, has come up to Matsuyama with foreign goods and curios to sell.

Grievsky, who was with Skobeleff at Plevna, and knows what happened after that surrender, says that the Japanese cannot possibly care for these 40,000 prisoners, and that we shall all suffer for it.

"It will be rice and fish for the whole lot of us before long," says our prophet of woes. "The situation will soon horrify the civilised world. When the Germans could not manage the problem in 1870, and our own Russian army, with the sovereign and his staff at hand, could not do well by 30,000 Turkish prisoners at Plevna, what can these people do?

"When the Turkish surrendered at Plevna they were marched out to the open fields beyond the town, divided into three herds like cattle, and sentries marched around them. It was midwinter then, also; wet snow on the ground, damp, cold, miserable Balkan weather. Fortunately, there's no snow at Port Arthur, they say; dry cold and bright sunshine,—a climate like Peking's.

"At Plevna, our own Russian soldiers were short of winter clothing and blankets, and were glad to get into the town and the shelter of Turkish houses and barracks. Imagine, then, the poor Turks in the open fields in December without shelter or covering, and no food at all, for three days and nights! It was terrible; but it was war. Hundreds died of exposure and starvation; for there they stood or lay on the wet snow—sick and wounded as well. Each morning, they moved the droves to fresh pasture ground, in lieu of cleaning—and picked up the dead and helpless. All the dead Turks were stripped of their clothing, for our own men needed it, and we buried them in trenches *pêle-mêle*. It was terrible! but what could be done? Skobeleff was off on other work, and the others were—not zealous. Finally, they did get some food for the poor creatures, and enough tents for the sick. It was twelve days before they could begin to march them in herds the twenty miles over to the boats on the Danube. Now, let us see the Japanese do better.

"Thank God, Kondrachenko died before this came!" cried Grievsky heart-brokenly. "Ah! Kondrachenko, my dear brother; not you, not you! The others should have died first. You made the fortress strong. You would have held it. You would never have surrendered. When you died, the fortress died. And where did Kondrachenko die? Not in a headquarters armchair. Not at the club. Not at the supper table, champagne glass in hand. He died in the casemate of his own fort, beside his own guns, crushed by an infernal Japanese shell. His officers knew then that the siege was done, the spirit of the garrison, the soul of resistance gone. It was only for the others to die there like him—or surrender. And to surrender was so much easier—and more comfortable, of course, for a *Stoessel.*"

Saturday, January 31st.

After we had worked ourselves up to the last degree of sympathy for their sufferings, the men from Port Arthur arrived. A sad-faced, woebegone, broken-hearted lot of sufferers? Not at all! There marched, there strutted forth, from the little white railway station, the smartest lot of officers I ever saw parade the Nevsky!—a gala party in full-dress uniforms, clanking their swords and blowing smoke rings to the sun. Was this the downfallen, the degraded garrison of a great fortress?' Not at all. It was the triumphant arrival of distinguished winter tourists. Well-fed, superior beings they were, looking down on their curious surroundings. They sauntered at ease, stood in picturesque groups, bowing over their cigarettes; and the nice, kindly Japanese, who had come so full of sympathy for the poor *horios*, were nonplussed. I was too.

These were not prisoners. Oh, no! These were not the men I had in fancy seen slinking and crouching, hiding from the light of day, fearing to meet a Russian's reproachful eye—not the men I had fancied extenuating, explaining, and fleeing from the irate Grievsky, lest he throttle them on the spot. The revulsion of feeling was so abrupt and complete that I felt myself verging towards hysterical laughter; and I fled from the sight. It was not a dramatic scene at all, this landing of Port Arthur's proud garrison in Japan. There was nothing tragic or soul-stirring about it at all. Verestchagin could not have made an historic picture of it. One artillery officer brought his little daughter, who had been his companion in one of the high forts all through the siege. The mother died as the siege began, and when the surrender came, where could he send her? With whom? General Nogi consented, and the little daughter of the battery came to Japan. Another artillerist brought with him his tiny nephew, three years old, orphaned

131

of both father and mother since June. Poor baby! Poor mite! Wide-eyed and joyful in his miniature Cossack uniform, complete to felt over-boots, leather and fur coat and tall fur cap, he trotted along beside an indulgent Japanese officer.

A few of the rank and file were pale and sickly-looking, sad-faced and silent; but these were bleached from long service in covered trenches, in casemates and galleries underground, not from starvation or scurvy. All these were sad and silent, partly from dull fear of what might befall them here in an unchristian land, and from the habit of silence which the continued roar of guns and shells had imposed. They formed in lines, were counted by smart little Japanese officers who barely reached to their shoulders; and, at the word of command, these huge creatures in fur bonnets and sheepskins, moved off briskly, obedient to one master as to another. The people in the streets looked on open-mouthed at these hairy, furry giants, who so overtopped them. And the contrast! Seeing our giants beside these pigmies, I kept asking myself again and again—How had it happened? How could it be?

They did not bear themselves as captives. Not they. They walked like kings. Kings in exile. Yermoloff, in his fur coat and *gros bonnet*, would have made four of those who stood guard over him, and children gaped with awe at our giant defender of the Two-Hundred-and-Three-Metre Hill.

One Artillery Officer Brought His Little Daughter

CHAPTER 25

Dark Days

Sunday, January 22nd.

These have been exciting days. All that we have wondered about is known, all the mysteries are laid bare. Grievsky is a merciless judge and prosecutor, and the poor officers in bandages might well wish they had been left in the Port Arthur hospitals. Every technical detail and problem is dwelt on by the hour, every feat of engineering must be sketched for him and diagrams made. There were no sallies, but he repels all the attacks over again, and as an engineering chief, his heart is in the trenches, the galleries, *caponieres*, and redoubts of the forts. The working of searchlights and shooting of fish torpedoes by naval men do not meet with his approval. That was unwarranted trespassing on engineer's ground by those sailors. "Ugh! I'd like to see them shooting any of their water toys from my batteries."

A poor lieutenant, now in No. 6 ward, was on the bridge of the next ship when the *Petropavlovsk* struck the mine. He heard one explosion, saw the ship stagger, wallow, and push her nose down into the sea. He saw the crew leap from the decks; he helped rescue them, even that bawling calf of a Cyril Vladimirovitch, who was a good swimmer and not hurt, yet who bellowed and roared until he was saved; who fought off and prevented the rescue of many a better fellow. "Save me! Save me!" he bellowed in fright, "I am the Grand Duke Cyril," and he kicked away the wounded sailors as he climbed in the boat, beat them away with an oar, and beat the boat's crew until they did as he bid and rowed him to land, and left the wounded to struggle and drown.

"No one seems to have seen Vassili Verestchagin after the ship went down. Ah! My God! to think of his being allowed to go there, to risk his life with that fleet. To lose him, was to lose one who had value in the eyes of all the world. Vassili should have lived to paint the scene, with Cyril beating wounded men away from the life-boats. Cyril! worthy descendant of that Glottstop-Holstein tribe! Cyril will demand the life-saving medal now, I suppose. Did he not save his own life? Give him a St. George! and the St. Anne, by all means!

"*Ah! bas!* My compliments to the Imperial Russian Navy!—Even to that Rojestvensky idling by the coral groves of Madagascar."

Four Russian surgeons came over with the sick ones, as there were not enough Japanese surgeons and interpreters. The Japanese were surprised that the surgeons were not Jews. "Yes," said the interpreter at the barracks to me, "all the surgeons are Jews except these, just as all the engineers are Poles."

It is cold now, cloudy and gloomy—the "grey days" of Rome. The wooden houses are as cold as stone palaces, and much more draughty,—and all is woe. Vladimir frets and grows feverish again, after we had thought the tertian entirely broken, and he sleeps but little. One knee is still rigid and useless; his spine is agony when he walks or tries to lift his knee, and he can only shuffle his feet over the floor. All my massage and efforts seem useless, now that this penetrating damp cold has gone in to his joints. The officers begged that something be done to make the barracks more comfortable; for draughts suck up through the thin floor and walls, where the thatch roofs join loosely. All are sneezing and coughing. We made a tent or canopy over Vladimir's bed, which kept him secure from cold currents while he lay there; but he was exposed to a dozen draughts when he lay on the long chair.

It is absurd that, here in semi-tropical Japan, with palm trees and oranges on every side, and my camellia hedge in splendid bloom—that we should feel the cold indoors as we have never felt it in Russia. The floors are always cold to the feet, for the wind has full sweep through the open air-space beneath and up through the cracks. The longer the ingenious, portable oil and charcoal stoves bum, and give out comforting heat, the more the pine boards shrink, until one sees the sky in hair lines all along the walls. It is impossible to save the pneumonia cases, and I watched one poor Siberian to his death the other morning, when wet snowflakes preceded a chill, rainy day, that seemed the dreariest we had known.

When I had made Vladimir safe and warm for the night, and was leaving, Nesan came out from the chemist's room with her bottles, and walked with me past the chancery, to tell me that the chief-surgeon had been ordered to command the great hospitals at Dalny. This was the last blow.

I waved my hand to Nesan and ran out into the darkness and rain, unable to repress my tears. The *coolie*, crouching under the lee of the guardhouse, called to me to wait, while he lighted his paper lantern and turned the back of the *jinrikisha* to the driving rain. He tied me fast in the tiny interior with the rain apron; and, chuckling cheerily at the misadventures and the weather, pattered with bare feet down the shining, wet road. His worn rubber coat showed one thin, rain-soaked, blue cotton garment beneath it; and the bare knees caught the lantern light as they swung back and forth with the regularity of pendulums. Still chirruping like a cheerful bird, and laughing, as if the raindrops he wiped from the edge of the hood were precious things, lucky jewels, he was gathering, he helped me out at my door. I looked at him, as the *shoji* slid open and sent the full lamplight on the ugly little scrap of a man. He was old, since all the young *jinrikisha coolies* have gone to the war, or over to Ujina to enjoy the high wages at the government stores; yet he was cheerful and happy, contented with the hardest lot that I can think of for a human being. "You have no trouble, I can see that," I said to him. "A full pipe and a rice bowl, and the dark, wet, cold night is the same as sunny noonday to you."

"*Okasama*, my only son went to the war. He died at *Ni San Rei* (Two-Hundred-and-Three- Metre Hill) that last time. I am old and my wife is feeble, and this *kuruma* feeds us all—all—my son's wife and his three children. Although the little box (cremation ashes and relics) came three weeks ago, I have not yet had the priests say the prayers at my house, and his friends go with us to the temple. I have known much sorrow, truly, *Okasama*." The old *kurumaya* bowed with the grace of a noble, proudly. With dignity, he lifted the paper lantern and hooked it to the shafts. It was a reproof that covered me with shame.

"Stop! Stop!" I said. "Come for me in the morning at nine o'clock, and I want to send now some little things to your son's children. Anna, make ready plenty, much, a big Japanese supper for three times three little children, and give *kuruyama* san some hot tea first. He waited so long in the rain for me, he is cold and hungry. Do not forget that."

My feet of lead dragged me to my room, when the soft-spoken, purring little housemaid had changed my shoes. I sat there in the cold, forlorn, alone—alone. Vladimir sick and alone too—far away in the cold. Alone! A black night of sorrow encompassed me. I thought of the old *kurumaya*, the sick wife, the lost son, and the family dependent on the one feeble old man. And he so cheerful and courteous, while he sat cold, wet, and of course hungry, waiting for me in the rain. I began to weep quietly, and when Anna came in and asked why, I burst into violent sobbing and alarmed her with a nervous collapse that I have not approached in many, many years.

It was Anna who went out In the morning at nine to find the American pope, and ask how I should relieve the old *kurumaya*; or rather, how much money, and in what form I could put it, to meet the expenses of the honourable, military funeral. It must not come from me, a Russian, but anonymously, through some Red Cross member. Would one of them do it for me? or ask Madame Takasu to do it?

In the end, I sent twenty, immaculate, new one-*yen* notes, folded in pure white paper, accompanied by a great bouquet of green *sakaki* branches; and the next Sunday there was a funeral, with the local band in attendance, starting from Madame Takasu's own courtyard, where the priests held a short service over the little wooden box that came from Port Arthur. The old man marched in stiff silk *hakama*, leading a sedate, splendidly-striding boy of eight, as chief mourner and guardian of the tablets. A concourse of friends trailed away through the town and across the belt of fields to a temple near Dogo, and the funeral party from the castle barracks sounded the bugles and rendered the final honours there.

I shall not tell Vladimir of this for a long time, and I hope his brother officers may never find it out. I do not like their attitudes at times when I am only trying to be just to these people, who are kind to me beyond all that I could ever have imagined.

CHAPTER 26

From Port Arthur

Sunday, January 29th.

The *contessa's* pretty postcards come daily, and Lyov is for the most part steeped in reveries and interested only in his own convalescence. He sits up in a long chair each day, and one arm is free of its bandages and is subject to my massage treatment. He says he shall ask to be sent to Kioto, as soon as he is able to leave the barracks.

The arrival of all the Port Arthur officers at once last week was like the arrival of the Court at Yalta. Each day, someone has a surprising rencontre. Andrew Y—— was half smothered one day by a visitor who cried: "Oh! Uncle! Why, Uncle! I did not know that you were in the army again!" And it was his nephew.

"Saints above!" cried Andrew, stupefied. "No more did I know that you were in Port Arthur!"

They all have photographs which tell the story better than words, for, although they were permitted to bring away only a portmanteau and a travelling rug, all came out with their pockets stuffed and their clothing filled with traps.

"I was a standing column of photographic prints and film negatives," said one officer; "and my lens was such a good one that I put it in my pocket and will buy a new camera over here."

Many mourn for their books, pictures, and musical instruments, which they had to leave behind. "Oh! it did break my heart to leave my pictures," one told me. "I had them brought out from my Kronstadt house as soon as I was billeted for Port Arthur, three years ago. I paid insurance on a value of 50,000 *roubles*; and then—I had to come away and leave them all on the walls. Leave them for the Japanese to use as targets, I suppose. That is what the Prussian officers did to the paintings in French *châteaux*,

"We were all limited in the amount of luggage, but luckily it was cold weather and we could wear two and three sets of clothes. It was like a fete day review, when we left Port Arthur. Every one wore his best uniforms, and there was elation and excitement in just getting out of that hole, where we had seen such horrors. No one had luggage save the Stoessels. And, Mother of Mercy! how the *Barina* had made good her last opportunity! She had a little garden and cow, you know, and some chickens; and headquarters milk and eggs sold at rising prices all through the siege,

"The first anyone suspected of Stoessel's intention was when the servants brought word that the *Barina* was packing her trunks. She brought away with her twenty-two boxes, and the rest of us, each only a rug and portmanteau. The regulations said, 'Retaining their swords and carrying the same baggage allowance as Japanese officers of corresponding rank'—which is sixty pounds only. Stoessel asked General Nogi, at the dinner table, after the signature, if the *Barina* could take all her own things away with her, and the old Spartan said chivalrously that Madame Stoessel should take what she pleased without regarding regulations—other ladies, with children, the same. Nogi prearranged those things like a kind father. Every officer's wife with a baby had a soldier allotted her as servant. Others, a soldier to each two children.

"The *Barina* packed up everything in their establishment, and her twenty-two trunks so filled up a railway wagon that twenty Cossacks, who ought to have been in that wagon, had to ride on the platforms. But not a trunk would she carry for anyone else. Not she. Not a picture, an embroidery, or old Peking treasure would she take back to Russia for any one of their own staff. We all went down to Dalny on the one train that morning. The six officers of highest rank were to ride in the one railway carriage; but, when old Smirnoff found that he was to ride in with Stoessel and the *Barina*, he said loudly: 'No, no, I will have nothing to do with that general,' and jumped into the carriage crowded with orderlies. And Bieli and the others with him! The Japanese were fearfully embarrassed. They had not prearranged any such scenes. They did not know which to apologise to first. Smirnoff waits until he returns to Russia, and then Stoessel's sword of honour and Black Eagle of the *Kaiser* will look very small.

"We held a council on the 27th, and as there were ample provisions, enough for two months at least, we voted not to surrender. Stoessel did not fear his council of generals and colonels. Oh! No! But there was someone he did fear; one who commanded him to

139

surrender—'She-Who-Must- Be-Obeyed'! In fear of the *Barina*, by stealth, without letting us know, he sent the messengers out to Nogi. We were watching, and when his Cossacks rode out toward the Japanese lines and began to display a flag of truce, a dozen binocles were on them. They telephoned down from Wangtai to headquarters to ask what the parley was about. No one at headquarters knew. The next morning we all knew. We all saw the procession of shame ride out to surrender. 'The general surrenders, the fortress does not,' said Smirnoff. And Smirnoff was right. Smirnoff was in command of Port Arthur, of the fortress. Stoessel should have surrendered only himself and his Siberian troops and gone out. I am sick of all these horrors, of the sight of death, the smell of blood and corpses. If I ever get back to Russia, I shall leave the army. I am tired of war."

Another friend commanded the battery on the Golden Hill above the harbour entrance. "For a year I lived on that hilltop. Everything I saw; all save the first part of the night attack by the Japanese that caused the war. I was down in the city that night"—and we interrupted with laughter in which he had finally to join. "What sights there were from my Col d'Or! I miss my lookout, my great sweep of sky and sea, and the horizon with its Japanese ships, now that I live in a damp temple with low, overhanging eaves, and see only a stone path, some gravestones, and a granite image of Buddha sitting in the rain.

"And what devils those Japanese were! Fear! They don't know the word. Came right in under our guns, into the muzzles of the guns of the lower forts, to sink their ships! That American who tried to sink a ship in the Cuban harbour to block the Spanish fleet was only one, and only tried it once. Here were Japanese by the dozen, the hundred, coming at it again and again. I wish we had some naval officers of that same kind; someone who could have followed Togo's fleet and discovered his naval base. To think that Togo kept his ships as near us as the Elliot Islands! and Starke and Oukhtomsky never found it out!

"Ah, it was beautiful up there on my Col d'Or! Moonlight and searchlight made sea and land as bright as day. Then star rockets and burning parachutes! It was *fête Vénitienne* all the time. I have seen all the spectacular side of war.

"I watched Makaroff go out and come back, and watched his ships manoeuvre about just below us, to allow them to work their way back into the harbour, one by one. Rascheffski had his camera out, for he had long been waiting for just that chance at the whole fleet in the open. Oh, everything was quite right that day—the sun just high enough, and the sea so calm! They were racing signal flags up and down, giving the orders to each ship, when I saw the *Petropavlovsk* give a queer pitch, a jerk. The officers on the bridge threw up their arms, and others ran out of the towers and gun-turrets. The ship gave another jerk, the water boiled around it, and the muffled sound of an explosion came up to us. 'Great God!' cried Rascheffski, "she has struck a mine!' and he whipped out his plate-holder, turned it, and drew the slide. As he touched the bulb, a heavier boom sounded, and a cloud of black smoke closed around the *Petropavlovsk*. I could not breathe nor utter a sound, as I realised that the flagship of our fleet, our admiral, and our grand duke were in that black cloud on the water; that the huge iron ship was sinking, and the wounded crew drowning before my eyes. I saw the black nose of the ship rear up and then dive down. The smoke drifted away, and then men and wreckage came to the top.

"I turned away for a second, all my nerve gone with the horrible sight witnessed in just two minutes and a half. And that cold-blooded devil of a Rascheffski was putting away his last plate-holder! While everyone else on that parapet was transfixed with horror and speechless, Rascheffski had been exposing his plates, clicking his camera as coolly as at a review.

"'How fortunate that I had my plate-holders full,' he said, 'I have made six exposures!' He had taken one picture and was ready for another, when the *Petropavlovsk* gave her first rebound from the mine. The same afternoon he developed and printed, and the pictures went on to his Majesty at Petersburg, and all Europe has since seen them. We have prints from them, too.

"It was a great time for photography, there at Port Arthur. Those materials never gave out. You see the prints here of the successive stages of the bombardment—of the officers' club in May, and the same club in December!—Ah! those last days at Port Arthur! The sad pictures of the *Sevastopol* at bay outside the harbour! Each night our searchlights showed those devils of Japanese nosing around her with their torpedo boats—wolves around a dying stag. And then we saw the wounded Sevastopol dragged out and sunk, at the foot of our hill!

"And now, it is all over. We are here."

CHAPTER 27

The Course of True Love Not
Smooth in Japan

Tuesday, January 31st.

The surrendered officers all grumble at their crowded quarters
and—at the cold!

Oh! how these grizzled, old Siberians complain of the cold! of
the rigors of a Japanese winter! with the thermometer ten degrees
above the frost point! When it is forty degrees by my English thermometer, they shiver and gather in the sun, like so many Neapolitan
lazzaroni. They put all the officers out in one common ward for three
days, while carpenters sealed up the cracks and joints in the flimsy
woodwork and made the place snug and comfortable. And that was
an experience!

At the time of the surrender, General Nogi said that the Port
Arthur officers should retain their swords. At Matsuyama the commandant required them to deliver up their swords, as the regulations
for prisoners of war required it. He could not let prisoners go armed;
and as none of the officers previously here retained their swords, he
could not make such a distinction for the Port Arthur men. The officers protested, and the commandant telegraphed to the War Minister
at Tokyo. Word came back that they must be disarmed, like the other
prisoners, and their swords put in safe keeping until the end of the
war. Any resistance was, of course, useless, but some of the young officers foolishly resisted, against the protests and advice of senior officers, and were disarmed by force, and are now imprisoned; others broke
their swords and threw the pieces on the ground; and some laid the
swords on a table and turned away.

"You may take my sword behind my back, like a thief. I will not

At General Fock's Headquarters, Nagoya

yield it," said one. Those who had the swords of St. Anne wept, kissed the swords of honour their sovereign had given them, and removed the red-and-white sword knots, to wear as decorations on their breasts. I think it was chiefly bad management and bad manners which made all the trouble. As Vladimir says, the chief-surgeon could have gone, taken the swords away, and left every officer his friend; but the commandant is of another type and school, arrogant as a Prussian, hard, tactless, and almost contemptuous in manner to these new captives, to the "surrendered officers," as all call those who came from Port Arthur, in distinction from the "captured officers," who were here before January.

One poor fellow wailed to Grievsky, "We know the Japanese all despise us. They think us cowards to surrender and come here as prisoners. By their code, we should all have committed suicide when Stoessel sold us out. But we Russians have not the courage for cold steel in the stomach, just because a battle or a fort has been lost."

With three hundred idle, unhappy, homesick, heartsick officers here, I fear more trouble. All are depressed, morbidly sensitive, and their nerves are on edge. They are looking for insults and humiliations; and of course they find them or imagine them. They will not see anything that the Japanese do for them in the right light. They persist in attributing hostile, sinister motives to them, and credit them with a wish to insult and persecute them.

I can talk my one or two stray visitors into a more reasonable frame of mind, but I cannot get at, nor harangue, the whole three hundred in the temples and quarters in town. If they would only let me go around and visit them at each place—each *étape* Grievsky bitterly calls the places of detention—I am sure that I could pacify some and put them in a better frame of mind. It would be better if there were at least one of our own higher and older officers here to have some authority and control over these young hotheads, someone to appeal to, to act as arbiter and spokesman. But here are only a few colonels, and the rest are all majors, captains, and lieutenants.

I asked the surgeon why they do not send the two crazy officers back to Russia, as they did the seventy crippled and infirm men in October? But he says: "No! No! Too many would go insane, if that was a way to get to Russia. We cannot be too sure about these two, sometimes."

The reaction after the tremendous excitement and long nerve strain of Port Arthur is too much for many of the newcomers. Many wish now that they had given parole and gone to Europe. Although

144

our officers are not such sportsmen and athletes as the English, they complain bitterly of the want of exercise.

"Think of it! Forty of us walking up and down, up and down among the crowded gravestones, taking our turns at sentry go. I wish I had gone with Stoessel. I never did care about this war, anyhow. *La guerre n'est pas gai!* I was on the point of going to give my parole, when I heard that old Fock was actually going as prisoner to Japan. After that, I had to play heroic too. Old granny! When Fock urged the council to surrender in September, the first time we lost Two-Hundred-and-Three-Metre Hill, he had had his fill of war and battle then; but Kondrachenko and the brave ones were so fierce that he never proposed it again, although he would have been glad to do so at any time. They were all hard on him, except Stoessel and Reiss. Fock is afraid to go back to Russia, so he sticks to Smirnoff as his only hope; shares his same fate, copies his brave conduct. Yet Smirnoff won't speak to him! And there they are both at Nagoya! Each has an archbishop's palace to live in, and we, the victims of Stoessel and Fock, are crowded together here like Siberian convicts. No landscape gardens, no tennis courts for us."

The Japanese find that the rank and file cannot get on peaceably together, because of their differences of race and religion; so that, even in the hospital, they must separate them, and put the Jews, Poles, Finns, and the Baltic provincers by themselves. Then we have Circassians, and every kind of a Central Asian you can think of in Cossack dress, on to Lyov's Buriat Mongol, with the placid face of Buddha—that Osip, who ought to wear a *lama's* brocade robe and say his rosary. His face is so serenely the Buddha of Japanese art that I long to gild his face, lacquer him, and put him in some temple.

The Japanese show marked favour to the Jews, Poles, Finns, and Baltic provincers, because they do less fighting and more reading and writing than the others; use more paper and pencils and notebooks; take more baths, wash more clothes, and try to occupy themselves. I said this to the interpreter one day, and he said the Japanese ought to be kinder to these non-orthodox ones because they were treated so badly in Russia and in the army! Madame Takasu even told me that the Finns and Baltic-ers are Christians (meaning Protestants), the same as the American missionaries.

Two Russian ladies, who have lived in Port Arthur all through the siege, wives of engineer officers, have asked to come here to live. The interpreter told me, and he significantly added: "They are from Baltic

Gen. Fock

EACH HAS AN ARCHBISHOP'S PALACE, LANDSCAPE GARDEN AND TENNIS COURT

provinces, *Okasama*. They are real Christians, Lutherans they call them!" One of them has a daughter, sixteen years old, who served as a hospital nurse during the last week of the siege. The other brings a little baby, born during the last weeks of the siege. Thirty such siege-born infants were sent to Nagasaki, and good, kind, old Nogi let the mothers choose thirty soldiers to go on with them to Russia as nurses.

And now for our romance, a real storybook kind of romance. When one wounded officer reached the quarantine station and read the orders for steam baths ashore, he sent word that as his orderly was a woman she could not go ashore with the Cossacks. The Japanese drew long faces, they stood aghast. Romance of that sort did not appeal to them. "Not Cossack! Not man! *Naruhodo!* Not wife! *Naruhodo,* these Christians are queer!" There was a tragic parting on deck. Officer and orderly kissed and embraced and wept loudly, regardless of the Japanese onlookers. The orderly was quarantined after all the transports were gone, and they have sent her to the poor French Consul in Kobe. She waits, the consul says, until the Blessed Virgin shall intervene, for he can do nothing.

"Ah, I am here in prison, and my bride is in Kobe," wails the poor fellow as he lies in the hospital.

Vladimir is not sympathetic, and in his dry, extra-dry manner advises me to let the thing alone, not to mix myself up in this affair, which is not our affair. But I still hear that weak and fretful voice repeating it: "Ah! I am here in prison, and my bride is in Kobe."

CHAPTER 28

Daily Life

Thursday, February 2nd.

We were talking, at tea today, of the little Amazon who followed her lover down to Port Arthur and into captivity, and which seems so romantic to me, in this twentieth-century time. Loris told of so many "maids of Saragossa," in Macedonia and the Balkans, that I had to recede from my heroics over the little Siberian. They cited so many cases that it seemed as though Russian women were all "warriors bold." Several of the battery commanders had their families living with them in the high forts around Port Arthur. The officers said it was safer there; they wanted their families with them, if anything happened; and the air was better on the hills through the summer.

Children lived in the forts; romped in the casements and galleries, and around the magazines; played tag over the cannons, and got in the way of the gunners during action. They were delighted with the novelties of warfare, wanted to work the machine guns, to see the fish torpedoes swim in the air, and to turn the searchlights. They waited up to watch the star rockets and parachutes, as if for illuminated fetes. There was also a sergeant's wife, who wore men's clothes and fought as a soldier at one of the forts. She was an expert shot, and when her husband was killed she stayed at the sights in the trenches until she had killed one hundred and seventeen Japanese, before she herself was shot by a Japanese sharpshooter.

Besides the titled women who went to Siberia and devotedly did all the routine work of their Red Cross and *zemstvo* hospitals, I hear of mounted Red Cross nurses, hardy Siberian women, who scour the battlefields for the wounded. I think Russia will wake up to and discover the real value of Siberia after this war, as England learned to appreciate her colonies after the Boer war.

I marvelled at this presence of women in the battlefield, until Von Woerffel, not to let his arm of the service be left out of the honours, said that each battleship carried Red Cross sisters of charity, and that, when the fleet made its fiasco of a sortie, August 10th, it had not only carried the usual nurses on the ships, but the wives of many officers who volunteered for nurse's duties, in order to escape to Vladivostok. I could hardly believe this. Certainly there is no such *Pinafore* business in the English navy; for I know my English uncle could not take my aunt with him on his own gunboat from Cowes to Deauvllle—a few hours' trip on a summer's day. But Von Woerffel assures me that it is so, and that the commander of the *Peresviet*, who is at Ide-bude-machi, can assure me that his wife was on board during all that 10th of August flight, fight, and retreat. She was down below, while the big guns were firing, and Japanese shells were striking.

Think of it! What a place for a woman! And think of the discipline maintained by an admiral who would permit a *Pinafore* party on a battleship in action—or at any time! No wonder our navy has made such a pitiable showing all through the war; that this lagging Baltic fleet imagined Japanese torpedoes in the North Sea, and was shooting at shadows all the way from Libau to the Channel. If we get out of this without a war with England, we will be fortunate. It's a mercy Lord Charles did not attack, when he had them all in one fleet near Gibraltar. We of the army do not take the Russian navy seriously any more. I asked a Port Arthur man what chance Rojestvensky had against Admiral Togo.

"The same chance exactly as if he came in forty-four steam launches, cargo-lighters, or Volga barges. For the good of Russia and himself he had better turn around now and go home, with a whole skin and all his ships above water. Rojestvensky is a fussy, old martinet; his officers all hate him and would not obey his orders half the time; certainly not after that devil of a Togo began to be noisy and unpleasant with his infernal prearrangements. Sea power is not in our line. It is not in the genius of our race to go on the water. No, nor in it either; as you see here in Matsuyama, when sick and well have to be pushed into the baths once a week. That's another count in the Japanese contempt. They despise us because we are beaten, because we do not commit suicide; and because our Cossacks are so dirty, and do not like to bathe in boiling water every night."

Every able-bodied civilian in Port Arthur had to do military duty with the volunteers, and there are many tales told of what happened on this account in "Stoessel's satrapy." Even the manager of the Russo-Chinese bank was ordered to duty. He protested, and so Stoessel said: "Very well, I give you charge of the abattoirs." Abattoirs supplying horseflesh only! All Port Arthur roared with laughter, and the volunteer protested. "Then," said Stoessel, "you can report to Colonel Yermoloff for duty in the trenches on Two-Hundred-and-Three-Metre Hill."

After the surrender, the volunteers had to answer the roll-call like any of the regular troops, be counted, and march the six miles to the railway station. Among these volunteers were many secret agents of revolutionary societies. The Siberian Army has many such agitators, and here in detention, they distribute their revolutionary literature freely. Grievsky thinks the Japanese should not permit that, and gets furious when Vladimir says his point is out of all rational order; that of course the Japanese will allow the captives liberty in that respect, as Japanese soldiers can read anything they please. Even in war time, their Japanese temporary censorship of the press does not equal what we have in Russia in time of peace; and there are no books barred out, to judge of what I saw in the bookstores at Kobe; and any books we order they send us.

The Lafcadio Hearn books that I ordered for holiday gifts were brought to the barracks by one of the headquarters clerks, who did so because he was anxious to tell Vladimir that he had often seen that great genius when he, the clerk, was a student in the Imperial University at Tokyo. "He was my revered teacher," said the youth proudly, and we made the most of his visit.

We had a laugh, too, at Akimoff, who went through the ward as interpreter for the Protestant missionaries, distributing tracts and picture books to the invalids. The children in the mission schools in the treaty ports have made these picture scrapbooks by thousands for the Japanese soldiers in hospital, and these have now greatly diverted our poor Cossacks, to many of whom pictures of European life are quite as foreign as to the Japanese. But the tracts! They have been provided to win poor ignorant Russians away from the "gross superstitions and idolatry" of the Orthodox Church! Some of the tracts in Russian text, en- titled as temperance lectures, proved to be revolutionary literature, and were promptly burned by the horrified missionaries.

Then the Japanese authorities abruptly shut down on the activities of a supposed philanthropist who was at the bottom of this way of reaching our stupid *mujiks*. This terrorist agent, masquerading as a benevolent old doctor, was even offering to take to America at the end of the war any real cultivators of land who would settle in the further states. If they would only go with him, how well rid Russia would be of the lot, and how well it would serve America! Her philanthropists got the Doukhobors, and they have quite enough of them, I hear.

I go to the English service once a week at the mission house, and the officers are now arranging a little chapel at the hospital, where the Japanese Catechists of the Greek Church will hold services regularly. Hitherto, they have visited from ward to ward, and confessions and burial services have been their chief occupation. There is much scepticism, of course, wherever two or three really educated Russians are gathered together; and Nimidoff, who is blunt and frank to a degree, has a way of setting fire to the irreligious opinions of the others. After one long bout, when he had led in denouncing the Church, as it now exists in Russia—all mummery—simply, an instrument for extorting money from and coercing the ignorant—they nearly reached the point of putting Christianity itself aside as an outlived delusion.

"Oh! if the procurator-general could only hear you!" Esper exclaimed.

"Oh! Damn the procurator-general! The old fiend! He belongs to the Middle Ages anyhow. He would burn recalcitrants and unbelievers at the stake today, if he dared. His prison for priests is worse than burning; and there is Kavkaz and the Trans-Baikal for the others. I will distribute all the Protestant tracts I can get hold of here. I think it would be a good work, a real missionary service, to convert the imprisoned army in Japan to any true Christian religion."

"But what did you do in camp, with your troops, if you feel that way?" I asked.

"Oh! it is part of the tactics and drill—military regulations. I put my men through the Mass and service just like any other manoeuvre. Pile up the drums and make an altar for the priests; cross myself, just as I salute another officer; habit—habit—I have often made the sign of the cross when I meant to salute, on the Nevsky, and often saluted, absent-mindedly, when I should have crossed. It is automatic—that's all there is in it. We kneel with our heads on our sword-hilts, and the men's heads on the rifle-butts at service in camp, and the priest chatters lines that my men surely do not understand; nor do the popes themselves, half the time. We kiss the book and march back, keeping step with the feet, crossing ourselves with our hands—both automatic. We march to battle crossing ourselves, because all the rest do. Some say their prayers honestly, I suppose, but not many of my class. And who has respect for a pope anywhere, or even for a pope's son." And how Christian is it for our popes to lead the attack with the crucifix, at the front? Ah! don't talk to me! Our beggar of a pope at Telissu was as keen on the fight, had as real a blood-thirst as any Cossack. He screamed and shouted, and waved his big cross; and when our men broke, he beat them with the crucifix, drove them back, made them stand their ground. We never could have retreated in such good order, if it had not been for that fighting pope. He and his cross saved us for once, even if he had broken one arm of the cross, when a Cossack dodged, and the holy club came down on a rock. To the devil with Pobedonostseff, and his whole bigoted tribe!"

CHAPTER 29

The Exiled Student

Friday, February 3rd.

I was down in the street, buying cotton cloth for Andrew Y——'s tailor shop this morning, when I heard a cry of: "*Matushka! Matushka! Tyotushka!* You! You! Here! In Japan !"

Of all the surprises I have had, none equals this of finding Sandy von Rathroff, my own godchild, among the Port Arthur officers. "For Heaven's sake, Sandy, tell me how, how you got here.?" Where is your uniform? What are you doing here? How did you get away? In mercy's name! This surpasses all. Oh! You *mauvais sujet!* Here! of all places! Oh! your poor mother, now—"

Sandy stood there smiling, as happily as if it were all a *fête*, while I was quite unnerved by surprises of so many kinds. The moon-faced sergeant, who was escorting his little flock around the shops, came up at the sound of our excited voices, and his presence brought me to my senses enough to explain to him in full that this was my long-lost nephew, whom we had all considered dead in Siberia. We had, truly.

"Tell him the whole thing. He's a good sort, different from the other Japanese at our place. They say they are better to the Jews, the Poles, and the disloyal ones; and I want any credit I can get on that last score." When I had talked the sergeant into security we sat down on the red benches, and Sandy told me rapidly, in German, all that had happened to him since his exile.

"Yes, aunt, I am more unreconcilable than ever. I shall always be the enemy of Nicholas Alexandrovitch and all his following, although I have worn his uniform and taken his pay. Very small pay, aunt, only sixty *roubles* a month—less than a Japanese *sous-lieutenant* gets. Well, *tyotushka*, since Mr. Stripes, that is what we call that sergeant of ours, since he will let us talk, I must tell you all I can now, for I shall not get out for a walk for another week. There are so many of us in the temple and so few sergeants to chaperon us as we walk abroad. Oh! it is quite like a young girls' school, a convent brood taking a gentle promenade. '*Baissez vos yeux, mesdemoiselles*,' the French governess used to say to my sisters when they passed the Yacht Club. Oh, dear! will I ever be there again .''

"I shall come to the hospital at once—as soon as they will let me, I mean. To think that you are here! But, to begin with myself; now, *ma tante*. After I was seized, with the students who had been in Kazan Cathedral—while I had not been in there at all—I was shut up in the fortress for weeks. You know how my family worked for my release. But old Von Plehve, curses to his soul, and all his agents, swore against me, and I went with the *rota* to Irkutsk. They assigned me to the town of —— near ——. It is supposed to be on the railway line; but it isn't by eighteen *versts*. Well, I had to live; and the best thing was to get on with the authorities so well that I could escape—get over to China in some way. I taught school. I took the classes away from the drunken pope, and taught the little Siberians to read and write, some arithmetic, and some geography. The pope sobered up now and then, and told them Church history.

"Ugh! What discomforts! What hideous surroundings! What people! What drear winter nights I passed! I was desperate many a time. But I held my tongue, made friends with the authorities, and saved every kopeck I could of what the family sent me, and all I could earn. I should need money when I could escape. So I had one thousand *roubles* on me when the war began. And I danced a *tarantella* of joy. In the confusion, I could surely get away and make my way into China, I thought.

"Our governor advised me to volunteer for military service in Manchuria, as I would be made a sub-lieutenant at the start, see some good fighting, and get amnesty after the war. We expected, you know, a quick march down the coast, and to do all our little fighting in Japan. I wish you could have seen the troops I commanded! Raw Siberian infantry, of course, for me. Such a lot of cutthroat brutes you never saw; No jail-yard of criminals could match my Siberian riflemen. All had bullet heads and retreating foreheads—prognathous skulls, and nothing in them—eyes like elephant's eyes. Ugh! I am glad to be away from the sight of them. Thank the saints they are sent somewhere else in Japan, and I don't have to see those two-legged dolts any more, and bother my head with their soup and cartridges. I don't know that they hated me as I loathed them. Poor things! They were not to blame that they wore the *Czar's* uniform and carried his gun. They are dragged off at the end of the knout for conscription or mobilisation, and treated like cattle. *Kanonen-futter* they are. I am not sure they have souls. They seemed no higher in the scale to me than horses or camels—camels that talk, and can scratch—and get drunk, if there's any bad vodka around.

"Well, they sent me to Port Arthur, and there I stayed from April to the end of the siege. I intended to surrender as soon as I could get near the enemy, but I never had the chance. My trenches were never near the outposts; and I think my men suspected me. Two others got across and surrendered; but no such luck for me. I had to endure all those horrors and discomforts. Ugh! the smells in those trenches! the corpse smell in the air, everywhere, all the time! And the hospitals! I had to go to look up my wounded men, in decency's name. I wish I could forget it all. It sickens me now, whenever I think of the hospitals beside our barracks. And the noise! I believe that was worst of all. The roar of those Japanese shells! *Ach Gott!* It was like the end of the world. A thousand thunderclaps in one. Night and day, it was one *bang-bang and roar-r-r!* It took one of these Japanese shells to make the stone-deaf to hear.

"And then! Go up on the highest forts and look, and you couldn't see the first sign of a Japanese or his outworks. Not a gun, nor an embankment, not a trench, nor a line of earth, nor a sand-bag in sight. The pigmies would come up out of the ground to attack, and come on until they could push grenades in the mouths of our big guns in the casements. In all the world, there was never anything like it. It was uncanny. Nothing in sight, only shells shooting over from the hills and dropping down out of the sky. No fort, no gun, no gunner anywhere in sight. Somewhere on a hill-top, there was a little gnome In a pit, with a telephone wire, telling his gunners to fire higher or lower, so many degrees to east or west. It gave me the creeps.

"I did not admire the Russian commanders,—except Kondrachenko. He was a man. I would much rather have been with that old hero, Nogi, fighting on the Japanese side. And then, one day, Stoessel handed us over. Not a word did we have to say, any more than my Siberians had had to say as to whether they would like to be soldiers or not. I had full mufti always ready at Port Arthur, and I burned my uniform, all my peacock-coloured clothes.

"We live in a temple now. Queer notion! I should think they

155

would consider it a desecration to have Russians in the house of Buddha. Probably they will burn them down, purify by fire, when we are gone! *When* we are gone! Yes, I wish I knew when this stage would be over in my career.

"Here I am in Japan! herded in with a lot of men I despise, with not as much liberty as I had in my Siberian town. And when the war ends, I suppose I will be counted off like cargo again, and shipped back where I came from. There's no use in trying to do anything here. It's only when they ship us to Europe, that I can get away. All my efforts now are towards holding my tongue. I have asked to have a teacher of Japanese, but we are so crowded at Shin-so-ji that there is no room for a teacher unless he shoves some Buddha off his pedestal in the graveyard."

Vladimir's surprise was as great as my own, but he disliked the cold-blooded, calculating disloyalty of the young exile. "He is not a loyal Russian," said Vladimir severely, and at that I laughed. "How could he be? I don't believe I am one myself any more either."

Since the chief-surgeon left, the whole atmosphere has changed, and we chafe under many petty annoyances. Suddenly, there came an order to remove the cots, the wooden beds, from the wards—from all but the officers' wards. Many of the sick ones cried and protested, and all the nurses have been changed around to other wards, too, to the great sorrow and real injury of their patients. Nesan came from her new ward, to see if I would not explain to her sick Cossacks what was to be done, and quiet them a little.

"If you will tell me why it is done, I will come," I said. Nesan was embarrassed and plainly unhappy. "Oh! *Okasama*, it is the work of these small new officers in the chancery. They say Japanese soldiers lie on the floor, and so Russian soldiers must lie on the floor. But it is not so at Zentsuji. There every Japanese soldier, hundreds, thousands, all have wooden beds, like the Cossacks had yesterday. And so it is at Hiroshima, too. They are taking the beds up the hill to the Shiro, and Japanese soldiers are carrying."

And truly a procession of recruits were toiling up to the chateau with the hundreds of high cots, and hundreds of our sick men are crying and whimpering like children tonight. It is only a little piece of stupidity and assertiveness on the part of some petty official, but it is as unkind as it is senseless—a mere parade of authority. It is the old story of the *parvenu* in power, the upstart in control, the beggar on horseback, that we have evidence enough of in Russia. Our *zemstvos* and any estate owners, who try to do good for the villagers and peasants, constantly meet this same spirit.

The new surgeon is very eminent and skilful, they say. He speaks German, of course, for the Japanese believe medical science was evolved and can only be taught in Germany. But he is not the same as our old chief-surgeon, that *preux chevalier*, that fine flower of *Bushido*.

"Yes, he and General Nogi. I put them in the first rank, with any officer and gentleman in Europe. These others? No! There is not a real, a true gentleman, as Europe understands the word, among them. Only Nogi and Kikuchi to redeem these forty millions," is the way the captive officers talk. They are bitter against all in command in Matsuyama; and since the sword incident, there have been other regrettable affairs. Blows have been exchanged, and the Prussian martinet of a commandant has even struck un- armed captives, defenceless prisoners, with his sword.

CHAPTER 30

The Night Lodgers

Saturday, February 4th.

On visitors' day I went to Sandy's quarters, and I must own that he has a depressing *milieu* at Shin-so-ji. The forty officers are crowded together in the temple, and their exercise ground, the graveyard, is more closely crowded with grey stone monuments, tablets, and lanterns. The ranking engineer officers from Port Arthur are stowed like steerage passengers in the upper part of the temple library. They try to make merry over it, those six big Russians, who sleep and live where one thin shadow of a priest used to read and meditate. Sandy and the younger officers have bunks in the anteroom, and their interpreter is the worst I have yet encountered. Taciturn and suspicious, and woodenly stupid, he watches them all the time, as if espionage and not translation were his duty. He peers over their shoulders to see what they read and write, noses in to see what they are doing, and has his ears pricked-up listening to all they say. And how they loathe him! And how they long to wring his long, thin neck, and to beat him with their fists! If they only dared!

The gloomy interpreter stuck to my elbow, while Sandy showed me his quarters—his own bed in a big closet in the wall—and, when the officers in the *cabinet-de-luxe* gave me a chair and they sat on their rolled-up mattresses, M. *l'Interprète* stood near the door and craned his neck. The wrath of my hosts was at boiling point, and I spent my time assuaging them, in German. "At least," I said, "the war will soon be over. With Port Arthur gone, Manchuria is nothing to us anymore; and after the next big battle, whether we lose or win, there will be peace. The other nations of Europe are getting frightened lest they be drawn in; and the bankers, who rule the world, are opposed to continuing this disturbance of the Bourses. Be patient!"

"Bah! Peace now? No! A thousand times, no. I would rather stay here, in this little box, four years, ten years, rather die here, than have the war end now. There can be no end of the war, until we recover Port Arthur and wipe out the stain of Stoessel's surrender. This is only a colonial war. Russia itself is not affected. We fought a forty-seven years' war in the Caucasus. We can fight a longer war in Manchuria. No. No peace until there are Russian victories. I would rather stay here forever, than go free, than live—with Russia a vanquished power. Vanquished by these Japanese! beaten by an army of those!" pointing to a bow-legged old soldier, in patched and faded khaki clothes, standing at the gate.

Until last week forty more officers slept on the floor of the temple and a dozen or more slept on the broad shelves at the sides, where the images of the five hundred Rakans used to stand. Those in the library used to jeer down to the officers in *Na Dnie*, or *Le Font*, as they called it, after Gorky's sketch of the vagabonds' night lodgings in Moscow.

Esper came before I got away, and Madame P—— also arrived. She can come to see her husband here on the regular two days of the week when general visitors are allowed, and visit him in the chancery, or out in the graveyard. On sunny days, they put the samovar on the tombstones and have *al fresco* tea. Once a week, the captive may spend four hours with his family. Soon they will let him leave the temple and live with his family entirely. She is a Lutheran from the Baltic provinces, so naturally enjoys the good will of the Japanese.

An officer at Esper's temple collared the interpreter, cuffed his ears, and gave him the good shaking he probably deserved; but, for striking an official, the young hot-head is imprisoned for three weeks.

"The French prisoners in Würtemburg were shot for that very thing in 1870," I said, "and they were forced to work on fortifications all along the German frontier, as you know. They slept on the ground in tents, in rain and snow; they were herded in dark, damp casemates of the fortress at Ulm; and the French soldiers died in droves everywhere they were kept in Germany, because of their unsanitary surroundings, and for want of proper, of *sufficient* food and clothing, Germans themselves, and all Europe had to organise relief work to save them. Now the Japanese, you must admit, by contrast with what happened in 1870, are not as inhuman, as uncivilised, as unchristian as the people of your friend, the *Kaiser*, are they? You are well off. You are lapped in luxury, by comparison; so, give the devil his due, Esper."

"Yes, I can give the devil his due all right, but I cannot give anything to the Japanese. Don't ask me to try. You are not a loyal Russian to defend the enemy. No Russian ought to think and reason as you do. For Russia, right or wrong! is our watchword. And Holy Russia is always right, against pagans, heathens, Buddhists, and idolators."

"Andrew Y—— knows a *château* in France, where one of the *ex-votos* in the chapel is a piece of the black bread—half straw too—that the father of the *châtelaine* had served to him for months in the fortress of Magdeburg in 1870. Now, you have good bread here, do you not?" I asked.

"Yes, better than we had at Mukden."

"Well, then, the Japanese feed you better in this little faraway provincial town of Matsuyama, than the Prussians could or would feed the old Comte de —— in that large city of Germany. And they do this when The Hague ordains that you should be treated, as regards food, quarters, and clothing, precisely on the same footing as the troops of the government which captured you. You should be living on fish and rice, pickled plums and *daikon*, by the convention of The Hague, should you not? You have good white bread—made from the most expensive American flour, the missionaries tell me—soup, meat, vegetables, tea. You have clean, hot food three times a day; you have a clean bed, abundant covering and clothing, hot baths, more fresh air than you want, and a chance to walk in a narrow graveyard at any time, haven't you? And so has every Cossack here, hasn't he?"

"Yes, truly."

"Then the Japanese are kinder to their prisoners than the Germans?"

"Yes," he said slowly, while his colleagues roared with laughter at his discomfiture. "But then, you see, they have to. The conventions of Geneva and The Hague made sure that prisoners of war should never again be neglected and so shamefully treated as the French were in 1870. They wouldn't dare not feed and keep us well."

"But, Esper, it was after Geneva that Skobeleff took Plevna. What happened to the Turkish prisoners there? Did you ever hear?"

"Ah! Bah! Yes. But Port Arthur was not Plevna."

"No. Fortunately so. You were not all driven out into the open, snowy field and herded there three days and nights without food or shelter, nor kept in tents on scant rations for another week after the surrender, were you?"

"Good Lord, no!"

"The Japanese have not forced the prisoners to labour on new fortifications under the guns of the fortress, have they?"

"Not here in Matsuyama."

"No, nor elsewhere. Now you have virtually admitted that in these things the Japanese are more humane, more civilised, more enlightened, more Christian than the Germans, have you not?"

"Ah-h! No! No! Not yet. Have mercy! *Madame!*"

"And you admit that they observe the Geneva convention better than the Russians did at Plevna, do you not?"

"Ah! Ah! I cannot, I will not say 'Yes,' to that. You are all wrong in the way you approach your argument. I suppose I could love my jailers in time—love the sentries even, if they were not all bow-legged. Love the interpreter even, if he had thin lips, and round eyes set straight in his face. Until then, no, never."

CHAPTER 31

The Dull Routine

Sunday, February 5th.

I asked one Port Arthur officer what was the best thing he had seen during the war, the thing that impressed him most with the goodness of the world and the human race in it. He said: "The absence of the Japanese flag at Port Arthur. We never saw it, after the surrender, until we got down to Dalny. The Russian flag came down and the flagstaffs and buildings were left bare. We lived on in our same houses, waited on by our same servants, and the men remained in their barracks, until time to march to the Dalny train. Someone rowed over in the night and hung black streamers on the *Pobieda's* (*Victory's*) wreck. Poor *Pobieda! Pobieda!* What a name of irony! It was General Nogi's special order that no flag should be raised until Stoessel had left Port Arthur. There was much of *Bushido* with Nogi at Port Arthur. It is a pity we meet so little in Matsuyama."

Tears came to my eyes to think of such nobility of feeling, such chivalry, such considerate regard for a foe. Rare old Nogi! best exponent of *Bushido*. I cannot imagine Stoessel doing this, had the situations been reversed—nor Kuropatkin.

We have news lately of riots in Russia, and turmoil in many provinces. We are sorely puzzled as to how much truth is in it; how much more serious the usual winter disturbances are this year than in other years. Everything is exaggerated by enemies of Russia at this time, and the rest of the world does not know, and never interested itself to know before, that there are always strikes and small disturbances in every city, when the peasants have come in from the country to work in the factories during the winter. All this we owe to De Witte and his blessed industrialism that was to change and regenerate Russia. This affair of January 22nd in Petersburg, however, seems to be a little out of the usual, and we are all much concerned. That outcast, that degenerate, that Maxim Gorky, seems to have been at the bottom of it; and, in common with all decent Russians, I wish we might have an end of him and his ravings, his studies of the lowest life of our cities.

All countries and capitals have their slums, but why exploit them? and why do outsiders read such things and always talk about them, as if they were the typical, usual life of all classes of the whole empire? As if we all slept under old boats on the banks of the Volga! or slept in penny-a-night lodging houses! Bah! We read that Gorky is allowed thirty-four Japanese *sens* a day for his food in prison, and that he, a consumptive, is kept without fire. The newspapers hold this up as an example of how Russians are treated in Russian prisons, and draw contrasts with the situation here in Japan. I would not admit that this about Gorky's prison fare might be true, to the Americans who had asked me about it. I told them that it was probably a canard from some English newspaper, and that all Americans were mad about Russian prisons anyhow. He said that Americans only believed what Russians themselves wrote about Russian prisons.

Was it a true picture of the prisons in Tolstoi's *Resurrection*? Bah! We one and all cursed Tolstoi, but we could not say anything more. The French Consul says that last winter a dramatisation of *Resurrection* was produced at a Tokyo theatre, and announced as: "A Study of Russian Social Life and Customs!" Heaven forbid! Think of that! Think what Russia suffers in misrepresentation by her own writers. It really seems to be a conspiracy of all the world to misrepresent us, to put us wrong and show our exceptional worst as the typical average. It is useless to argue. I give it up. At times my allegiance weakens terribly, and I suppose for all the rest of our lives we must go on excusing and explaining and trying to put our half-civilised, our quarter-civilised country in better light.

At last our army at Mukden has begun to move. Two great armies, a half-million men, have been lying in trenches and caves ever since Kuropatkin's fiasco on the Shaho in October. The sentries have talked together, and the men in the trenches have shouted across, and none of us can understand this long inaction, this armistice. The Japanese have naturally preferred to crouch over their *hibachis* in the underground trenches; but cold is nothing to Russians, and our real campaign was to open in December. What is Kuropatkin doing? Mistchenko's raid down the Liao River to Newchwang did not accomplish anything, and did not cover a movement from Mukden, as we had thought.

Mistchenko only took a long, cold ride, and got a bullet in his leg, for his trouble. Another failure. And Cossack is now a name of derision to all the world.

The American pope said the other day that the greatest surprise to the world in this war, had been the harmlessness of the Cossacks; that they were now an exploded myth, an outlived delusion, a terrible bogy forever laid at rest; that everybody's teeth used to chatter when we said: "Cossack!" but that now the Cossacks seemed only good for whipping unarmed women and students, and shooting priests. A rather strong indictment, but true. I am afraid all Russia is coming to be an exploded myth—a bubble pricked—a decadent empire ruled by a race of degenerates.

All the white-robed, red-crossed company at the hospital have renewed their vituperations of Stoessel. Why, think you?

Some days ago ninety barrels of pickled cabbage arrived from Port Arthur. A spoil of war that will help feed this army of no occupation now idling in Japan. That everlasting Japanese pre-arrangement had no part in providing this cabbage. Stoessel did that. The high-smelling pickle offended the Japanese, who can endure their own *daikon*; and they asked Andrew Y—— to see if it was fit to eat, or if it should not be destroyed. "Excellent! Excellent!" said Andrew. "The men will be happy to have it every day, and the officers may like it once or twice a week!" But some pushed it from them with fury, and because of this captured cabbage flayed poor Stoessel alive again on a new count.

"What! I surrender with ninety barrels of this cabbage in the cellar? Never!" thundered Grievsky. He figured it out, knowing the precise Japanese ways of ratio and apportionment, how many hundreds of barrels there must have been in the storehouses of the surrendered fortress, if ninety barrels came to Matsuyama. "Surely, four hundred and fifty barrels must have gone to Nagoya, and nine hundred barrels to the Hamadera camp! Oh! the black villainy of that Stoessel! It grows worse and worse! *Kusai! Kusai!* (It smells! It smells!) the Japanese can truly say."

CHAPTER 32

The Finding of Tosaburo

Monday, February 6th.

Last night was the full moon night, the fifteenth night of the Chinese, or lunar year. Madame Takasu sent me word in the morning that the Jiu-Roku-Zakura, the Sixteenth-Day-Cherry-Tree, the tree with a soul, was actually blooming now in the dead of winter. As all Iyo will flock to see it—no, to worship it—for the next fortnight, we went early. As first-nighters, we assisted at this annual *première* of the old tree with a very charming company of poets and aristocrats, the same charming circle encountered at the *château* the night of the moon-viewing, in September. It is strange enough, at this season—in the dead of winter, when only camellias can stand the cold nights, and my beautiful hedge shows many a browned blossom every morning, and hardy plum trees are only beginning to bud—it is strange to think of a cherry tree blooming. It is plainly supernatural.

It is stranger yet to see that picturesque green glen of the lonely temple now alive with sentries and idling, strolling prisoners of war; for even the Cherry Tree Temple has been taken for a depot for *horios*—a forlorn, melancholy lot of soldiers from Port Arthur. It was not in harmony with the poetry of flower-worshipping to come upon these shaggy Cossacks and sailors, and shabby men of all arms and kinds. I looked at them critically too, they were so different from the suffering men in white *kimonos* at the hospital. And what a lot of criminals, cutthroats, and ragamuffins they looked to be! Not a comely, a joyous, or a smiling countenance there. I appreciate now the conventional Japanese smile when the heart is breaking, the smile when suffering intense pain, the smile when telling sad news. It is better than the gloomy Russian countenances we meet.

The officer in command came from the guardhouse, bowed profoundly to Madame Takasu, and offered to go with us. They had been a little in doubt, he said, whether to close the temple court to visitors, or to shut the prisoners inside during the blossom time. They finally concluded that either would be undeserved punishment. It is old custom in Iyo to make a pilgrimage to this tree, which first bloomed on the sixteenth day of the year in answer to a son's prayer that his dying father might once more see the *sakura no hana* (cherry blossoms). The dying man's soul entered into the tree, and the Jiu-Roku-Zakura is as famous as any of the classic Chinese *Twenty-six Examples of Filial Piety*. The people wish to see it in war-time more than ever, and are admitted to worship the budding branches; to clap their hands and say a prayer; to look over the parapet at the beautiful view; and to look their fill at the uncouth *horios*—peasants from a Christian country, who have no such refinements of life and thought, nothing so elevated in countryside customs as this divine flower-worshipping.

It was cool and fresh in the little valley, and when we had wound up the long path, and climbed the outer terrace steps, there stood the many-branched tree, all dotted over with brown buds bursting to show pink petals, while a few full flowers turned pale faces to the chilly sunshine. "How white it is!" I exclaimed. "Why, the cherry blossoms in Tokyo used to be rose-pink; as pink as my *tsubakis*." The lieutenant watched us narrowly, and Madame Takasu said very gravely: "It is because of the war. So much blood has been shed in Manchuria that even the cherry flowers are pale, without colour, this year."

I caught my breath; the tears came. Oh! these exquisite people! What other race or nation has soul and sentiment to such degree as to feel that even the flowers are blanched at the torrents of blood that have flowed in Manchuria! What a thought! How Japanese! Ah! that Lafcadio Hearn were living!

"How did you learn our Japanese language?" asked the lieutenant, and I gave him the name of my teachers in Matsuyama.

"But it is very difficult, our language. Had you never studied Japanese language before?" he persisted.

"Oh, yes, a little. Once before, a long time ago, I had been in Tokyo."

"Oh! Oh! Oh! was it at the Russian *Koshikan* (legation)? You must be my friend the *miya sama* (the princess) Sophia! I knew you. I knew you! It was long ago, when I was a little boy; but I remember. Oh, yes! I remember, and I still have all those beautiful eggs. I cried many, many days, when you went away without me. I wanted to go, as Saigo's son had gone with Russian minister's children to Russia, but you would not take me. And now—Oh! it is very wonderful! very wonderful!" and the little man began to open his card-case.

"But who are you?" I asked in surprise at this link in my past life reappearing, for his card in Japanese text told me nothing.

"Oh! you would not know me by that. I have new name now. I used to be Tosaburo, Higuchi's son, Tosaburo. Then I was only third son; now I am adopted son. I am Kato *san*; a lieutenant since the war has begun. Oh! I am so grieving, because they will not send me to war in Manchuria."

"Lieutenant Kato! My little Tosaburo! Impossible! Oh! *Molodetz! Molodetz!*" I cried.

"Yes. That is what you used to call me. And do you remember nice *sakura* (cherry) and *momiji* (maple) parties in Fukiage gardens with my mother? Well, she is gone, now; and Fukiage is not for the Kuges anymore. It is emperor's own garden now. No one can go there at all, to see the flowers in spring; only to Enriokwan; and that palace is pulled down. Oh! Tokyo is so changed since I was a boy."

"But Kato? Kato? You must be the *daimio* of Iyo now."

"No, no! Those are not my ancestors at Dairinji. My new family was not of Kato Kiyomasa, who went to Korea. Oh! No! There are many Katos in Japan. It is common name, like Ito, and Inouye, and Watanabe; and I am just one of those many Katos. There have been Hisamatsus, Matsudairas, and Hanabusas here as *daimios*, since the Katos. But your *miya sama*, your *knias sama*, where is he? Oh! Oh! a thousand pardons. I had forgotten all that at the Hibiya. I am so stupid—so sorry—so sorry. Please forgive. I am just like an Aino, you see, *miya sama*. I have lost all my civilised manners. Oh! Forgive me."

I told him my new name, and that I had also been adopted; that a Russian colonel, bandaged fast to his cot at the barracks hospital, had adopted me. His eyes opened full at that. And then he laughed, went off in a storm of glee, at the idea of my being adopted too, and having a new name. The years rolled away for a minute, and I played again and made jokes for my jolly little Tokyo neighbour. We had the jolly joke over again of my adopting him, and taking him back to Russia to grow up as my own *knias sama*, because there were two brothers older than he, and he really "was not needed in Japan," as he used to argue. And now, what a situation it would be if he were a Russian *knias sama!*—and at war with Russia! Or with Japan? Oh! No! No!

quite impossible, that.

The prisoners had slipped the paper doors, crowded out into the court, and surrounded us in a silent, staring circle, ten deep. Little Madame Takasu drew closer to me, as these heavy, stupid faces made a wall around us. "Oh! I am so afraid," she said, with an appealing smile—that wonderful Japanese smile of good manners, triumphant over all personal feeling. The prisoners looked as savage and ferocious, as untamed and uncombed as any barbarians one could ever meet. Pity stirred within me for the poor, idle, densely-ignorant, dumb creatures, driven to the army and war, as cattle are driven to pasture or abattoir, but no pulse of pride stirred at contemplation of them as my own nationals, as fellow-countrymen, as Russians. They were a frowsy lot, in disorderly uniforms, and every race-type was represented there, from the Laplander and Finn, and the flat-faced, broken-nosed men of the Volga, to the clear-cut faces of the Caucasians and Buriat Mongols. Men of every religion—Jews, Catholics, Lutherans, Armenians, Old Faith, Stundist, Orthodox, Mohammedan—were in that stolid, gaping mass that surrounded us, and whose odour was strong, peculiar, and distinct, as if they were horses or goats.

"Speak to them!" said the little lieutenant, and when I uttered a few words in Russian there was a show of life in the dull faces. "*A Barina! A Barina!*" they repeated with stupefaction, and looked helplessly to a petty, officer from the ships, who was their spokesman. Translating for my companions, I learned that they longed for something to do—some work to occupy, some musical instruments to help cheer the long days of nothingness. And then they naively asked about the tree. "Oh, so many Japonski have been here lately, and they all look and look at this one tree and talk about it. And yesterday, *Barina*, some old men with white beards came here, and they wrote all those notices you see hanging there, and tied them up and went away. I suppose they are going to chop down that tree, or sell this place, and then where will they send us?"

When I interpreted the Cossacks' idea about the poem papers, Tosaburo laughed amazedly at such ignorance of poetic custom. Poor Tosaburo was chagrined that he could not accompany two such distinguished visitors back to the city, but he was on duty, hard and fast, for three days.

"Yes, I am very honoured for one so young, of cadet school, for I command three military posts, you see; or, I am the *bonze san* of three temples. Just as you like. But my first day, I shall come to see the *knias sama*."

168

CHAPTER 33

A Little Victory

Friday, February 17th.

There were sounds of a *gogai* in faraway streets as I left the house this morning; but I had not a chance to ask the news, until I met the surliest of all the interpreters at the operating- room door. To my query he answered: "It is death of very bad man, your Grand Duke Sergius."

"No one in the world could agree with you better than I on that question," I told the astonished boor. He dropped his lower jaw, and the heavy rice-mouth with its big white teeth gaped wide open. Foiled of his purpose of insult, he moved off sullenly; and later, the American sister of charity, who was on duty, told me of the bomb-throwing within the Kremlin square. She thought it might be well not to mention it in the wards, although no order had been given; but I assured her that it would not be a cause of sadness and depression to any there; that in fact they would more likely rejoice and cheer up.

But the poor grand duchess, whom we all so admire! All the prisoners have enjoyed her bounty from the first. Only a few weeks ago, a large sum came to Andrew Y——, whom she deputed to act as her almoner; and his friends had their pleasure in making him explain every time that it was not Serge Alexandrovitch, but Elizabeth of Hesse, whose kindness was extended to them.

It would not do to record the treasonable sentiments expressed on receipt of this news, and there was sorrow for the grand duchess only that it was accomplished in such a shocking way. "Now my Cossacks may get their overcoats and shoes," said one officer tersely. "No more bales of Cossacks' great-coats will be sold at the Sunday morning Thieves' Market at Moscow." Their tongues once loosened, my patients talked so freely that I felt as if in a Geneva Nihilist assembly. It is amazing what advanced and liberal sentiments they dare voice, dare continually and openly discuss here in this freedom! And what contradiction! Freedom in prison! Freedom of speech in a pagan, Asiatic country, but not in our own Christian country! There is no censorship of what we read here, save as the censor cuts out notes of military affairs in the Kobe paper; and, what the censor cuts out for Dairinji, the censor at Oguri leaves untouched. The revolutionary emissary, brought from Port Arthur, so wearied his fellow captives with his philippics that they begged the Japanese to take him away. He and his big Baden-Powell hat have disappeared from Matsuyama, and he is now frothing his anarchist doctrines to a new audience.

All the books forbidden us in Russia are freely read and lent around here. There is liberty of mind at least in these paper and bamboo prisons. Many are seriously reading and discussing republican forms of government and representative assemblies. The Oxford Professor Bryce's book on the American Commonwealth is often brought me by those who want me to argue its English into clearer Russian. Vladimir and the old colonel say that all this seething of liberal ideas, all this talk of constitutions and parliaments is like the times in the last months of Alexander the Liberator's life. The old colonel wept the other day when he told how near Russia once was to attaining liberal rule and political enlightenment.

"To think how the constitution of Loris Melikoff was laboured over until that last midnight, when Loris Melikoff came home and said the greatest work of the century was accomplished—a greater work than the liberation of the serfs. The next day it was signed, and Alexander Nicholaivitch rose, rejoiced, and went for a drive, pondering on his *ukase* of the next day declaring this new constitution. I saw it with my own eyes, I held it in my own hands. I read it. I read it. I know it yet, every word," said the old officer excitedly. "And then—one bomb—one second—and Russia was hurled back to all this twenty-odd years of stagnation, of arrested development, of retrogression under Pobedonostseff's rule. Reaction, oppression, persecution, and darkest ignorance are the story of the years.

"Eighteen *roubles* spent on the army to each *rouble* spent on the schools! Millions of people living like dumb cattle, unable to read or to write! And this going on generation after generation when many of us are willing, but, yes, are actually prevented, forbidden, punished, for trying to teach the peasants. Children are excluded from the schools because of their race or religion, and *zemstvo* schools are hindered or closed. There seems to be no hope, no help for Russia. Von Plehve and Serge have gone to their account, but that archangel of evil, old Pobedonostseff, lives."

Beside all our regular social distinctions and classes, our order of rank and titles, there is a subtle line drawn here in Matsuyama that cuts through all the prisoner company of officers. It is as near to hearing Monnet-Sully as we can come when Grievsky, in some of his long tirades, beats his breast and says: "*We* who were captured in action, and those *surrendered* ones from Port Arthur!" And then, among the surrendered ones there is a line drawn between the military and naval officers. Von Woerffel tries to be a peace-maker and go-between of all kinds; for, although of the navy, he was not of the Port Arthur fleet. At his suggestion I have been to visit the temples, where the naval officers are quartered. Dairinji, near the railway station, has the largest company of fleet officers, and they gave me tea and good music.

They are very sure that the Japanese threat of raising the Russian ships in Port Arthur is an idle boast. Each set of ship's officers made thorough work of destroying the vessels, when the loss of Two-Hundred-and-Three-Metre Hill left the ships so many plain targets for Japanese gunners. They exploded dynamite inside, and fired mines and torpedoes from the outside, and none of the Russian battleships and cruisers will ever be raised and dragged over to Japan like captives in a Roman triumphal procession. To be saved that humiliation is something. All speak affectionately, even tearfully, of their lost ships. All have pictures of their ships in gala array, and as contrasts, pictures of those same ships sunk to their funnels and tilted at every angle as they lie with decks awash, resting on the bottom of Port Arthur harbour.

As Von Woerffel says, there cannot be much room left for the fishes now, it is so crowded with battleships, cruisers, gunboats, torpedo-boats, and dozens and dozens of launches and small boats, beside the wreckage of the Japanese blocking expeditions. The harbour is also paved with guns, rifles, revolvers, swords, and ammunition that were thrown there the night Stoessel signed the infamous surrender. The officers led and the men followed, until it was like the throwing of carnival confetti.

They are a very gloomy and depressed company, these sailors ashore. Their bandsmen, many of whom are now acting as officers' servants, weep for their abandoned musical instruments. It was unnecessary cruelty to thus deprive these poor musicians of their very breath of life and a part of their being, by obliging them to leave their

171

instruments behind. The officers, too, are sad without the consolation and distraction of music, and the French Consul is overwhelmed with requests for musical instruments. He spent much of the Queen of Greece's contribution in buying a piano for each "Prisoners' Base," for each *étape*, and piles of sheet music besides. The officers at Myoenji had more photographs than any of the others—innumerable views of the wounded battleships and cruisers, with their decks slanting to the tide. And the poor *Pobieda*! riddled from without, wrecked from within, the machinery a tangle of rusted rubbish, leaning to the *Pallada*—the broken dream of Russia's sea power.

Mikhail's cousin had pictures of his own fat-funnelled torpedo-boat, the ——, which was captured from the Chinese at Taku forts five years ago; and in which he had several times raced over to Chefoo by night and back again. "The Japanese tried to get my torpedo-boat at the Boxer time, and they thought they would get it again; but I settled all that when ordered ashore. They can lift her, but she will be an iron box with the bottom dropped out."

Sunday, February 19th.

We have many new cases in hospital now from this last fiasco of Gripenberg's—an advance straight at the Japanese front which carried him to Sandepu and Heikoutai. It was all hard fighting for three days in a blinding snowstorm; and then, as Kuropatkin did not send up reinforcements, Gripenberg had to march back again, passing his wounded, who had frozen to death where they fell, with no effort from the great army to even succour them. The jet-black, frosted feet and hands, that are brought here now, wring one's heart in pity. What wasted effort! What a senseless sacrifice of human beings! "The King of France with a hundred thousand men marched up the hill and then marched down again." An heroic march, a little victory; and then, defeat, retreat—and many prisoners brought to Japan.

How weary I am of this continued story of hesitation, incompetency, bickerings, and defeat!

The whole army blames Kuropatkin for his failure to follow Gripenberg's advance, and for his turning the Sandepu victory into the Heikoutai defeat. Nothing that Bertha von Suttner describes equals the horrors of this Heikoutai—this battle in a blizzard—when the surgeons' hands were frosted as they worked; when flesh and instruments froze as they touched together; and severed arteries were stanched without dressings. Ah! Truly! Lay down your arms! Lay down your arms!

Vladimir dwells now on the fact that the one success, the one advance of the whole war, was made by a general of German descent and traditions, one of the non-Russian officers to whom Alexander Nicholaivitch gave the important places, and whose superior intelligence, character, and ability even Alexander Alexandrovitch had to admit. No other Russian general has done anything but disgrace himself so far. No new stars have risen, no geniuses come forward, no great reputations have been made. In fact, reputations have been unmade; and Kuropatkin retains credit now only for his social qualities, his literary abilities, his French puns. The Poles have won all the honours so far. The best engineers, gunners, and surgeons were Poles, and one Polish officer on a torpedo-boat did things as recklessly brave as the Japanese away back in last March.

Sunday, March 12th.

Tosaburo made his ceremonial call on Vladimir, and the handsome chap made the most complete conquest of my *danna san.* Even Grievsky admitted that he was a true *bushi,* an ideal Japanese, the most charmingly polished and refined jailer he had ever met. I had such a pride in my *protégé* that both Vladimir and Lyov poked fun at me. His presence made a flutter in the chancery, too. Half the bureau escorted him to our ward, and even the surliest cub of an interpreter put on good manners for the occasion, and wanted to stay and interpret.

Tosaburo waved him off, in the magnificent way these long-descended aristocrats have, and said briefly to the *soshi,* "No! No! The *miya sama* can interpret for all languages," and the interpreter, looking bewilderedly around, finally brought his gaze to me and stood stock-still, frankly open-mouthed with astonishment. His brain was working over those words, *miya sama,* and their application to me, when Tosaburo, having clicked his heels together and made a military salute to Vladimir, and then a nice English handshake, turned and said a casual and quite polite "Begone!" And the interpreter vanished. The other officers came in, and limped in, to have tea with our unusual visitor, and a cloud of officials looked on from the entrance and passage-ways, saluting profoundly when he left.

CHAPTER 34

Mukden's Despair

Sunday, March 26th.

We accept the defeat of Mukden as a shameful fact; a last indictment of the Russian generals and the army; and we lose ourselves, as best we may, in the dimensions and details of the world's greatest battle. It is strange the comfort the megalomaniacs can get out of the fact that the front of the army was one hundred miles wide, the defeat a hundred miles long. It does not comfort me to consider that that mad, headlong retreat continued for one hundred miles.

For the wounded, my heart bleeds. Sad enough is the state of those who fell, and lay until the Japanese advance came and carried them off. It will be long before we hear how it fared with the thousands who were thrown hastily into cars and sent to Harbin, without fire, food, coverings, nurses, or doctors.

"We could not help it. The Japanese were upon us before we knew. We were worn out with three days' hard fighting, night and day, with a snowstorm and a blinding dust-storm; and we lay down at midnight five miles from the Japanese lines. We woke up to find all Mukden filled with Japanese and the Russian army ten miles away. They treated us well. Here we are. That is all. War is not *vaudeville*, but we felt very foolish that morning in Mukden." It was our usual want of information—and hesitation, hesitation, hesitation—indecision. The same old curse of Russia. If the dust-storm had not been in their faces, the Japanese would have arrived sooner, and we would have been a larger company. That is all. They had maps of the country, and we had not. In all the years in Manchuria, our officers had made no topographical surveys; and when they hurried up some maps for campaign use, they would have done as well for the Caucasus.

"If the map showed a mountain you might be sure that you would find instead a river too deep to ford.

Then another captive raged at what he called the "deception" of General Nogi. It seems that Nogi's army never went into barracks at Port Arthur, at all. That grim old besieger did not let his men weaken in the luxuries of our Russian Capua. He moved his men and guns, as soon as Stoessel's inglorious army had marched out; but he did not move them to face the Russian left, as our officers took it for granted he would do, and implicitly believed he had done. Having concentrated their strength to meet him there, they think it a breach of faith that he circled away off and fell upon their right flank miles north of Mukden. There is an officer in the seventh ward who tells of the panic that seized his men, when the Japanese sprang upon them unexpectedly, shouting in Russian: "We are Nogi's men from Port Arthur."

Vladimir and Lyov are sick with disgust that several of the paroled officers of the Port Arthur garrison were captured by Nogi's men at Sinmintun. They have been brought here, and Vladimir says no self-respecting man should speak to them. "*Parole d'honneur* means nothing to a Russian," the Japanese continue to say; for Port Arthur naval officers, who gave parole to take no further part in the war and were released, have been captured lately trying to run ships into Vladivostok. Long before that, paroled officers from the Russian gunboats at Shanghai, went around through China to Port Arthur, and met death on Makaroff's ship. What can one say when these things happen, and the paroled officers are captured and brought here."

I am sure many more concessions would have been made to us here, had it not been for the arrival of these dishonoured officers.

How I hate, loathe, the whole miserable business! And Russia has now suffered such continued disgrace and defeats that love of country may not be dead within me, but love of autocracy and reverence for our fatally weak ruler are not within me anymore. Poor hesitating, terrified, conscience- racked, nerve-torn sovereign! I pity you. Were there any hope for a stronger or better ruler, in any life next to yours, how fortunate it would be if you forsook the throne, and went away to live the quiet life of a country squire! But the burden is yours. You must bear it. You cannot pass it to those less worthy. You must lead Russia out of the darkness to light. The talk of the "Awakening of China" is paralleled by the same greatly-needed Awakening of Russia; and it comes more slowly.

Ever since the French Revolution, the wise ones have known that a change' must come in Russia. Force—brutal, pitiless force—has sup-

pressed all aspirations for liberty and enlightenment, and foreign con-
quests have distracted the public attention, as the gladiators and the
arena did in old Rome. But this war has roused some worthy men of
the nobility and bureaucracy at last to the point of boldness. Sviatapolk
Mirsky has done wonderful things already, and the liberty of the press
he has granted is a great step forward. Mertchensky now cries out for
peace since Russia has defeated herself. But out of defeat may come
the greatest victory. The thinking people, upright, intelligent Russians,
may take heart in their sorrows.

Grievsky has his laugh now, but it is a bitter laugh, a heart-broken
one, when he considers how the English have feared us all these years.
"If the Japanese can make a laughing-stock of Kuropatkin, can turn
all his boasts back upon his head, and make him personally run—run
from Haicheng, run from Liaoyang, run from the Shaho, and run last
and fastest from Mukden—Lord! what that cold-blooded devil of a
Kitchener could do, with an army of his little Goorkhas! Goodbye,
Ferghana and Kashgaria! Goodbye, Trans-Caspia!"

Thursday, March 30th.

With fifty thousand prisoners, they say, to come from Mukden,
many are to be sent to further *dépôts* to make room here. Several
have gone to Shidzuoka, near Fujiyama, but write back depressingly
of their housing there. A few occupy the villa of the old deposed
Tokugawa shogun, which is a labyrinth of small, dark cupboards. No
Cossack officer can stand upright in it, when he wears his *gros bonnet*.
The restrictions are severe in Shidzuoka; no daily newspapers are allowed, and the missionaries cannot come and go as here. The Japanese
petty official in brief authority is the same tyrant that the helpless
suffer from everywhere. I dare say the Russian keepers of the Japanese
prisoners at Medved are more severe, less *simpatica* even, than those
we chafe against here. They, too, might be capable of depriving the
prisoners of their musical instruments, lest music foster a martial spirit;
and might even prohibit card-playing at the hospital.

Some who have gone away write amusing accounts of the new
places of detention. In one city the prisoners are quartered in a theatre, and they have organised an opera company of their members.
They spend their days rehearsing the choruses and ballets of the grand
opera—*Les Horios aux Enfers*, as they call the spectacle they are about
to produce. The revolving stage and its effects amuse them, and they
plan to urge it upon Petersburg *impresarios*. At another town, they are

quartered in the pavilions of the public gardens, in the Zoo! for a fact. "Appropriately, they have placed us as curiosities in the Zoological Garden," one writes. "We have no more space nor liberty than our neighbours the stork and the bear."

All grumble and lament, save the few who drive themselves with study and work; studying Japanese, studying French, English, German; translating into Russian the English translations of Japanese fairy tales, novels, and histories; translating the many English and French standard books on Japan; as, except for Metchnikoff and De Wollant, our Russian literature lacks in general works, popular works on Japan, books of travels, impressions, analyses, such as the English have in numbers. If Lafcadio Hearn had but written in Russian, this war could not have been. Had the court and our intellectuals only read "*Bushido*," the war would have been prevented. We are being punished for our ignorance, that is all. The majority of Russians thought the Japanese no more than another Turcoman tribe—fish-eating heathens. That is all. This war was to be merely a hunting adventure for our Cossacks. They were to spit the tiny Kakamakis on their bayonets and toss them over their shoulders as lightly as so much hay.

Even in their treatment of prisoners, how wonderfully well the Japanese have managed with this great number of *horios*. The officers grumble that they are not allowed the freedom French officers had in German cities in 1870, where at Wiesbaden and Frankfort they lived in hotels. They forget that there are no hotels, as such, in Matsuyama, and that the government furnishes here as much privacy and more foreign comforts than any tourist can command in a tea house; while the rank and file are in a heaven of plenty, cleanliness, comfort, and idleness they never dreamed of before, and that contrasts sharply with the suffering, the cold, disease, and starvation of the poor French prisoners in Dresden, Magdeburg, Mayence, Ulm, and Augsburg in Christian Germany, in 1870.

CHAPTER 35

The Happy Day

Sunday, April 2nd.

Tosaburo came to my house one morning to say that he was going to Hiroshima, to meet his uncle who was returning from Manchuria by transport the next day. "And you know him too," said he. "He is also old *tomodaichi* (friend). He was only Colonel Higuchi when you were in Tokyo, but now he is Lieutenant-Greneral Baron Higuchi. He has done remarkable things in war with China; and was very remarkable ruler of Taiwan—of Formosa, I mean. Now he is chief-of-staff of Field Marshal Marquis Oyama, and he is greatest brains of all of our army. Our field marshal, you know, is quite aged and very portly, and he does not do such active things now. He has much spirit, but his body is not so boyful. He is the clan general, we call him, the Satsuma military chief. He is commander of generals, and all young generals obey him very peacefully. They never quarrel at our headquarters and oppose each other; and our field marshal rules like father of family, and tells how each battle shall be fought according to the plans of my uncle, the Lieutenant-General Baron Higuchi. It is my uncle who has made this greatest battle of all the world at Mukden. Truly. He is going now to Tokyo to tell about it himself—Himself tell it to our *Nippon Heika*, to the emperor."

"Higuchi! Higuchi! The young officer, with such very quick eyes and such very fine countenance, handsome like an Italian, we used to say? Is that the one?"

"Yes. Yes, that is the same one you used to call Italian Colonel. Exactly the same officer. I shall tell him you are here, and shall I ask him any somethings for you?"

"Oh! I am very content, Tosaburo *san*. Everyone is very kind to me. All I wish for, you know, is that the *danna san* may soon get well

178

enough to leave the hospital and come to my house to live. That is his fault. He is so slow. I say *Hiaku!* (hurry!) to him every day, but he is not obedient like my old *kurumaya*, you see." And we laughed at our small joke immensely.

"But, Tosaburo, why do they not let the Russian lady at Kobe, who was a soldier and surrendered at Port Arthur—why do they not let her come down here to see Captain X——?" and then that young sprig of Japanese militarism drew his shoulders up very square, made his countenance severe, and said: "Oh, *miya sama*, she is not wifes. Not truly wifes, you know. And the Japanese Government cannot allow shocking things, you know. If wifes, all right; come tomorrow. I have heard my high officers here, when they were talking with French Consul, say what it is. Really shocking."

"But, Tosaburo, here are two priests to marry them. Let her come here. Don't let them send her over to Shanghai."

"Yes. She must go away, they have told consul. He cannot marry without his general's permission, and that is distinguished soldier, General Stoessel, now wearing German *Kaiser's* merity sword, you see, in far country."

"Rubbish! Rubbish! General Smirnoff was his commander of fortress of Port Arthur. Will you please tell officers that? Only General Smirnoff's permission in a letter from Nagoya is necessary. Tell them. Truly I say so. Then the priest says ceremony, and it is all proper marriage, husband and wife. Not shocking, shocking, you young Englishman—you young Plum Pudding, as we used to call those pink-faced children at Kojimachi Koshikan."

Tosaburo laughed immoderately at the old joke, and, quick as could be, said: "Oh! Oh! I shall do it all myself. We shall have a little *Banzai* with it. We shall have a little marry party at barracks, just like that English lady, you remember. And we shall throw shoes and other vegetables—no, only rice, when they go 'going-way' as they called it. Oh! I remember that so well. We all thought it curious. And my father and mother I have heard talk much about that curious foreign custom since then. And since then I have seen several foreign marries. My English teacher in Tsukiji, she has had a marry in the foreign church there. I shall ask general here today for some orders, before I go to Hiroshima with the despatches. You see. You look. Soon Russian soldier-girl will come from Kobe, I know. I am sure. We shall have a marry party on my return. You and I shall be the *nakados* (go-betweens). Oh! Good!"

179

Monday, April 3rd.

I found them shouting "*Vivas!*" and drinking toasts to a newly ar-rived officer today, and they explained to me: "He had charge of those twin curses of war, the military *attachés* and the war correspondents. It was a duty to rightly earn one the St. Anne, and he was fairly promised that, if he would let his wards be captured. But he could not lose them. They always turned up safe, always escaped the enemy by a single hair. Luck had them in its keeping, until that night at Mukden, when they told them, at midnight, that we were pushing the Japanese back, that we had them on the run then. So they went to sleep; and waked, to find us gone and themselves ten miles within Japanese lines!—guests of another headquarters staff. It was worth his getting captured too, he thinks, to lose those beggars. He was caught himself at the Pass; and so, not having reported the irreparable loss of the strangers in person, he may not get his St. Anne."

Some queer sorts of officers have been brought to light by the Japanese dragnets thrown out to our army. I have been astounded to hear of military officers who could not read or write, as uneducated as *mujiks*. They are survivals of an old system, and of course would not have ever left Siberia but for this war. We take the ignorance of the rank and file as a matter of course, but we feel it as a bitter taunt when the Japanese order that those of the prisoners who cannot read or write shall learn to do so now. Japan cannot permit so many ig-norant members in one community! Those who can read and write must teach the others! At Marugame and Himeji prisons, the *Rurik* sailors have already learned to read, and B——, is a volunteer teacher already.

Another *bonne bouche* came from one of the Protestant mission-aries who made one of her schoolboys read to her, in English, the *gogai* that came out during the great battle. He reads: "Kuropatkin has telephoned to his emperor, 'I am inside of the Japanese. Please forgive.'" Grievsky appreciated this, but howls with rage to think that Kuropatkin is not literally inside of the Japanese—"inside of them as *we* are here—inside of a Japanese prison! Ah! He and his carload of icons came to dictate a treaty of peace in Tokyo! It will be at Tomsk, more likely. But I forget. He has taken oath not to retreat beyond the Urals. Quite true. Quite true. It is his distinguished, world-renowned successor, the well-known General Linievitch—'Papa Linievitch'—who will advance boldly westward! 'To Petersburg!' inscribed on his banners. Bah! a plague on all. Even the weather prophet, Demchinski,

180

can rail at them. He and Mestchersky are now our military critics, under Sviatopolk Mirsky's free press rules! Ah! Gott, *is* the world all mad, or am I?"

Tuesday, April 4th.

And now! Straight from the clear sky, as a bolt from the blue, comes an order for Vladimir to be removed from the hospital to my home! At once! For a fact!

While I was still at my luncheon yesterday, a bicycle messenger brought me a note from headquarters to come to the chancery at two o'clock, or earlier, if possible. In the agitation, I hastened there at once, fearing everything. "Oh!" said His Insolence, the official interpreter: "You are ordered to remove the prisoner, Staff-Colonel von Theill, to your dwelling, and there act as Volunteer Red Cross nurse. You must give your oath to observe the regulations prescribed as to visits, correspondence, and telegrams.

And the interview was over.

I could hardly utter my thanks, much less ask questions. To turn my tragic joy to real comedy, up stepped the *"Homunculus,"* as we call him, the *netsuke*, the *breloque*, the one whom Grievsky vows he will wear away on his watch chain. He is the tiniest Japanese I have ever seen, with almost no legs at all. Well, up rose this living *netsuke*, bowed, opened the door for me, and said: "I will show you the way!"

Oh! It was droll!

I walked slowly, thinking of myself as in a dream, and then I fairly ran, burst in upon Vladimir, and called him to "get ready quick, quick. Get up and come with me!" And he almost did so, in his sudden alarm at my irruption.

Soon after, the chief-surgeon came, and formally said to us: "By telegraphic order of His Excellency, the Minister of War, the Staff-Colonel von Theill is to be immediately removed to the dwelling of Princess Sophia von Theill, and to be treated with the highest consideration, at the request of Lieutenant-General Baron Higuchi, who sends his compliments and further messages by letter."

What an excitement there was there then! Vladimir's half of a man servant, the nurses and D——, all turned to and bundled up his possessions; and we were so wild with selfish joy that it was only when I saw Lyov's wistful face, and then noticed the others' blank dismay, that I realised how I was robbing them.

Within an hour Vladimir was bundled up, packed into a double *jinrikisha*, with many pillows around him and three coolies to pull, push, and steady him, and rode out of the gate ahead of me. Out into the open air! Out into comparative freedom and private life! His first outing since he was carried in on a stretcher, believing himself about to die.

Ah! Tosaburo! Tosaburo! My friend indeed! And the Italian colonel! *Bushido* is surely the living creed of my—enemies?

CHAPTER 36

At Home—Colonel and Mrs. Vladimir Von Theill

Wednesday, April 5th.

It was Tosaburo who had done it all—my jolly little *knias san*, and when he returned to duty, he came to see us straight from headquarters. He brought the letter conveying the formal compliments of his Italian uncle, who begged to be remembered, and to know how he could serve me, etc., etc. But everything was done; all that heart could wish for. I could only express my profound thanks again and again. Then everyone came to congratulate us; and Vladimir had hardly drunk in all his new surroundings, seen half of my pretty things, and only begun to look at the garden, when callers came. Every one called; from the governor and the commandant down to the last tradesman and coolie; and the startled house-boy asked Anna if he was to give a *thé complet* to every kitchen caller also. "By all means," said Anna. "This is our *Banzai*, our *matsuri*. A feast to everyone, certainly. The *Barina* would be very angry if you did not celebrate the *danna san's* coming home. Run and get more *mochi*, and more sugar-flowers quickly, and red rice in plenty."

We were touched to the heart by the simple gifts that came to us from all these humble folk. The *jinrikisha coolies* came with their headman to present a great bouquet of plum and quince blossoms arranged in classic style, and to wish good health to the *danna san*. The butcher, the baker, the greengrocer, the old eggwoman, the vegetable dealer from the country, the fishman, everyone who in any way purveyed to my little household, came to lay presents on the sunny *engawa*. Vladimir's blanched face in the long chair was a picture of pleased content and interest in all of them and their gifts of sugar, oranges,

183

eggs, towels, sweets, flowers. Whenever there were no Japanese in sight, I swooped down upon him with my caresses, my forbidden kisses, by thousands; for one could not be demonstrative at the hospital with other people always in hearing, and a curtain lifted at any moment without ceremony. To have him in my own home! *our* own home! all in my own care, every hour was rapture to even think of.

And this was a *home* at last—*our home*. With Vladimir within its walls, I should not care if I were never permitted to go abroad.

Anna would fairly have killed our patient with kindness, with all the delicacies of the Japanese market, all the concoctions that her life in Germany, England, Spain, France, Italy, and Russia had taught her to make in the kitchens of those countries. Poor Vladimir's thin face glowed with pleasure, from morning till night. He closed his eyes and opened them sharply, to see that things were what they seemed to be; he pinched himself to find if he were surely awake; and he threw salt, and did every known thing to capture and retain good luck beside him.

"Come here, Sophie, and stay beside me. I am afraid to have you out of my sight for a minute, lest something happen and you never return. We surely are as happy now as we ever were on the Janiculum. To look out at this little stage garden, this piece of painted scenery of yours, is pleasure complete. I should never dare step off the edge of this *engawa*, though. I don't know my way around among the pasteboard rocks and the milliner's trees, and looking-glass lake, as do these Japanese theatrical artists you've engaged for the day's performance to amuse me. If I stepped out there, my foot would go through somewhere, and the whole thing come down in wreck and dust. Ah! but it is perfect! A perfect illusion as one sits here and looks at it. Very like a garden. I only want a hand magnifying glass to study its detail. Ah! I see at last. The Japanese landscape gardener first held a Claude Lorraine glass in his hand, and made his garden in those proportions. Beautiful! Beautiful! and the angelic little pink *kaido* trees in their pots! Ah! it is too much! too much beauty!"

Friday, April 7th.

I went to the barracks today and I had such a welcome as quite turned my head. They had so much to tell me of how they missed Vladimir; and all that had happened in the forty-eight hours of his absence; how the new chapel was finished, and could not be consecrated this week because the priest had to go to Marugame to bury a poor sailor *horio*; of how Andrew Y—— would soon be put out to a temple; and the greatest news of all—how the girl-soldier bride was actually on her way down from Kobe! Moreover, these good gossips knew that a conscript regiment was to leave for Vladivostok tomorrow; another awful siege of horrors to begin, and that ten conscripts had been shot at Osaka for refusing to go to war, poor boys. Also, they had heard that the twelve thousand Japanese prisoners in Russia were to be immediately exchanged for all the officers and a few hundred of the Russian soldiers now in Japan.

All are anxious to return to Europe—Europe, where the political situation causes some of them more concern than the military mess in Manchuria. With the winter industrial strikes more severe than ever, rioting at every spot of mobilisation, the sovereign swayed by one faction and another each day, and his Mephistopheles cousin in Germany frankly deserting our cause and criticising us openly, the darkest days are coming to Holy Russia. We look at each other blankly, and wonder if the long-prophesied and justly retributive revolution is upon us; if Russia shall begin her era of Enlightenment only in bloodshed. But what other people in the world have secured their freedom and liberty without rivers of blood?

Only the Japanese.

Monday, April 10th.

Vladimir looked stupefaction when I said this the other night while reading him a curious little brochure: *Agitated Japan.* There was a little bloodshed to put this emperor in power, to restore him his rightful authority so long usurped by the military ruler, but the rights of the people and the constitution were voluntarily conceded them. The emperor promised them suffrage, a parliament, and a constitution within a fixed number of years, all of his own accord, and he kept his promises to the letter. Many residents think the Japanese not yet ready for parliamentary government; but, with a restricted suffrage and an upper house of peers, there are safeguards, and the people are learning.

When the emperor declared the new order, he addressed a rescript to his people on education, a remarkable paper, in which he hoped that soon there would be no village with an ignorant family, and no family with an ignorant member. And to see the flocks of school children on the streets with their books every morning, that hope must now be realised. The emperor foresaw that universal education was

185

necessary to a modern, enlightened order, to make his people able to compete with western nations, and there has been a fury of education for these forty years. Compulsory education is a complete misnomer, for the people clamour for more schools and for higher schools, and they are given them. The Japanese borrowed the free school system outright from America, and all the empire went to school. Since western learning was so necessary to compete with western people, they set to and acquired it. There was no Pobedonostseff to forbid and to close schools, limit the number of pupils, exclude the Jews, and forbid the Poles and Finns to learn their own language.

Instead of thirty-two thousand school teachers for that many new schoolhouses in Russian villages. Von Plehve gave thirty-two thousand secret police to spy upon the villages, and see if any reform agents or ideas found entrance. We have wise statesmen and educators—philanthropists, who strive with all their influence against the police and the synod, to lift the cloud of ignorance that rests upon the Russian peasantry, an ignorance so dense, so appalling, so sickening and hopeless that I have no heart in considering its alleviation—but, all who would do good to Russia, and save the ignorant from the evil of socialist ideas, are hampered and hounded, terrorised by janitors in the cities, by Von Plehve's police in the country, and there is no hope in us. We feel the hopelessness of the struggle, our helplessness; yet we know a change is coming. But long before that may the war end, or Vladimir get an exchange with one of the Japanese officers at Medved.

Vladimir smiles grimly over the news from Russia that we read daily in our Kobe newspaper. Since the Zemsky Sobor was permitted, then forbidden, and finally let assemble to present a petition for reform and a constitution, the official mind at St. Petersburg has been a mere shuttlecock. Since "Vladimir's Day," that unfortunate 22nd of January, rescript has followed upon rescript from the irresolute, softhearted sovereign at Tsarskoe, who hides in his guarded palace like the *sultan* in the Yildiz Kiosque—even more a prisoner, more in fear of his own subjects, perhaps; since the *sultan* does go guarded once a week to Selamlik, and Nicholas does not stir abroad at all. There were rumours of flight from palace to palace, of the desperate illness of the infant *Czarevitch*, all of which are fortunately contradicted.

But the autocratic government wavers from day to day, and in our frightened hearts we wonder if it is not surely tottering; if this is not the end of the dynasty—Nicholas, the last of the Romanoffs. The few family letters that come to any one from Petersburg direct, are full of forebodings. One of the officers at Oguri has word of the sacking of his estates by the peasants; and another hears that his student son was killed in a charge of Cossacks in Moscow streets; and the old colonel hears of the death of his son in a sortie in Manchuria. Cheerful thoughts some of my patients have to help their convalescence! Another weeps as he looks at me, for he has not had a word or letter from his wife since he came here, ten months ago. He knows the man who fills her life—a brother officer who could control his exchange.

The soldier-girl bride has come down from Kobe! She stays at a Japanese tea house, near where the other Russian ladies are living, on the other side of the *château*, and it begins to look still more like the romance of a yellow-covered novel. His Japanese smile was a loud chuckle, all the while Tosaburo was telling me about her. "Oh! I wish you would look, and tell me how you think. I cannot say that word beauty, when I see her; but maybe you will tell me. She has short hairs like a man, or just like a widow. Oh! She does not look like you," and, with childlike *naiveté*, Tosaburo put his finger on his own well-cut nose and flattened it down to *mujik* type, and squinted his eyes smaller. We both laughed, and Vladimir declared it enough; that he saw her, as in a photograph.

Tosaburo only knew that she had arrived; that the French Consul in Kobe had had her supplied with proper clothing—a *trousseau*—and that they were at their wits' end at the headquarters here as to what to do about it all. "*J'y suis et j'y reste*" was her motto as much as Alexeieff's. After some days she was permitted to regularly visit her lover, and he was promised a transfer to another city where he should live in his own private house, with his faithful bride. I saw her several times, in the shops and on the street; I met her, too, at the barracks; and then, one day, Tosaburo told me that they had had "the marry party" in the little chapel at the barracks, and that they had gone off with twenty officers to a city on the west coast. Exit Romance! Cupid without wings.

CHAPTER 37

Love Laughs at Prison Bars

Sunday, April 23rd.

Word has come down from the higher officers at Nagoya that the *Czar* will not ask for the exchange of prisoners; that: "*He—does—not—need—his—officers!*" but, that he "Prays God will soften the pains of captivity, and quicken the arrival of the time when they may return home!"

It came to me like a blow in the face.

"Let Nicholas himself quicken the time of our return," said Vladimir—"Exchange us, or make peace—Peace on any terms he can get, as Mestchersky says—Port Arthur gone, Mukden gone, the fleet gone, Kuropatkin fallen, and Japanese prison lists and parole lists our army's best register, for what should we further expose our incapacity and rottenness? for a few flour mills and a frozen harbour? Let us get back to Russia, and conquer ourselves, defeat the real enemy entrenched in the palaces and ministries of Petersburg."

Today the consul appeared for his domiciliary visit, as he called it, having been surprised to find us gone from the barracks. "M. Siemenoff goes to Kioto next week, I suppose you know," said the consul, smiling, and we both started with surprise.

"No! No!" I wailed at the thought of losing my special charge and *protégé*. "But *Madame la Comtesse*, what happens to her?" I asked.

The consul broke out in a great laugh, shrugged his shoulders, and made gestures with both hands; and then my slow wits wakened, and I joined in Vladimir's and the consul's laughter at my stupidity.

Oh! Those clever young people! How dull we old people grow. Of course the consul is Cupid's messenger, the *Deus ex machina*, who arranges all, whom the *contessa* consults. And we had thought the silence so ominous! Only the daily postcards coming, with no messages on them at all. Telepathy, of course.

And while we have gone on in our little routine here, immersed in ourselves and our daily small happenings, the *contessa* herself has been down to Hong Kong, and the Russian Consul has cabled to Petersburg for official and family sanction, the permission of the commandant of Lyov's *corps du garde*, to the marriage.

"Then," I asked, "how did that shower of post cards keep on coming from Kobe if the *contessa* was in Hong Kong?"

"Ah!" said the agent of romance, "my office boy did that. A large packet lay ready addressed on my table, and when he dusted my desk each morning he took the top one off and put it in the post box. That saved him from dusting it, you see, an automatic beneficence."

Also he gave us the news that Captain Siemenoff is to be removed to the Kioto district, and there permitted to dwell with his own family. His family! His family! Vladimir and I laughed. I wanted to rush to the barracks and see Lyov at once, but it was late, the consul was weary and wanted to rest the hour or so with us, until time to take the train to Takahama for the evening boat to Kobe. And anyhow, as he described it to me, Lyov was steeped in joy and reveries so profound that no one could disturb him.

"He can be happy alone with himself now," said the consul. "You need not go near him. But ah! *la comtesse!* What cleverness! what force! what ability! Such a clear head. She is more like an American almost. And it was the old American minister who has helped and advised her. Her own uncle, *M. l'Anglais,* would not hear to it at first. He would forbid the banns; he would not permit them to be posted in any British edifice in Japan, nor would any Church of England clergyman perform the marriage, he declared. And *Madame la Comtesse* announced her prospective baptism by the Russian bishop in his guarded retirement at Tsuruga Dai, and that her Russification would be concluded by a Japanese, priest in the Greek church at Kioto !"

"The American minister conducted the negotiations, the *pourparlers.* He argued with the islander uncle, and temporised with the scandalised islander aunt, who wrung her hands and cried: 'Oh, what will the Japanese say?' I suppose she will never get a special decoration from the Crown now. So this brave old man from the Virginias faced the English aunt and bearded his colleague, the English lion of an uncle; consulted with my chief, and even went down to Kioto to see how the convert was proceeding with her novitiate. He told me to 'hustle,' if you comprehend that droll word; and I have hustled, he has hustled, she has hustled, and it is only the distinguished prisoner who has been idle and has not hustled—*Tout le monde ont hustlé*. Heavens! What a bride! What beauty! What distinction! What ability! and riches, besides!

"The uncle has only now insisted that there should be an antenuptial contract, in which Captain Siemenoff should waive all participation in her estate. There have been cablings and signatures of papers in numbers at Tokyo, and today Captain Siemenoff has signed away any control of her property in Canada. I have brought the papers, and your Lieutenant Kato has witnessed the signature. He pledged himself also to bestow upon her certain properties in jewels upon his return to Russia, and *voila!* It is all. It is finished. It rests only for Captain Siemenoff to reach Kioto with his confreres in captivity, to give his pledges for observing the regulations while in separate residence; to meet *Madame la Comtesse* at the church altar, and then drive to the villa at Fushimi, which I have leased for her."

Friday, April 28th.

I have been to see Sandy von Rathroff, and, having sent word ahead, that young agitator was awaiting me among the tombstones, with *samovar* and teacups ready. He had even a lemon to grace the occasion, and we had a nice little *tête-à-tête* under whispering pines on the softest of spring days. With Lyov gone, Sandy becomes my particular charge.

Now that mild weather has come, the casts are off Vladimir's knee, and he is ordered to sit erect in a chair properly, and begin to walk. The dressing gowns are cast away, and my invalid emerges from his chrysalis, and dines in a dinner coat like any other gentleman. Half of trading Nagasaki has moved up to Matsuyama with its wares for foreign custom, and the tailors and, shirt makers are doing a great business. Modern curios, hideous coarse embroideries, rubbishy metal and lacquer work, and gaudy porcelains have come in quantity to tempt the idle officers; and, oh! sad commentary on the *horios'* taste and knowledge! are bought up rapidly at prodigious prices.

CHAPTER 38

The Russian Armada

Sunday, May 31st.

The departure of Lyov last week has left us a little sad. He was a link with our past life, and represented to us our happier days, when Russia was a great power, and we were but a pair of discontented Finnish subjects sulking, as our former colleagues thought, in idleness in Rome, because Vladimir had not received the envoyship so long due him and so clearly promised him.

The two fleets have left Cochin China, have joined, and are approaching Japan. We are all tense with excitement. Von Woerffel and his naval friends are wrought up to such a pitch that a street peddler's cry nearly throws them into spasms. They hardly sleep at night, feeling that the crisis approaches, that the whole war now hangs upon Rojestvensky; that there must be victory and our release—or defeat and our release by a shameful peace. All Dairinji is a debating club, and those naval *horios* argue all day and all night upon the probable course of the fleet after it leaves the China Sea. "But suppose he meets Togo's whole fleet when he tries raiding that bay full of unarmoured transports at Dalny!" says Vladimir, when Von Woerffel has outlined a plan of action for the Baltic fleet.

"Ah! he expects to meet it somewhere, does he not? He has not come out here to avoid Togo's fleet, and only make a practice cruise. Let him do some damage first, to make sure. It is a pity he could not run into Kiaochau and help the *Czarevitch* out. Soon his uncertainty will be ended. Victory for the Baltic fleet, and our term will be short. Defeat—ah! we may prepare to stay here forever—forever then."

Poor Sandy von Rathroff is keyed to the same pitch of excitement as the rest of us, at the coming of the long-awaited deliverance, and at times is loyally Russian. I rallied him in a shop the other day on his plan of going to America when he is released, remaining there as a teacher of languages, and marrying some heiress with dollars and a big estate. Poor boy! he gets woefully homesick and heartsick at times. We spoke of Japanese patriotism, the pure love of country, and he burst out feelingly: "That is what I envy the Japanese. If I only could love my country! Instead, I have only hatred for Russia, for those who rule Russia, who are Russia. Sixty thousand of the best blood and brains of Russia were unjustly and brutally driven out of it in two years by Sipiaguin. Sixteen thousand intelligent men were exiled from Petersburg that spring they arrested me. Ah! it is sickening to think of in this era of civilisation.

"We are no better than the Persians or the Afghans, as far as honest or intelligent government goes. We persecute learning, education, intelligence. We punish and degrade where civilised countries honour and promote. We send all the brains and ability of Russia to vegetate, to drag out useless, embittered lives in the Caucasus and Siberia. Physicians, surgeons, even artists and musicians are exiled at the whim of some ignorant, drunken *mujik*, temporarily exalted by a uniform. Von Plehve is type of them. His creatures are no different from him—base ingrates all, who like Von Plehve would denounce and ruin the humane couple who took him as a starving waif, reared and educated him. In all Russia, there seems no figure worthy of respect. Autocracy has sunk to the lowest dregs; and the very scum of the well-dressed, but truly ignorant classes, are in office, are ruling everywhere in the empire."

Tuesday, May 30th.

Our suspense is ended. The usual thing, quite the expected thing, has happened. Rojestvensky has failed—so egregiously, completely, abjectly, that we are content to know the bare first facts without detail or explanation. As if there could be any explanation!

Admiral Togo's telegram is enough:

"The main force of the enemy's Second and Third Squadrons has been almost completely annihilated. Therefore, please be at ease."

"Please be at ease! Please be at ease!" What a complete, all-embracing, final expression is this of the Japanese admiral! What a convincing message to sovereign and people!

Friday, June 2nd.

Poor Vladimir, who had improved greatly in his general tone of late, is now sunk in the uttermost despair. He has taken to the long chair, and lies with his eyes closed half the time. They are reddened and swimming with tears, and he has slipped back weeks, months almost in his physical condition, in these three days. The street sounds, the bells of the *gogai* boys, cause him pain, and I can see him quiver as the joyful clang and clash of the bells of the fleet-footed news runners approach, pass, and die away down the street. We have no wish to go out, to walk anywhere, to look upon the radiant Japanese faces and the sunburst of decorations, the unbroken lines of flags and lanterns, and red and white striped festal curtains that now line the streets. We have no wish to meet our countrymen; to note the signs of woe in their faces; to talk over and speculate upon this last crowning infamy and disgrace.

There is no longer question of how it could happen. We know too well that it is the same old story of unpreparedness, want of prearrangement, of unfitness, inability. Rojestvensky was as a child with a fleet of toy ships, when he sailed head on into Togo's trap, and let the Japanese batter him by day, and torpedo him by night, and gather up the fragments of the great fleet and bring them to Sasebo. Not since the destruction of the Spanish Armada in Europe, and of Kublai Khan's fleet here on these very same shores, has there been anything approaching this one-sided naval battle. Victory was all to the Japanese from the start, and the work went on like a *battue* of pheasants in an English park.

And the surrenders! Oh! disgrace of all disgraces. Nebogatoff hands over a fleet of ships, and lives on! Surely the Japanese are right in their contempt of those who fear death more than dishonour. Soon we shall have some of these precious Baltic-ers here. And how shall we receive them?

We hear that the Cossacks and sailors at Choenji sent up a mighty cheer when they heard of the defeat, because—it meant the end of the war and their speedy return to Russia! They are talking eagerly now of the return to Odessa, and of what they will see and do on the way. While we—do we really want to return to Russia? Do we want to see again the spires and domes, the Neva front of the palace, and the Nevsky? In all truth, no. Both Vladimir and I, without acknowledging it to each other, seem to be drifting away from all love for or loyalty to Holy Russia. Each month here has loosened the tie, laid bare, at all this long distance, the traits in Russian character, the features of Russian life, the principles—or want of principle—and things that are most antipathetic to us in Russia's corrupt, mediaeval government—things which everything in us resents and revolts against.

Now, less than in the happy years just gone by, could we consent to live in Russia, or Vladimir to wear the uniform of office, to uphold and defend the *Czar* and his government. Already, I long for the quiet comfort of my little place in Devon, the pleasant social order of English life, and all that such a stay means to us after this year of sorrow and humiliation. I should be rejoiced were Vladimir a British subject; our lives and future secure; Russia a dark and unhappy past.

Chapter 39

Two Futures

Saturday, June 3rd.

The consul gave us the luncheon hour yesterday, and he brought us the news of the strange marriage in Kioto, at which he and the English Consul were present. The consignment of *horios* reached Kioto one day, the preliminaries were arranged the next; and on the third afternoon, Lyov, a Japanese officer, and a Russian general went to the Russian church, met the *contessa's* party there, and Japanese priests performed the ceremony. The *contessa* had brought her poor uncle to tolerating the idea, and Madame H———, after oceans of tears and upbraiding, had made the best of it.

The American Excellency had come down out of pure good nature, but was haled back to Tokyo the night before. He wanted to see what sort of a *rara avis*, what unusual specimen of a *horio*, it could be, to induce a rich, young, and beautiful woman,—of title and good family, with no encumbrances, with everything in the worldly sense to gain by remaining single or waiting,—to hasten to marry a prisoner of war, a subject of a defeated, discredited empire, officer of a beaten army.

The French Consul, acting as the Russian Consul, took over "Mira Foresta, a British subject; widow; aged twenty-five years; religion, Greek Orthodox," as a Russian subject. He said the solemnity of all, including Lyov and Mira, made it more like a funeral than a wedding.

For them, all is rose colour, naturally; and they are full of bright plans for the future, which the speedy conclusion of the war makes possible. They can happily forget everything at this moment. We, and the others, cannot.

Sunday, June 4th.

It is touching to see the sorrow in every face we know so well, and to recognise how every hope and dream has fallen since Rojestvensky's defeat, and Nebogatoff's surrender. Of all the Kamramh harbour full of vessels that was so nearly France's undoing, a few refugee ships at Manila, a stray torpedo boat at Shanghai, are all that fly the Russian flag. The rest are at the bottom of the sea, or handed over to the Japanese by cowardly officers who feared their own crews more than the enemy; who obeyed the Japanese signals more willingly than they obeyed their own admirals. Better that Russia had never attempted to be a naval power, than to end in such a fiasco.

Sandy is of course in a ferment of excitement since the hopes others had based on the arrival of the Baltic fleet are now so completely dashed. He foresees a speedy peace and his own escape to the land of liberty across the Pacific. Many are counting as surely as he on shaking free from their allegiance to Russia, and the current of our monotonous life here has been strongly stirred. Everyone has plans, and many have such forebodings and anxieties as it touches me to see.

All the news from Russia tells of discontent, uprisings among workmen in the cities and peasants in the country. The Great Awakening is surely at hand, the Revolution, the *Débâcle*. Paul Lessar's death, which occurred a few days before Rojestvensky's terrible fiasco, was another blow to Vladimir, although we have really been so long expecting it. We are thankful that he was spared this last ignominy. Poor Paul! Even had your life lasted a little longer, the guns of Togo's victory would have closed it.

Tragedy would seem to be heaped on tragedy, if there were not touches of comedy in even the Rojestvensky promenade towards disaster. In one breath, these surrendered officers from the Baltic fleet tell of the insubordination, the incipient mutiny that reigned on every ship. How Nebogatoff's captains had no sooner gone to his flag-ship to arrange for surrender than the officers left behind looted the ships' safes and threw overboard the moneys they could not carry. They admit, too, that they did throw the wounded overboard, because they were cumbering the decks, making it slippery, and unnerving the gunners with their screams and groans.

They naively lament that the hospital ship having been apprehended in carrying troops, despatches, and ammunition, was seized by Togo, and brought in with the other prizes. Then the youngest and best-looking sister of charity asked to be allowed to go to the Sasebo naval hospital and nurse her "uncle." This incident is detailed in the Japanese and in our Kobe newspapers in all sincerity, and if it has been cabled to Petersburg, one can fancy the roars of laughter at the naval club and in all the salons. And how the treaty-port papers jeer at the whole promenade of this "Mr. R. J. Ventsky" from Libau to Sasebo!

Although confined to their ships' decks ever since October, when they left Russia, these new *horios* complain most loudly about the restrictions of their places of detention, and of their inability to roam the streets at all hours. It grates upon them most of all, that their out-door day should end at six o'clock, and the long, long evenings are their distraction. Cards and hard drinking fill the hours as best they can; a very few study and occupy themselves in rational ways; but the most of them, knowing little of shore life save the routine of club and admiralty yards, are at their wits' end.

Tuesday, June 6th.

"The game is up, the cards are shown, and Russia's boasts prove mere bluff," says Sandy scornfully. "Hereafter, I should blush to call myself a Russian. I am not—I ceased to be, when Sipiaguin unjustly threw me and my classmates into a criminal's prison, and then exiled us to the Trans-Baikal. Fortunately, that in the end was the means of getting me here, where I can fully measure to the fraction Russia's right to be called a Christian and civilised nation. When I get to America, it will be more apparent still. I am thankful my name is German; although of course in a republic I shall have to drop the von and be known as Citizen Rathroff . Ah! that will be good to vote, to elect a ruler, to help govern! even if I must be waiter at a *café*, or drive a tramcar, or carry bags at a railway station to earn a living. And then, you know, there are such wonderful chances over there. If some Mademoiselle Dollars does not admire my pretty eyes—I am not bad-looking, as you know—I may achieve millions by myself and go back to Petersburg to dazzle the Nevsky in the guise of an American bil-lionaire. Even come as Ambassador! even have the chance to spit upon Von Plehves and Sipiaguins as I go by. Ah! those are my castles in America!

"Ah, America, my new country—of thee I sing!" he exclaimed, trolling the air of "God save the Queen" in his joy. "I am cultivat-ing these American popes now most assiduously. I am asking how to travel there, where they live, how they live, how much it costs to live there—how much clothes cost, and beef and bread. I don't dare say a syllable about tobacco and spirits. It would shock them, and lose me all my fountains of information. Ah, *Matushka*, you do not know how many others in this very Matsuyama are planning and dreaming, as I am planning and dreaming! I know, by all the signs which I think I am concealing myself. We all know better than to speak aloud. We shall meet, nevertheless, a very considerable number over there, when the peace has been made.

"Ah! will the day soon come? Never too soon to me. In how many months will it be that I stand in Washington's country, and become a citizen—a fellow-citizen—of the great Roosevelt? Oh, if our Nicholas had been a strong fighting man like that!

"Truly William of Hohenzollern is right when he says the Japanese are the scourge of God, like Attila and Napoleon, and that the Russians lost because they were enervated by alcoholism and immorality. Oh! you should hear the loyalists at my lodgings discuss those speeches of the *Kaiser* at Wilhelmshaven and Strasburg! They do not so much mind his fling at Russian Christianity and its deplorable state—that truth does not cut them like his comments on the military. After advising Nicholas how to run the war, he takes to criticising us. Perfidious! Like his truckling to the Japanese after the truth about Port Arthur was known, and declaring that he only wanted peace and his own home empire. To prove that, he walks into this Morocco affair, and is within one hairline of war with France. *A bas* with the universal genius!"

CHAPTER 40

"Peace! Peace!"

Thursday, June 8th.

Surprise treads upon surprise—Sandy's hero, the American Roosevelt, has intervened and asked both Russia and Japan to name commissioners and see if they cannot agree to make peace!

In my first gasp of astonishment, as the cook burst excitedly into our presence, with the little pink *gogai*, crying, "Peace! Peace! The American emperor says: 'Stop fighting! Stop fighting!'"—in the first moment of shock, I could hardly stand upon my feet. Good news is so unusual to us, anything pleasant coming by *gogai* has hitherto been so unknown, that I quite lost my head for the moment.

Vladimir lay sleeping, dozing in the warm soft afternoon air of the June day, but the fanfare of the *gogai* bells in the street soon roused him. "Vladimir! Vladimir! The Peace! The Peace! It has come. God has given it to us at last."—And I burst into uncontrollable sobs.

Vladimir, dazed, rose slowly to a sitting posture, and tried to stand, but he tottered on his weak knees and sank to the long chair again and buried his face in his hands. In silence, we sat and listened to the chime of *gogai* bells, as the newsboys ran about the town, and the sounds echoed down the long stretch of the moat and against the *château's* hillside. We must have sat in this way for fully ten minutes, when the house-boy slid the door panel, said: "Kato *san!*" and sat back on his heels with radiant countenance, as Tosaburo clattered in with all his accoutrements—no time to lay aside his sword belt at the door.

"Oh! Oh! I have come! I have come as fast as I could, to be the first to make you the present of good news, but I see that *gogai* bell has told you all. Now it will be peace, and we shall be best friends."

With joyful faces, we sat and talked it over and over; how It would be done; where the conference would meet; who would be the commissioners to negotiate; and how soon we should get away from the little Iyo city, where, really, now that it draws near an end, our stay—has—been—a—happy—one!

Thoughtful Anna slid the door and entered with a tray, and the house-boy held the sparkling bottle of cheer swathed in the white robes of peace.

"A flag of truce! A flag of truce!" said Vladimir, pointing to it, and Tosaburo burst into chuckles of joy at the joke. We clicked glasses and drank to the white angel of peace *per se,* and to the American Roosevelt, who has forced the situation upon both combatants. We drank to the last dancing bubble, and then Vladimir whirled his glass overhead, with the fire and gaiety of youth, and tossed it out on the garden stones—I threw mine also, and frantically embraced him in the presence of Tosaburo.

The gardener heard the crash and stole to a gap in the shining green hedge; the cook peeped forth from another green frame; and the boy and *amah* peered across from the dining-room door.

"Come! Come!" cried Vladimir, motioning to the staff. "All must drink a *Banzai* in *champagne-saké* with me, and celebrate the end of war." And in proper form, they ranged themselves, accepted the glasses from Anna with easy grace and profound bows, and let her pour them frothing to the brim. Vladimir made the toasts, to "Peace," to "the emperor in Tokyo," and to "Roosevelt in America," and then led the *Banzais.* The gardener, as elder of the company, responded for them with graceful thanks. They bowed profoundly and shuffled away, chuckling and cheerful.

Sunday, July 16th.

Days and weeks have passed, and the Japanese Peace Envoys are only departing to meet Sergius de Witte! in Washington!

Blank astonishment has overwhelmed every Russian, when, after several names, De Witte's was announced. "I would rather die here, rather stay here years, than make inglorious peace now," sobbed Captain M———. "And to gain my freedom through Sergius de Witte! Oh! this is hard!"

The Angel of Peace could only be believed as posing to the world's admiration for a deceitful moment, and wore sinister mien in the garb of Sergius de Witte. None trusted her—him—the high-handed *genii,* whose railroad and industrial policies were to recreate Russia, but instead, have ruined her. First the Trans-Siberian railway; and then a war to hold and keep the railway.

"I should not be here but for Serge de Witte," growled one. "I mortgaged my last estate to a Jew, and put it in his cursed industrial shares. They paid me forty *per cent*, and then fifty *per cent*, and then— since 1901, nothing! Before I could redeem my lands I was penniless. I rode back from Paris in third-class cars by night. I applied for service on the frontier. They gave me a Siberian regiment of railway guards at Harbin. We were moved to Port Arthur, and there my career ended. I have very truly served twelve years in one. And now, I must owe my freedom to Serge de Witte! A curse on him! What has Nicholas Alexandrovitch come to, that he chooses him? A post worthy of our ablest diplomat, for the cleverest, wiliest ambassador, and he gives it to the station master. Ah! It is a loan, not a treaty, that he seeks."

Thursday, July 20th.

Poor Nebogatoff and his men are in the saddest plight of all, every one now turning cool glances and sneers towards them, because of Nicholas' displeasure. They are prisoners and they are not prisoners. Having surrendered, they were offered the same privileges as the Port Arthur officers, and Nebogatoff cabled, asking authority for those who wished to do so to go on parole. The sovereign ignored the message, and it was repeated. Then the French ambassador at Petersburg was cabled to present the case, and for answer, Nebogatoff and all his officers were stricken from the rolls of the Imperial Navy! deprived of their commissions, degraded, disgraced without regular form of court-martial. Their dismay, their sorrow, and their chagrin are pitiful to witness. As they cannot any longer be considered prisoners, they are men without a country, without an occupation even, since Vladimir says the average of them could never get employment in any mercantile marine, hardly on Volga barge service.

It is a sad situation, a dilemma none could ever have foreseen when Nebogatoff's council of officers voted that resistance was hopeless and the surrender of two thousand useful lives better than giving them to be battered by Japanese shells and drowned among the rocks of the Korean coast. They have not done anything nearly as iniquitous and cowardly as Stoessel in his surrender, yet he gets a sword, and Nicholas, pitiless in the bitterness of his chagrin, visits his wrath upon these poor naval men.

Sunday, July 23rd.

One of the American popes has been to Kioto, and seen the Siemenoffs at their Fushimi villa. "A honeymoon in captivity!" he exclaimed. "Why, Captain Siemenoff can stand captivity forever. He loves his prison—and his fellow-prisoner! They are the most ideal pair of lovers the sun ever saw. They have a beautiful Japanese house on a hill, with fine old screens and *fusuma*, and a garden that is a copy of the Sambo-in garden; and the house is already a godown. It is fairly crowded with the curios Mrs. Siemenoff has bought. She is a good customer of the Kioto dealers, and will soon be a dangerous rival for you, Mrs. von Theill. You must be glad that she chose another field, for you could not both have gleaned here.

"Captain Siemenoff says the military and police need not trouble to watch him. The art shops of Kioto do that, day and night. 'I slide the *shoji*,' he says, 'in the morning, and there waits a Japanese Smile and something tied up in a blue cotton cloth. "I am of Ikeda," says the smile, and produces things that send my wife into ecstasies, and she buys them all before breakfast. He goes, and another bundle and smile come to the front of our garden stage. "I am of Hayashi," says the smile; and his end is like the first. A third smiles loudly, and says: "I am of Yamanaka," and he discloses more Japonaiseries and Chinoiseries, and *Madame* gives another chit. "I am Kita," "I am Shimizu," "I am Fukuda," say other smiles all day long. Then there are ancient men of Fushimi, with voices like foghorns and manners like velvet, and a man of a million wrinkles from Nara. He must have sat for the picture of old Longevity. When *Madame* makes *moues* at his prices, he creases a few more wrinkles into his visage, and her soft heart relents. They all cheat us and overcharge us; but we like it. We enjoy life so much that that is even part of the enjoyment.

"'What do we collect? Oh! everything, everything; from screens and bronze goldfish bowls to *netsukes* and dolls, toys in gold lacquer; everything—porcelain, pottery, tea jars, tea bowls, paintings, prints, pewter, brass, wood, leather, sword guards, brocades, embroideries, dolls, fans, rosaries—All, all! Being human, everything human interests us. We have spent days at the potter's, turned the wheel, shaped the bowl, glazed, fired, and acquired it. We have lived beside the lacquer artists, magnifying glass in hand. We have had painters by the score hold day-long *séances* on our mats, and give demonstrations and art tournaments for us. We have had jugglers, dancers, fencers, *jiu jitsu* experts, wrestlers, and archers to delight us in our own compound. The high priests at the temples are our dearest friends. They condescend to take ceremonial tea with us; and show us all the inner treasures.

202

The policemen at the Art Museum run to tell us and show us when an exhibit is changed, and all the children and toy venders at Inari are our special cronies.'

"I assure you, Mrs. von Theill, those two young people are so absurdly and completely happy at Fushimi that I doubt if they pay any heed to the course of events. I was with them for two hours, and we did not once discuss the peace conference. Out of the evil of this war has come good for them."

CHAPTER 41

After the War

Sunday, August 6th.

If war is a fearfully slow business, so is peace.

There was interminable delay before Nicholas would agree to negotiate—interminable delay while he played with Mouravieff and Ignatieff, and finally chose De Witte—and interminable delay before they finally left Petersburg. So has passed all of June and now July, and the plenipotentiaries meet face to face. We have drifted along, living with slack interest from day to day; depressed and stupefied almost by two months of saturating rain and dampness. Typhoons and the edges of typhoons have smothered and drenched us, and already there is concern for the rice crop. It started badly this year, and I can see that the green belt of rice fields around the city is not as luxuriant as it was last summer. A few weeks of dry, hot weather now in the *doyo* can save it, they say.

Sunday, August 20th.

I let my journal lag, during the suspense and delay until the peace-makers reached America. And then followed day after day of nothing-ness—nothingness in the cable reports our Kobe paper printed. I al-most wondered if Vladimir were dissembling, he seemed so indifferent to the day's news that he had always so earnestly discussed. Incidents went by without ruffling or depressing him. Nothing stirred his apa-thy. Saghalien was taken and overrun by Japanese troops, the garrisons offering as little resistance as the Baltic fleet; and whole garrisons were brought over to swell the total of the Russian army in Japan. "I shall never discuss peace until a Russian army is landed in Japan," said our most boastful and incompetent general—and the army is truly here—seventy thousand strong.

The Black Sea fleet, which proved as worthless and undisciplined from admiral down to coal-heaver as Von Woerffel had said it was, has mutinied and held Odessa in a state of siege for a week, and the Sevastopol admiral did not dare descend upon the *Kniaz Potemkin* lest his battleship crew mutiny also, toss him overboard or shoot him. The whole mutiny on the *Potemkin* was so like *opéra bouffe*, that Sandy Rathroff laughed, and Vladimir and I had to laugh too, as if it were the fleet and mutiny of another country. And Tosaburo, our own courteous Tosaburo, when appealed to, read and roughly translated the screaming farce from the *Mainichi*.

"Oh, translate that again, please," begged Sandy, "that about the ladies with the red parasols promenading on the quarter-deck with the *corsair* chiefs. Oh! Delicious! Delicious! There must be a comic opera of that incident. And then, they fled to a Roumanian port and surrendered when they had eaten up all the provisions. How characteristically Russian! An army travels on its stomach—and so do Revolution and Reform! Oh! *Svoboda! Svoboda!* (Liberty! Liberty!) what jokes are perpetrated in thy name!"

Sunday, September 3rd.

Early this gloomy, suffocating, grey Sunday morning, we rode to the Dogo side of the *château* hill to the garden of a banker, who had some wonderful *asagaos* in bloom. This is the second season now that I have seen the great *cloches de matin* open their enchanted *corollas* in Japan! Our own gardener has grown us some beauties this season, has ravaged Iyo, and sent to Kiushiu and Nagoya for precious seeds. At Dairinji they have a flower show of their own, and by carrying the pots into a dark room, they keep them to enjoy until quite late in the day.

Our banker had put mat-awnings over and around his shelves of flower pots, so that even at nine o'clock his single *cloches* were only a little limp. We sat admiring when Tosaburo joined us. "What news of the peace?" we eagerly asked, and our host made a gesture and lifted his eyebrows in despair, at the reply of no further progress. The deadlock, as it seems to be, has lasted these three days, and the suspense is as great as for the conclusion of any battle. De Witte will not yield territory nor pay indemnity, although he at first conceded every other point the Japanese demanded, with such alacrity that it was apparent that he knew the negotiations would fail in the end, and that these surrenders would not be held against him. Quite as we all prophesied, these first negotiations are to fall through, and we must wait and drag on our lives, while more defeats bring Nicholas to his senses, and a second conference assembles. Then more parley and preparation, and nearly a year will be gone before we can leave Japan. My hopes have undergone so many alternations since the conference began, that I am dulled and indifferent. As easy to go as to stay; and now, in this wilting, typhoonish weather, after the incessant rains of the long hot summer, even the effort of thinking about our packing and plans is an exertion, and is shirked.

When we were leaving the garden, Tosaburo suggested that we go with him up to the signal station on the first terrace of the *château* and get a breath of air. Extra *coolies* pushed our *kurumas* up the long slope to the first high terrace overlooking the city and the far sea. The air was motionless, stifling, and so thick and heavy with dampness that it was an effort to draw it into the lungs. The *coolies* streamed with perspiration, and glistened as if their golden-bronze skins were freshly lacquered.

The banker and Tosaburo talked more intently, as they looked out toward the sea—toward an indefinite, grey, hazy space between hazier grey hills where we knew the sea must be. It was all grey, colourless, monotone landscape—no *notan*, no contrast of black and white, of distinct light and shade, no clear silver lights. It was all sodden, dull, and leaden-tinted; a bullet-coloured landscape, done in half-defined washes with a big, wet brush.

The banker looked westward and to the south, and shook his head in impatience. He asked Tosaburo if any weather report had been given out since the first one of the morning, and both went over to the old *samurai*, who was rubbing and petting the gun with which he announces exact noonday to Matsuyama. The *samurai* reached into his tiny sentry-box and brought out a paper; the two visitors leaned in and regarded the barometer, and all three talked earnestly.

"Another typhoon coming, I suppose," said Vladimir. "I must say I am weary of weather. I have been steamed in this typhoon atmosphere since early June, and three months of rain and hot mist has softened my very bones. Ah! for the bracing dry wind of a desert! Hot, hot, and dry—dry as the sands themselves. One week of Ferghana, and I should be a giant in strength."

"Is the typhoon coming this way?" I asked Tosaburo.

"Yes, when it left Formosa, we thought it would turn in to the China coast, like the other. But it is coming nearer to us now, and will

LOOKING TOWARD THE INLAND SEA, FROM CASTLE TERRACE

be at Nagasaki this afternoon. We shall get it in the night, I suppose. Look to your flower-pots tonight, Asagao *san*," he said to the banker, who was the picture of gloom.

"We shall have the peace tonight also," said Tosaburo, with a fierce smile, as if bracing himself to some disaster. "Japan will sign at once. We shall yield the indemnity, probably. Our rice crop is totally ruined. The bankers will decide the day. Our assets are millions less in these hours since the glass began falling, and it will not be profitable to keep on fighting. We have Saghalien and Manchuria; and that will do." His face grew rigid, and he smiled the Japanese smile.

"*Saio de gosarimasu*," said the banker gravely, and left us.

"And the barometer decides the peace?" asked Vladimir wonderingly.

"Yes, the barometer, the typhoon, the rice crop, and the bankers— they are all bound together in the sum of our national prosperity and riches. It is decided. You will have your Christmas in England. All the *horios* will go home before the chrysanthemums bloom; and our soldiers will come back from Manchuria before the snow flies at Mukden. I shall not return to the field with my uncle, as his *aide*." A great sigh, a setting of the jaws, and then the Japanese smile, the courageous smile that hides grief, sorrow, and disappointment, put a mask over his face.

Sunday, September 10th.

A chime of *gogai* bells rang through the streets. "Peace! Peace!" the people cried joyfully again, as they sprang upon the bits of pink paper. Very quietly, without comment, they went back to their mats. There were no *Banzais*, no fireworks, no flags, no lanterns, no rejoicings of any kind. Although not official, London despatches said that the pact was concluded without De Witte paying a *sou* of the enormous indemnity he was trusted to scale down! And half of Saghalien awarded to each country! The London news stood for days without denial. Dismay and indignation drove the Japanese to sullen speech or gloomy silence; and, strange to say, at Dairinji, the Kokaido, Oguri, and in the hospital wards, the Russian officers denounced the peace as furiously as they knew how, and denounced De Witte more violently still.

The Cossacks, the riflemen, the Siberians, and the sailors cheered, as they did for Togo's victory over Rojestvensky—for the same reason—that it meant the end of the war and their speedy return to Russia! Vladimir and I wait quietly without excitement, for we know that we are soon free to go—to Russia? God forbid! To Russia—where a terrible era, the fearful awakening of those half-civilised ignorant peasants, and those savage, brutalised workmen, must now come. From those horrors we shrink. In the revolution and the reconstruction, we cannot take part. Vladimir has served his country well, but the tie is almost broken.

Monday, October 9th.

Enviously our brother *horios* looked upon us, believing that Vladimir and I would leave at the earliest moment, by grace of Tosaburo's uncle. "No, we shall probably be the last to leave," said Vladimir. "We are comfortable here, and we shall both wait, if we may, to see the sick and wounded safely out of the hospital."

Everyone else is impatient, and for them the days seem to drag. Poor M—— and his four companions, who have been in prison for these months because of their repeated attempts to escape, have re-appeared, pale, sad, and listless. Theirs has been a real imprisonment, thanks altogether to their senseless and repeated folly.

The Americans have sent us their home papers to read—nothing is censored or forbidden now—and Vladimir has been lost in their hundreds of pages.—He reads them all, for such peace-making never was before. He shudders and gasps, beats the air and beats his brow, and calls me to listen to this and to that. He calls all the saints to witness that there never was such peace-making before.—Peace of the new diplomacy! Peace of the Twentieth Century! Peace as she is made in America! Peace as she is hammered out at the American Cronstadt! All the traditions are broken with. Japan and Russia have not made peace—nor wanted it. Oh, no! That terrible American President, *Il Strenuoso*, he has made it. He wanted it, he would have it. And I believe him capable of locking the conferees in a room and starving them into obedience.

No gentle peace was that at Portsmouth. Shades of Paul Lessar! Could you only have lived to sit with Vladimir and read this astonishing history they have just made in America! What a feeble "Iron Wrist" is yours, compared to this chilled-steel wrist of this Roosevelt!

Vladimir has laughed. He has thrown back his head and roared, as if it were a burlesque or a comedy he were enjoying, and not the fate of nations in a balance lightly poised—poised until the terrible Roosevelt hit the scales with his steel wrist and left Serge de Witte dumfounded with the clumsy muddle he had made of it in the beginning.

But who could have dreamed of such a turn in the orderly course of negotiations, as this irruption of the American President! Fancy such an incident in Europe! Hardly Napoleon ever equalled it in highhandedness! And we can none of us do anything nor repudiate it! Oh, it is the strangest thing in all the world! Never more will a peace conference go to America. The Americans are too literal. A peace conference is for the purpose of making peace, they argue—therefore. Make peace! Quick! At once! Immediately! Oh! sooner than that, even; if the Roosevelt happens to be ruling.

In our heart of hearts not one of us, not a Russian nor a Japanese, believed that peace would result from this conference, nor did we want it just yet, while realising the need of it. Both armies in the field protested. Both emperors yielded to Roosevelt's first request, for appearance's sake only— as a matter of etiquette, to maintain *les convenances*, and pose properly to the world—to save face. It was such a well-managed farce, we thought, that diplomatic promenade from two ends of the earth to the American Cronstadt. It must have been hard to keep straight faces when they all entered the council room.

Serge de Witte yielded everything, knowing they would soon reach the *impasse* and retire—and William of Hohenzollern had confused the situation hopelessly by his melodramatic meddling and— but the unexpected happened. To the amazement of all the world, to the horror of all of the old school of diplomacy, that terrible M. Roosevelt would have none of their *non possumus*. He telegraphed, he sent messengers and notes; he haled them from their beds at midnight by that last invention of the devil, the telephone. Could the wires have permitted, he would have helloed in the ears of both Emperors—by their baptismal names—*tutoyed* them orally, as he even did by cable; arguing, harping on, and repeating his wish for peace, oblivious to denials and rebuffs.

Oh! it has been dumfounding. Never was Son of Heaven nor our Anointed Autocrat bullied and coerced by any outsider like that. Nor would any living person have dared to do it save this plain Twentieth Century Citizen Roosevelt! Oh! William of Hohenzollern, where are you now? A greater one has risen up!

Well, this "Steel Wrist" Roosevelt fought for peace as knights jousted of old. He struggled for peace, as if it were a football on the field. He argued for peace like Maître Labori for Dreyfus. And he won, to the amazement of the world. "Another day's delay," says Vladimir, "and I believe that American President capable of bursting into the council room, knocking their heads together, and holding them by their throats until they signed a treaty of peace."

And now, to save us, we cannot see which side he has favoured—both claim his favouritism, both repudiate and revile him. It is all beyond us. We wait to meet the diplomatic world in Europe, and learn the truth, the inside springs which are known only to those of *la carrière*.

Sunday, October 22nd.

The Russian hospital ship Mongolia will arrive next week at Taka-hama, and I shall be so glad to be useful in helping to get my poor patients away. They will be taken over to Vladivostok first, and then by Red Cross trains to Russia.

We have had amusing times with the social amenities. Vladimir and I have been on good terms with all the authorities, and as soon as the actual peace gave us an excuse, we had a round of dinners for the Japanese officials and residents, and the foreign residents who have been so uniformly kind to me for all the past year. Then the conscience-stricken commandant wished to proclaim his cordial intentions, and invited all the three hundred and twenty Russian officers to a banquet by the sea, and—three hundred declined. *Donnerwetter!* but there was wrath at that.

Then the American sister of charity gave a little dinner, and the higher Russians officers went and sat amicably with the Japanese civil and military officials under the flag of Roosevelt, the Peace Angel. Cheered by that, the Japanese general took a hand, and invited the higher Russian officers to dine. Under stress of arguments by Vladimir, Grievsky, and the American sister, they accepted; but on the very day of the dinner some thirty fell suddenly and grievously ill, and civilian worthies filled their places. We were incensed beyond words; for, if the Japanese military were willing to part amicably and to strive for good feeling, our officers should have responded.

"He took away the sword that General Nogi left me," said one. "He struck me with his sword when I was unarmed, at his mercy," said, another. "He unjustly punished me for the stupidities of his interpreter," said another. "But we like the Matsuyama townspeople, who have been uniformly kind, courteous, and sympathetic to us; and we want to express it to them. What shall we do? What can we do?"

"Go and ask the American sister," said Vladimir. In a few minutes they reappeared to tell us that the Red Cross ladies were having a bazaar at a tea house garden at Dogo in the afternoon, to raise money for some destitute soldiers' families, and the American advised them to go there and spend.

"It is precisely our chance," shouted Esper, who posted off with extra coolies to carry the word to every officers' mess to go to Dogo, and spend, spend, spend, as long as the little Japanese ladies had a tea-cup left.

It was like a procession out the Dogo road that day, and the *breloque* railway carriages were crowded. The garden was jammed, and the little women had soon no time to bow to their *horio* acquaintances, so rapidly did the money flow in upon them.

"Five thousand *yens!* Five thousand *yens!*" said Madame Takasu, excited beyond all her Japanese powers of repression, when the money had been counted. "And we never dreamed that we should make two hundred yens even. What shall we do? What shall we do? It is so wonderful. And all the time the *Shoko sans* (officers) have been giving to our poor through the American sister of charity! I only know today how the Russian officers, in gratitude to her, have been contributing all of this year to the support of her home for factory girls. Ah! it has been a good fortune to Iyo to have you Russians here, and to learn your goodness."

CHAPTER 42

Sayonara!

Sunday, November 19th.

Our hospital ship has come and gone; has returned again, and sailed away with the last fevered and crippled and ailing Russian. The barrack wards are empty, and long rows of bedding hang airing in the rich autumn sunshine. With the *Mongolia* came Countess I——, Countess I——, Countess B——, and others, whom I had seen depart from Petersburg on the first Red Cross trains. For nearly two years, now, these devoted women have been actively working in hospitals and on hospital trains. Several of them were at Mukden when the great battle began, and made their escape with the fleeing army on foot, their places in the ambulances given to the wounded whom they succoured on the way. Such experiences as they have gone through surpass all belief, and I look upon them with awe, with the reverent respect due to beings above and apart from all their class and order.

All of them show the strain of work and war, of horrors, hardships, of suffering witnessed and endured; all of them are aged and saddened in these terrible months since I saw them. They are eager to return to Russia. They foresee some terrible years for us all. De Witte has launched his reforms; a constitution and a parliament are promised. All Russia has hurled itself into a carnival of license and wild excess in the name of liberty. The empire is in uproar, and no one can foresee the end.

As the hospital closed its wards, the little Red Cross nurses went to their homes, and the officers have made each departure an occasion for a demonstration of friendship and respect. We all went to the station to see them off, and presented them with bouquets with inscribed ribbon streamers, and escorted them on board their ships at Takahama. To Vladimir's and Lyov's special nurses, Mira and I have sent money gifts that will be delivered to them by the post office at their homes; and both have the heaviest grey crape *kimonos*, gold *obis*, and painted neck-pieces that Mira could send me from Kioto—a complete ceremonial dress for each dear little woman, who has worn the nurse's uniform for so long a time.

And photographs! I have given Vladimir's picture in his Red Cross *domino*, and in his white duck clothes, by the dozen—to all the nurses, to all our friends and neighbours; and also to all Madame Takasu's little circle of poets and beauty-worshippers, with whom Vladimir and I together sat in the castle keep and watched the September moon rise clear and golden beyond Dogo's hills—the soft, soul-compelling, gentle moon of peace.

Tosaburo has gone, his temples are empty of wistful *horios*, and the priests are purifying, in the hygienic sense. Later come the rites of purification by salt and fire, by symbols and long Buddhist ceremonies. The hammer of the carpenter, tearing down fences, inner partitions, and bunks, is as continuous as when they were building so hastily last winter for the Port Arthur garrison. The Iyo troops are returning from Manchuria, and the shrill *Banzais!* of the street crowds affect me differently than when they went with marching regiments going out to the war, going to death, and to deal death.

We are to keep in touch with Tosaburo until the last moment, so that I can see his uncle when he passes through to a triumph in Tokyo—Vladimir and I are now going to spend a fortnight in Kioto to see the Siemenoffs and their *mise en scène*. Sandy goes with us, Andrew Y—— having secured this privilege and detail from Daniloff. We are full of plans, busy with plans; but in my heart I am desolate at leaving, and I cannot look around my little home and garden without my eyes filling with tears. This has been a home, a haven. It has all been for the best. "*Hœc olim meminisse juvabit.*" Truly it is so.

Sunday, December 3rd.

We have seen Kioto; and Lyov, and "the prisoner's bride," in their exquisite chalet on the slope of Momoyama; and have watched sunsets together from that hilltop whose view could well enchant the great Taiko. Some of the Siemenoffs' treasures we have seen, too, but not all; as many had been boxed to make room for the later inflow of everything rare and beautiful that the *contessa* and her scouts could lay hands on.

And those boxes—where will they go? Over that we have had

214

long discussions, and Lyov's future seems an uncertain thing. The old Russia will not claim him either, I fear. First, he will apply for a long leave before returning for retirement; for, with his knee, he can never be a dashing dragoon again. The *contessa* proposes that they go first to America, and stop the winter in the Californias, where her mother's brother has an orange and olive estate in the south. After that.? "We will find you in England, I fancy," she says.

★★★★★★

"I have been everywhere," said Andrew Y——. "I wanted to see the Japanese in the back provinces, for I feared that Matsuyama was a trick, a show town, and Iyo a show province put upon us—something like those theatrically clean towns in Holland, you know. I wanted to catch the peasants lying in pigsties, with untidy fields. But, no. It is the same everywhere. The same little thatched cottages made to order for sketch classes; the same little shrines along good roads; the same neat little geometrical puzzles of tidy rice fields; every valley and every hillside planted to the last inch, as far as water can reach; and plantations of trees like a model forestry school all over—in every province— along the railway—miles away from the railway. It is no trick. I give it up. As an exhibit, it is *hors concours*. Put it under a glass case, and let me go away and think awhile. Maybe I am dreaming, and it is not so different from the rest of the world. Maybe all the world has come to look like Japan, in these ages that I have been here."

"Yes, and I thought it a trick, too; so I asked the head nurse where she lived, and I got leave, and went one hundred and forty miles in *jinrikisha*, and on foot, across Shikoku to Tosa province," said R——. "I stayed in their house—they wouldn't let me go to a tea house—and all their friends, all the doctors and nurses from far and near, came and showed me how charming and courteous are the real Japanese people—the non-military class, who have not been corrupted by Prussian drill. Heretofore, I had only met those tainted by Germany and its ideals. Now, I believe in *Bushido*."

★★★★★★

I went to the Hiogo railway station to see Tosaburo's uncle pass through with the field marshal, on their way to the triumph in Tokyo. I demurred at being present at such a scene, but Tosaburo insisted, and said he had already telegraphed down to Okayama warning his uncle of my presence. "There will be many foreign ladies and Japanese ladies there, but my uncle will wish to see you, his old friend."

In the crowded station, I was lost, save for Tosaburo, whose glittering full-dress uniform and face glowing with patriotic enthusiasm were a sight to inspire one.

And such *Banzais!* when the train paused in the vast Hiogo station! Enough to lift its arched iron roof. All eyes were upon the field marshal but mine, which sought and found the fine Italian countenance, the sharply-cut features, the flashing eyes, and the inscrutable smile of my old friend the staff colonel—now the lieutenant-general and chief of staff—the brain and soul, and moving spirit of the Ever Victorious army. Briefly I made my thanks to him, and acknowledged my deep indebtedness to Tosaburo, my friend of early days, my protector of later days; and, with felicitations on the blessed peace, we parted. I found it impossible to convey to Vladimir any conception of this living force, this human dynamo, this animating spirit that so overpoweringly impresses one when in the presence of the outwardly calm, reserved, repressed, yet smiling man, who is—the world's greatest general! The Twentieth Century God of War.

December 11th.

The Siemenoffs and ourselves are returning independently at our own expense through America, through grace of Daniloff and the home authorities, with long leave for recuperation. Sandy von Rathroff, to his great relief, has leave to go *via* America, also. We are making him a little dot that will keep him until he finds his footing in the New World, where he means to make his "escape," as he calls it, from us, and under a new name begin the life of an American citizen. Vladimir pleads with him to resign in proper form for his family's sake; but the boy is obstinate, and his hatred of Russia seems to increase daily. He believes in, and he gloats over, the reports of riots at Vladivostok and Harbin, and the hideous happenings in Odessa and the south. "Live in such a country? Be of such a people? Never! Leave this sunshine, this beautiful country and all its chrysanthemums, for the gloom of Siberian barracks, or the town where I lived my years of exile? No! No! No! *Civis Americanus sum,*" and the young hot-head wraps an imaginary *toga* around him and strides down the deck like Henry Irving.

I have been reading to Vladimir that favourite chapter of his in *Kokoro,* where in liquid prose, in language as smooth as melted velvet, Lafcadio Hearn begins so musically: "*Hiogo, this morning, lies bathed in a limpid magnificence of light indescribable.*" I look over to the massed roofs of Kobe climbing steeply to the green hills beyond, out to the soft expanse of pearl sea and the blue heavens above; and, without a sound the water eddies around the stern, the Awaji shore slips around to our starboard side, the Sanuki mountains rise and recede, and our prison life is ended.

LEONAUR

ALSO FROM LEONAUR
AVAILABLE IN SOFTCOVER OR HARDCOVER WITH DUST JACKET

THE WOMAN IN BATTLE *by Loreta Janeta Velazquez*—Soldier, Spy and Secret Service Agent for the Confederacy During the American Civil War.

BOOTS AND SADDLES *by Elizabeth B. Custer*—The experiences of General Custer's Wife on the Western Plains.

FANNIE BEERS' CIVIL WAR *by Fannie A. Beers*—A Confederate Lady's Experiences of Nursing During the Campaigns & Battles of the American Civil War.

LADY SALE'S AFGHANISTAN *by Florentia Sale*—An Indomitable Victorian Lady's Account of the Retreat from Kabul During the First Afghan War.

THE TWO WARS OF MRS DUBERLY *by Frances Isabella Duberly*—An Intrepid Victorian Lady's Experience of the Crimea and Indian Mutiny.

THE REBELLIOUS DUCHESS *by Paul F. S. Dermoncourt*—The Adventures of the Duchess of Berri and Her Attempt to Overthrow French Monarchy.

LADIES OF WATERLOO *by Charlotte A. Eaton, Magdalene de Lancey & Juana Smith*—The Experiences of Three Women During the Campaign of 1815: Waterloo Days by Charlotte A. Eaton, A Week at Waterloo by Magdalene de Lancey & Juana's Story by Juana Smith.

NURSE AND SPY IN THE UNION ARMY *by Sarah Emma Evelyn Edmonds*—During the American Civil War

WIFE NO. 19 *by Ann Eliza Young*—The Life & Ordeals of a Mormon Woman During the 19th Century

DIARY OF A NURSE IN SOUTH AFRICA *by Alice Bron*—With the Dutch-Belgian Red Cross During the Boer War

MARIE ANTOINETTE AND THE DOWNFALL OF ROYALTY *by Imbert de Saint-Amand*—The Queen of France and the French Revolution

THE MEMSAHIB & THE MUTINY *by R. M. Coopland*—An English lady's ordeals in Gwalior and Agra duringthe Indian Mutiny 1857

MY CAPTIVITY AMONG THE SIOUX INDIANS *by Fanny Kelly*—The ordeal of a pioneer woman crossing the Western Plains in 1864

WITH MAXIMILIAN IN MEXICO *by Sara Yorke Stevenson*—A Lady's experience of the French Adventure

CPSIA information can be obtained
at www.ICGtesting.com
Printed in the USA
BVHW031647300323
661466BV00004B/60